BOOK ONE

WICKED GAMES

M.J. SCOTT

Praise for M.J. Scott

The Shattered Court

Nominated for Best Paranormal Romance in the 2016 RITA® Awards.

"Scott (the Half-Light City series) opens her Four Arts fantasy series with the portrait of a young woman who's thrust into the center of dangerous political machinations… Romance fans will enjoy the growing relationship between Cameron and Sophie, but the story's real strength lies in the web of intrigue Scott creates around her characters."
—*Publishers Weekly*

"Fans of high fantasy and court politics will enjoy The Shattered Court. Sophie is such a great heroine…"
—*RT Book Reviews*

The Forbidden Heir

"This story was packed with action, political intrigue, scheming, and high stakes."
—*Alyssa - Goodreads reviewer*

"This is a marvelous book. The world building is unique and complex. The characters are well developed and likable and there is intrigue for days. If you've read the first book in the series it only gets better in this one."
—*Lissa - Goodreads reviewer*

"'Forbidden Heir' is a great rarity: a sequel that I liked better than the original book."
—*Margaret - Amazon reviewer*

Fire Kin

"Entertaining…Scott's dramatic story will satisfy both fans and new readers."
—*Publishers Weekly*

"This is one urban fantasy series that I will continue to come back to…Fans of authors Christina Henry of the Madeline Black series and Keri Arthur of the Dark Angels series will love the Half-Light City series."
—*Seeing Night Book Reviews*

Iron Kin

"Strong and complex world building, emotionally layered relationships, and enough action to keep me up long past my bedtime. I want to know what's going to happen next to the DuCaines and their chosen partners, and I want to know now."
—*Vampire Book Club*

"Iron Kin was jam-packed with action, juicy politics, and a lot of loose ends left over for the next book to resolve that it's still a good read for series fans."
—*All Things Urban Fantasy*

"Scott's writing is rather superb."
—*Bookworm Blues*

Blood Kin

"Not only was this book just as entertaining and immensely readable as Shadow Kin—it sang in harmony with it and spun its own story all the while continuing the grander symphony that is slowly becoming the Half-Light City story.... Smart, funny, dangerous, addictive, and seductive in its languorous sexuality, I can think of no better book to recommend to anyone to read this summer. I loved every single page except the last one, and that's only because it meant the story was done. For now, at least."
—*seattlepi.com*

"Blood Kin was one of those books that I really didn't want to put down, as it hit all of my buttons for an entertaining story. It had the intrigue and danger of a spy novel, intense action scenes, and a romance that evolved organically over the course of the story.... Whether this is your first visit to Half-Light City or you're already a fan, Blood Kin expertly weaves the events from Shadow Kin throughout this sequel in a way that entices new readers without boring old ones. I am really looking forward to continuing this enthralling ride."
—*All Things Urban Fantasy*

"Blood Kin had everything I love about urban fantasies: kick-butt action, fantastic characters, romance that makes the heart beat fast, and a plot that was fast-paced all the way through. Even more so the villains are meaner, stronger, and downright fantastic—I never knew what they were going to do next. You don't want to miss out on this series."
—*Seeing Night Book Reviews*

"An exciting thriller . . . fast-paced and well written."
—*Genre Go Round Reviews*

Shadow Kin

"M. J. Scott's Shadow Kin is a steampunky romantic fantasy with vampires that doesn't miss its mark."
—*#1 New York Times bestselling author Patricia Briggs*

"Shadow Kin is an entertaining novel. Lily and Simon are sympathetic characters who feel the weight of past actions and secrets as they respond to their attraction for each other."
—*New York Times bestselling author Anne Bishop*

"M. J. Scott weaves a fantastic tale of love, betrayal, hope, and sacrifice against a world broken by darkness and light, where the only chance for survival rests within the strength of a woman made of shadow and the faith of a man made of light."
—*National bestselling author Devon Monk*

"Had me hooked from the very first page."
—*New York Times bestselling author Keri Arthur*

"Exciting and rife with political intrigue and magic, Shadow Kin is hard to put down right from the start. Magic, faeries, vampires, werewolves, and Templar knights all come together to create an intriguing story with a unique take on all these fantasy tropes. . . . The lore and history of Scott's world is well fleshed out and the action scenes are exhilarating and fast."
—*Romantic Times*

About Wicked Games

My mother was a wicked witch. Her spells brought nothing but trouble. Since her death, with no power of my own, I've stayed far away from magic . . .

In a San Francisco struggling with earthquakes and rising seas, where technology can do things that are close enough to magic, Maggie Lachlan is a computer whisperer. The one they call when no one else can find the elusive bug bringing a complex system to its knees. They call her the TechWitch. But she knows there's nothing magical about what she does. It's just hard-earned skill.

So, when billionaire Damon Riley, owner of the world's biggest virtual reality gaming company, comes calling with a problem that his entire empire of geeks can't fix, Maggie leaps at the job. Riley Arts is the kind of place she feels at home. All tech. No magic. Except, perhaps, for the undeniable chemistry she has with the man in charge.

But she never imagined stepping into one of Damon's games would break a spell she didn't know she was under and free the magic her mother said she didn't possess.

Now she has a demon hunting her and the magical world she knows nothing about to navigate. To save herself—and the world—she needs to learn fast.

Because, when it comes to magic, the games are wicked. And losing can be deadly…

Copyright © 2018 by M.J. Scott

Visit M.J. at www.mjscott.net

All rights reserved.

All characters and events in this book are fictitious. Any resemblance to real people, alive or dead, is entirely coincidental.

No part of this book may be reproduced in any form or by any electronic or mechanical means, including information storage and retrieval systems, without written permission from the author, except for the use of brief quotations in a book review.

Published by emscott enterprises.

Cover design by Deranged Doctor Design.

For my darling Dad.
This is the first book of mine he never got to see and I'm not sure I'll ever get used to that.

Chapter One

My mother was a wicked witch.

An ill-wisher, a doer of dark deeds.

Trading in false hopes, broken hearts, and the not-so-pretty side of human emotion and gullibility.

She liked me to be seen and not heard. She liked magic that served her best interests. And she liked her men tall, pretty, and well acquainted with sinning.

She would've liked the guy standing next to me.

Even if he was a simulation.

He looked like he knew all about being bad. In all the good senses of the word. Tall, dark-haired, and sculpted by a perfectionist. But avatars—skins—can look like anything you want. In real life, he—or she—was just as likely to be a toad as a prince.

I turned back to the game menu, raising my avatar's hand to flick through options. Pretty or not, I hadn't expected company in *Nightruns*. The game was old. Several gens old. Uncool.

I'd retreated here for that precise reason, hiding out from Nat's coaxing to join her and her team in the latest Phobos offering.

I'd wanted peace and quiet. Time to think.

Which, yes, meant more fool me for coming out in the first place. But Nat was never easy to resist. Though she did know better than to ask me to play any game with magic. I'd known the real thing and seen what it could do; I had no desire to relive it virtually.

But tonight I had no desire to stumble after her and her friends in an unknown game. Nat was a pro. I wasn't. There'd be hundreds of thousands tuned in to the game stream. I didn't want to hold Nat back, nor did I want to sit around and watch her on the screens. So I'd headed for the more obscure parts of the club's catalog.

"You like classics?"

The question startled me. I twisted toward my companion. He studied me with improbably blue eyes, making me wonder again about the real face of whoever was running this skin. "Sorry?"

"Classics?" He gestured at the menu shimmering in the air. "Everyone here tonight seems to be trying to get a slot in the Phobos launch, yet here you are, back in the dark ages."

His voice, like the eyes and the body, was too good to be true, deep and slightly roughened.

Definitely overcompensating. Still, that didn't mean I couldn't enjoy the scenery, given it was so nicely packaged in tight black clothes that hugged every pixel. "Newer isn't everything. Anyway, I'm not much of a gamer."

The avatar raised one dark eyebrow. "What brings a non-gamer to Decker's?"

"I'm with friends. They're pros." And could get me comped on the entry fee and game price, which was how my currently slender credit balance could withstand playing in a club like this.

He nodded. "Ranked?"

I shrugged. "Some." I didn't want to get into a boring conversation about the leagues and rankings and upcoming competitions. If he was a game-head, then I'd find somewhere else to hide out. I reached toward the menu in case I needed the exit fast.

"Made a decision?"

I pulled back. "No."

"How about Kingmaker? The palace run? If you feel like company, that is?" One brow quirked a challenge onto that perfect face.

I hesitated. The palace run was my favorite level of Kingmaker, full of the sorts of traps and logic puzzles I enjoyed. Zero magic. I'd been planning on tackling it alone, but a bit of competition could spice things up. Besides, it might be fun to beat pretty boy. "Pairs or head-to-head?"

He smiled, and I had to give points to whoever had designed his skin—the avatar was an advanced lesson in sheer male beauty. I smiled back before I could stop myself.

"Competition is always more fun." He ushered me toward the menu. "Ladies first."

"First to the crown jewels?" I asked, dialing the time to night. Moonlight made playing sneak thief more fun.

He nodded. "I'll be waiting for you."

"We'll see about that," I muttered, then pressed Go.

The walls of the palace shimmered into view and I flung myself into a run, heading for the first challenge point. Pretty boy dropped out of sight behind me. I smiled and then sped up, sinking into the moment, losing myself in the game, enjoying the familiarity, even if the simulation didn't feel entirely real at times and the ageing graphics had a tendency to flicker at disconcerting moments.

My breath sang in my ears as I traversed the darkened corridors, climbing balconies, solving the puzzles guarding each new stage, and dodging guards. Occasionally I caught glimpses of my opponent, muscles rippling under the sleek black shirt and pants as he vaulted over an obstacle or stretched for a handhold.

He was doing pretty well—okay, *really* well—but I thought I had him. If I was reading his route right, he was taking the long way around. He was toast.

Or so I thought, until I dropped onto the balcony above the throne room, creeping carefully through the line of booby-trapped gilt chairs, to find him leaning against the railing looking down at the sumptuous room below with the well-satisfied expression of a king surveying his domain. His avatar didn't even look rumpled. Maybe he didn't like the realism of sweat and heavy breathing, but Nat had built the skin I wore and she was a purist. I knew it showed every inch of effort I'd put into my route. I stopped myself from reaching up to smooth my hair back.

"I wondered where you'd got to," he said with another damnably perfect smile.

I bit back an annoyed retort and looked down at the throne. The crown and scepter we were supposedly here to steal still glittered against the black velvet seat. "Too scared to make the drop?"

"Actually, I wanted to talk to you, Ms. Lachlan."

"How do you know my name?" Alarm prickled my spine, and I backed up a step.

"Easy." He lifted his hands from the railing, holding them out palms forward. "I don't mean any harm."

"How do you know my name?" I repeated, flexing my hand. One quick slap of the release button—the virtual reality equivalent of a safe word—and I'd be out of there.

"Your reputation precedes you," he said. "I've been hearing the names Maggie Lachlan and TechWitch a lot lately."

My mouth dropped open. "You want to talk business?"

"Does that surprise you?"

"Most people just make an appointment," I pointed out.

"I like to know who I'm dealing with. Besides, this is more fun." He hit me with the smile again.

I found it a little less perfect on the face of a mysterious stalker. "I like to know who I'm dealing with too," I said, letting my tone frost a little. "So you've got about five seconds to tell me your name or I'm out."

"Sorry. Where are my manners?" He held out a hand. "I'm Damon Riley."

I sat down on one of the spindly gilt chairs with a thump. It squealed a protest, but I didn't care.

"Game halt." Damon snapped his fingers and the balcony disappeared. The lobby reformed around us, my chair morphing into a plain black cube.

"*The* Damon Riley?" I asked, more to myself than to him.

Those wickedly blue eyes twinkled. Their effect was even more annoying when I realized—having, like everyone else on the planet, seen his picture many times in almost every form of media—that the shade was close to the real thing. His avatar was nudged a little from reality, just enough to hide his identity, I guessed, but not too far.

"Yes. You know who I am," he replied.

It was more a statement than a question. I wondered briefly what he would do if I said no. Probably leave. Unless you were a hermit or otherwise out of touch with the world, you knew who Damon Riley was. "Sure. You own Righteous."

Somehow I managed to sound casual, as if I regularly had people who made world's richest insert-noun-of-choice-here lists come looking for me in game clubs.

His mouth curved again. "I thought you said you weren't much of a gamer?" He sounded amused.

I realized why. Most people would've said Riley Arts. Only the hard-core fans called his company Righteous. "Like I said, I know some pros."

Pros whose heads would explode if they knew who I was talking to. I pictured Nat's expression when I told her I'd played against Damon Riley. Exploding heads would just be the start.

The gamers called the company Righteous because it was. Riley's games were the best. No argument. He was the man who'd developed *Sorcerer's Apprentice*, the must-have game of all time. Almost a cult. It had made him his first million or fifty.

Since then, he hadn't looked back. Riley Arts did both games and game-tech now. Their latest home virtual reality console had sold out worldwide approximately two hours after its release. The games usually took less than that.

"Right." He rested against the railing, stretching out his long legs. "That would be Ms. Marcos and her crew?"

I nodded, my brain trying to catch up with what was happening.

Damon Riley. I didn't have the foggiest idea why someone like him would be coming to me for help. I didn't usually work with his sort of company. My somewhat specialized skills were generally more in demand by boring industries that lacked their own tech gods. Riley Arts had to have more computer geeks per square foot than almost any other company in the world. Why on earth would he want me?

"Yes, Nat's my roommate. Call me Maggie," I added. Ms. Lachlan always made me nervous. Every time the police had knocked on our door in my childhood, they were looking for 'Ms. Lachlan.' Back then, it had been my mother who wore the name, not me, but the sound of it still made me twitch somewhere deep in my gut.

"Of course."

The muscles along the back of my jaw clamped down. I recognized that cool, self-assured tone. Every rich kid who'd ever made my life hell in any of the twenty or thirty schools I'd passed through sounded like that. Like they could snap their fingers and life would provide whatever they needed.

My experience was more like snap your fingers all day long but life would still hand you whatever the hell it wanted and laugh as it knocked you on your ass.

I forced myself to relax. Working for Riley Arts would be

great for my career, no matter how aggravating Damon Riley himself turned out to be. "I guess that's enough of tiresome small talk. Which brings me back to why you're here."

"Your name was brought to my attention."

He waved a hand and a cube like the one under my virtual butt rose out of the featureless white floor. He took a seat, pushing back the sleeves of the shirt. I caught a glimpse of gold on the underside of his right wrist.

An interface chip.

Nice. Better than nice. Covetable, cutting-edge technology. Still almost exclusively the domain of the power players of the virtual entertainment industry. Of which Damon was indisputably king. No wonder he had one, even on his avatar.

Nat had a chip, courtesy of a tournament win a few months back. Me, I couldn't begin to afford one. Even if I could—and I'd had my moments of tech lust drooling over the specs—I wasn't sure I wanted one. The thought of something plugging straight into my central nervous system made me, well, nervous.

Luckily my clients didn't yet expect me to have one. By the time they did, I figured the tech would be tested enough to overcome my instinctive caution and I might be able to afford it.

Of course, if Damon Riley hired me, I'd be able to afford several of the damn things and still have enough left over for my other, more pressing expenses.

"Who gave you my name?" I gave him my best "hey, give me a job" smile. He smiled back, and my pulse hitched.

Just an avatar. Yes, in real life he was plenty pretty too. Not quite as sleekly perfect as the skin, but it wasn't too much of an exaggeration. The real man was tall and dark and built too. But in real life, if I played this right, he'd be a client. Maggie's rules of life included a strict no-lusting-after-the-paycheck clause.

Especially no lusting after the way-too-sure-of-himself paycheck.

He leaned forward, and I mirrored his action automatically. *Damn.*

"Like I said, I've been hearing your name a lot lately."

"And you also heard I was friends with Nat?"

His eyes twinkled. "No, I'm afraid that was something my team dug up."

"You had me investigated?" My jaw twinged again, and several muscles in my back joined in the protest. Twinkles and sinner's smiles be damned, I didn't like people poking around in my business.

"I believe in thorough preparation," he added, not sounding even the slightest bit apologetic.

Paycheck, I reminded myself as my teeth ground a little tighter. "Mr. Riley, you can be as prepared as you like, but unless you tell me what the problem is, I can't help you."

His eyes narrowed. "Who says I have a problem?"

"Maybe the fact that you've hunted me down in a club on a night off and took the trouble to meet me anonymously?"

"Maybe I was just curious to meet the woman who calls herself a TechWitch."

"TechWitch is a business name, not a description. Marketing. Something you understand very well, if the evidence is to be believed."

I didn't like the name. It was something one of my earliest clients had said in recommending me, and it had stuck. It was, like I said, good marketing, nothing more, which was why I'd kept it. And I was sure Riley's investigators had told him as much. He was beating around the bush. Or lying. Or maybe both. Growing up with Sara—my mother—had left me with a well-honed bullshit meter, and the needle was starting to waver.

"So you don't claim supernatural abilities?"

I frowned. Was he serious? Or still trying to avoid getting

to the point? "Not at all. I'm very, very good at my job, but that doesn't require magic. As I'm sure you know."

Sara's laughter echoed in my head. How could anyone think I had power? My mother's disappointment—or disgust, rather—had been perfectly clear when I failed to show any signs of power after I turned thirteen. Overnight I became strictly an annoyance and a burden to her, not that she would've won any mother of the year awards before then. I was spared knowing just what she might've eventually done about that burden when she died a few months later.

"Why? Did you want a witch?"

His face went still. "No. No. Just the opposite, in fact."

Some of the tension riding my gut eased even as my curiosity piqued. Damon Riley wasn't a fan of magic either? One point in his favor. Though he was happy enough to include it in his games, so obviously it wasn't completely a no-go. "So what do you want? You do know what I do, right?" I threw his words back at him.

"Yes. The term 'computer whisperer' was mentioned."

I didn't let myself groan. I'd been dumb enough to give the interview to the tech reporter who'd coined that little term. I lived with it, but I didn't have to like it. "That's not the term I'd use."

"What would you use?"

"Troubleshooter, usually. Do you have some trouble that needs shooting?" I cocked my head, waiting for the inevitable questions.

Troubleshooter was a simplification. I was more a cross between cyber engineer and cyber therapist.

I found the problems that technically shouldn't exist. The systems that just didn't seem to like each other. Pieces of code that, in isolation, should've worked perfectly but caused unforeseen complications and glitches when put together with other pieces in adjacent systems.

Despite the cold hard facts that computers were machines

and had no feelings, I knew from experience that they did get moody. True, by any test yet devised, no one had yet created a true artificial intelligence. But as each generation of cyber tech became more complicated, more powerful, more autonomous, and we humans generated more and more data to feed them, the systems became . . . touchier. And I, God knew why, had the knack of soothing them. Untangling the knots no one else thought were there.

I assumed I got my cyber skills from my unknown father; Sara had been useless with any sort of machine.

Damon studied me for a long moment. "I might have a systems integration issue in our accounting department."

The needle shot into the red zone. Financial packages—other than the ones used by massive international banks—were not usually particularly temperamental. I could count the number of times I'd been called in to consult on one with less than five fingers. And a bookkeeping problem wasn't important enough to send Damon Riley looking for me in a game at Decker's, where there'd be no record of us meeting.

I didn't like being lied to.

"Riley Arts must employ more geeks, nerds, and tech heads per square foot than NASA, Wall Street, and the CIA put together. If your people can't solve an issue with your financial package, you should fire them. How about you tell me the real problem?"

"No—"

"I don't appreciate having my time wasted," I interrupted before he could spin another lie.

He held up his hand, giving me an even better view of the chip glittering against tanned flesh. Interesting that his skin reflected that particular bit of what I had to assume was real-life detail when it blurred others. "Let me finish. Not here was what I was about to say. I don't discuss confidential matters in unsecured venues."

I folded my arms. "You're the one who came to me. And

at the prices this place charges, I'd think their security would be top of the line."

"Not secure enough."

There was that master-of-the-universe tone again. "Then why did you come?"

"I believe in knowing who I'm dealing with. And being discreet."

"Well, it was nice being stalked by you and all, but I have to get back to my friends." I stood. My chances of landing this gig seemed pretty remote.

He rose too. Apparently he had nice manners when he wasn't being irritating. "Can you come to my office on Wednesday?"

Do this all over again? Why?

I shifted a little in the game chair, aware of my back sticking to the slightly sweaty fabric of my shirt in the real world, but held my avatar still as I tried to figure out if he was playing an angle. "Why Wednesday?" It was still Monday, unless our game had taken more time than I thought. If he did have the sort of problem I might be able to help with, surely it would be a priority.

"I have business in New Zealand tomorrow." He tugged his shirtsleeves down with two sharp movements. "Unfortunately. I will, of course, pay for your time."

Ah. Payment. He'd found my Achilles' heel. The problem with being very specialized was you had to wait for the very specialized problems to come along. And while I did well enough, there had been a distinct lack of computers throwing temper tantrums lately, and there were other demands on my finances.

Which was part of the reason why I was out on a school night. I was sick of cooling my heels at home, worrying about my lack of billable hours and what that meant for my debts. The prospect of cold hard cash flow was even harder to ignore than my curiosity about what might be going on at

Righteous. It couldn't hurt to at least find out what the mysterious issue was, even if the boss had pushy and demanding and driven written all over him.

"I'll have to check my schedule," I said finally.

"Is that a yes?"

Check on pushy. "It's 'I'll have to check my schedule.'"

He gestured and a data entry screen appeared in the air before me. "Go right ahead."

Pushy and not used to being kept waiting. Not my favorite traits in men, or clients, but traits I would put up with for a chance of a job at Righteous.

I crossed to the screen, switched it to secure mode—which meant the visuals would be blurred for him—and called up my calendar with an irritated twitch of my hand. As the image appeared, I settled for glaring at it in lieu of glaring at him.

Nothing had magically appeared to fill the next four weeks since I'd checked that morning. I was still negotiating over a potential trip to a province in Liberated China to see what I could do with a state-of-the-art manufacturing plant that was behaving in a less than state-of-the-art manner after that, but getting a visa was proving to be a bitch. Apart from a few local follow-up calls, my dance card was empty.

Plenty of time to take on a new client.

Ample space in my bank account to be filled.

Not that Damon Riley needed to know that.

"I'll have to move some things around," I lied. I hadn't learned a lot that was useful from my mother, but "never appear too eager" had been one of her life rules. She used it on men and marks. I used it in business negotiations.

His mouth quirked, making me wonder exactly how deep his investigations had gone. Money could buy a lot of supposedly secure data these days.

"That's fine. I'll get my assistant to schedule some time on Wednesday and confirm with you."

Wednesday. After his little jaunt to the southern hemisphere. Across the planet and back in a day. Obviously he didn't suffer any side effects from suborbital travel. Personally, it made me feel like I'd been on a three-day bender without any of the fun parts. And the travel drugs that were supposed to help only knocked me on my ass. Lucky for me, most of my clients were only too happy for me to travel via less expensive means like regular planes.

But at least I had until Wednesday to do some digging of my own into Righteous and the man at the helm.

"That will be fine."

Damon offered his hand. "I look forward to it."

His fingers closed over mine, and I couldn't help wishing it wasn't just two avatars touching.

He hit me with one last smile. "If you'll excuse me, I'm going to duck out the back way. Early start tomorrow."

His avatar vanished before I could reply.

I hit the release and yanked my headset free. Light stabbed my eyes and I blinked rapidly, ignoring the rush of dizziness from too quick a reentry as I clambered out of the game chair and pushed my way out of the curtained-off solo alcove.

The sounds and smells of the club slammed into me after the relative peace of the game, a rush of reality that made me wonder if I'd imagined the whole thing. My eyes scanned the crowd, but there was no sign of anyone who looked like Riley. And there was none of the excitement that an appearance of the gamers' guru would cause. He really had slipped away. Easy enough to do. He'd probably been in one of the private suites on the upper levels.

I fought the stupid surge of disappointment even as my hand tingled, remembering the touch of his avatar.

"Mags! There you are. Where have you been hiding?" Nat pushed a drink into my hand. I took a swig without thinking, then cursed. It was an Insomniac. *Crap.* I didn't sleep well at the best of times; I didn't need to add triple-refined syncaf to the adrenaline already riding my system.

I passed the drink back. "You know I don't drink these this late."

She blinked at me, then looked down at the glass. "Sorry." She gave me her "victory is mine" grin. "I wasn't thinking."

She must've won her bout if she was drinking Insomniacs. She only used caffeine for hard-core victory parties.

"You won?" I asked before she could ask me where I'd been again. If she found out, I'd never get out of the club. I'd have to repeat every detail to her and all her friends. Then they'd probably want to replay the game tape and endlessly critique every move. And I had the feeling that Damon Riley didn't appreciate anybody who couldn't keep their mouth shut.

"Crushed them mercilessly," Nat said.

We high-fived. Nat's team was climbing the ranks steadily, and I loved watching her kicking butt. But even as I grinned at her, I tried to think of a way to make my excuses and leave. The clock was ticking. I had thirty-six hours to try and find out as much as possible about Damon Riley.

And thirty-six hours to convince myself that I shouldn't already be looking forward to seeing him again.

I reached for the Insomniac. At this point, I needed all the help I could get.

Chapter Two

By eleven o'clock Wednesday morning, I'd managed to work myself into a fine state of nervousness. Slurping on my third syncaf of the day, I stared across the road at the front gate of the Riley Arts campus and tried to psych myself into going inside. My datapad had already chirped thirty-, twenty-, and ten-minute warnings at me.

My feet stayed firmly rooted to the pavement as I watched the faint flicker of the shields above the fence in the sunlight, trying to peek through the electric haze at the low buildings scattered like white-and-glass jewels among green trees and greener lawns.

Serious money had been spent establishing this place. Or reestablishing it. My day and a half of digging up all I could about Riley had told me that he'd been one of the first companies to push to redevelop downtown. Before the quake, there wouldn't have been a piece of property this large for sale in the heart of the city, but afterward, well, no one knew where was safe to rebuild, or if they even should. And no one wanted to build skyscrapers. Not that there were skyscrapers here—none of the buildings were more than a few stories high

—but Riley had put his money where his mouth was nonetheless.

Looking into the flawlessly manicured grounds, nobody would know there'd been a wreckage of a city here just ten short years ago. Not a leaf or blade of grass out of place as far as the eye could see.

But part of me couldn't help interposing the image of the aftermath over the scene. Which was why I rarely came to this part of town any more. It was mostly like this now, big corporate headquarters mingling with the new memorial park and buildings rebuilt to resemble the originals to bring in the tourists. Tourists wearing optics and engrossed in the augmented reality feeds sent out from the memorial plaques, oohing and aahing over images of the old city overlaid over the new.

Worse, some of the memorial plaques projected holo images rather than AR. The last thing I needed was to catch a glimpse of one of those. I had my own memories of Old SF. Once upon a time they'd been happy. Now they just mostly reminded me of all that I'd lost.

But there was no memorial plaque here. All that stood between me and the inner workings of Damon Riley's empire were the gleaming gates and a sleek glass and metal security checkpoint. I still stood frozen, my confidence overwhelmed by nerves running riot.

The man had managed to rebuild practically an entire town's worth of property in five years. I couldn't even get one lousy house back up. I was playing out of my league.

The last drops of syncaf ran down my throat, and I tossed the cup at the nearest recycler. It squeaked and crunched, and I wondered if Riley might chew me up just as easily.

"Stop being a wimp, Lachlan."

My research on Riley had confirmed first impressions. He played the affable, charming computer geek humbled by his good fortune in the media and online, but his business record indicated someone who was single-minded in achieving his goals.

Someone who didn't suffer fools gladly and who protected what was his.

Lucky for me that I didn't like to be foolish.

Though if I stood here much longer, I might melt in the midday steam. Frizzed hair and running makeup weren't exactly the first—or second, I guess—impression I was aiming for.

"Just another client interview." I sucked in a breath, straightened my jacket—resisting the urge to check that I hadn't eaten my supposedly immovable lipstick—then headed across the road.

The gate guard looked like he had sumo wrestlers in his ancestry. Sumo wrestlers with sumo-sized attitude, judging by the way he looked down his nose at me until I announced I had an appointment with Mr. Riley. Apparently those were the magic words, earning me a respectful smile once his data screen confirmed I wasn't lying.

We did the inspect-the-ID dance—palm scan and plastic—and then the guard took a truly hideous digital picture of me, which the tiny ident tag he punched onto my jacket collar would project on demand.

Tiny circuit lines surrounded the tag's equally tiny lens. If I'd had to guess, I would have put money on it being some sort of locator device. No moving around Riley Arts without them knowing exactly where you were, apparently. Fair enough. In Damon's place, I'd protect my secrets closely too.

To complete the process, the guard zapped a set of directions to the building I needed to my datapad, informed me that the map and my access permission would be deleted in three hours, and let me through the gate.

Inside, the air was slightly cooler, which meant the shields went overhead as well. Expensive, though welcome as I walked for what seemed like miles following the map to my destination—the tallest building on campus, five stories or so of elegantly curved glass and wood. I vaguely remembered rapturous articles about the design and the eco-friendliness of the whole campus when it had first opened, but I was too nervous to appreciate much about it other than it was big and the lobby was light and airy and oddly free of any of the things you might expect a gaming company to litter its offices with.

Luckily, the concierge at the front desk was friendlier than the security guard. I guess if you made it through the gate, you were deemed safe. One glance at the image projected by my tag as she scanned it, and then I was ushered to an elevator bank and given detailed directions on what to do when I reached the fourth floor.

The elevator disgorged me onto a sea of gleaming floorboards and I halted, trying to get my bearings. I shouldn't have bothered. Before I could take another step, a very tall woman, whose expression was far too efficient for her carefully trendy clothes and blue-streaked hair, stepped through a door that opened in the opposite wall.

"Ms. Lachlan?" Pale gray eyes gave me the once-over. I got the feeling she didn't miss much. And maybe didn't approve of me.

"That's me," I said, trying to give her my best I'm-harmless smile. "Your boss is expecting me."

Her answering smile was tight. "I'm Cat Delaney. *Mr.* Riley's office is this way."

You can take the suit off the assistant, but you can't take the assistant out of the suit. I doubted many of Damon's employees called him Mr. Riley—tech companies were notoriously informal—but I couldn't fault her for being professional.

Her heels tapped over gleaming floorboards as we walked. She stayed a little ahead of me, which gave me the chance to check the place out and try to get my bearings. This floor wasn't as sparsely furnished as the lobby. The bare brick walls were broken into sections by strips of vertical gardens, the green providing contrast to the massive framed pictures hung between them. The black-framed images were an intriguing mix of stills from Righteous games and other pop culture memorabilia both old and new.

Every so often there was a door and a floor-to-ceiling pane of glass that allowed glimpses into the offices. Some had clusters of desks and some only one, but all of them were in use, if the sheer volume of gadgets and gizmos and wacky desk ornaments was anything to go by. No actual people were in evidence, but the casual feel of the place eased my nerves. Maybe Damon Riley would be easier to deal with on his home turf.

"Where is everybody?" I asked.

Cat kept walking. "Recognition hour. They'll be finished soon."

She didn't offer any further explanation, and I didn't ask. "Recognition hour" sounded like the sort of compulsory touchy-feely corporate team bonding that made me happy that I worked for myself.

The long corridor turned several times, following the lines of the building. Finally we reached a set of huge wooden doors. At first glance, the designs carved into them looked vaguely like they might have decorated the walls of an old temple in some hot and humid country. But on closer inspection, the figures revealed themselves to be stylized versions of famous characters from Righteous games.

One side of my mouth quirked reluctantly. I didn't want to find the man and his sense of humor charming.

"This is Mr. Riley's office." Cat placed her hand on the scanner beside the doors and they swung inward. "Go on in." She made a little shooing motion.

I got the feeling that keeping Damon Riley waiting was a Very Bad Thing in her book. In my book, it was tempting to linger just on sheer principle. Taste in men wasn't the only thing I'd inherited from my mother—contrariness ran deep in my veins too. Though I'd never been sure if it was Sara's contribution or just Gran's sheer Irish stubborn-headedness.

Neither was going to help me land Riley as a client, if indeed that was what I wanted to do.

The jury was still deliberating on that one.

But I did want to hear what he had to say. The more I'd read about Riley Arts, the more interested I'd become.

"Thank you," I said politely, then walked into Damon's office.

The room behind the doors was not much smaller than my apartment. If Cat didn't get enough cardio walking from her desk to Damon's office, then she'd be able to make it up just crossing from the doors to his desk.

I hovered in the doorway, feeling dwarfed. Arching ceilings and the sweep of floor-to-ceiling glass that formed the far wall of the room spoke of wealth, power and authority.

The décor took a little of the edge off. It didn't really look like any other CEO's office I'd ever been in. Sure, there was the standard desk and conference table made from the same dark wood as the doors, but they shared the space with a pool table and an antique pinball machine. Several surfboards leaned against one wall, and a giant screen dominated another. In front of the screen was a neat semicircle of squishy bright red leather recliners that I suspected might be game chairs in disguise.

What was missing was the man himself. I'd assumed, from Cat's desire to get me here on time, that Damon was waiting for me. Apparently I'd been wrong.

Unwilling to just stand inside the doorway like a nervous kid waiting for the principal, I walked over to one of the recliners, trailing my hand over leather that almost melted under my fingers, trying to adjust my mental image of the man to the room. Which one was the real him? The surfboard collector or the business genius who staged stealth interviews in virtual reality?

"I keep another meeting room for the really boring meetings." Damon's voice—deep and warm—made me jump.

Crap. Apparently his avatar's voice hadn't been a simulation.

He stood in a doorway I hadn't noticed in the wall with the surfboards. Dressed in jeans and an open-necked shirt, he didn't look quite as polished as the avatar, but he still looked expensive. Expensive and damn good. The reality had laugh lines bracketing those blue eyes and a slightly crooked nose. Somehow it was more enticing than the simulation.

"Nice to know I'm not boring," I managed.

My brain tried to work that one out while trying not to notice the low down flutter caused by his smile. A flutter that only increased as he reached me and I caught the scent of soap and cotton and something subtly spicy.

Real

Male.

Inviting.

Potential client, I reminded myself firmly. "How was New Zealand?" I asked. It seemed a safe enough question.

"Productive." He gestured toward his desk and waited until I'd seated myself in one of his visitor's chairs before sliding into the sleek ergonomic contraption on the other side.

Productive. Was that code for "I got what I wanted"? I doubted he had many unproductive meetings if that was the case. But asking that wouldn't be so safe, so I settled for a neutral smile and stayed silent. Letting the client speak first was always a good tactic.

"I'm glad you decided to come today," he said. "You're probably wondering what this is all about."

Denial was pointless. "I'll admit you piqued my curiosity."

"Good." He pushed a button, and a section of the desk slid aside to reveal a data screen set in the wood in front of me. The document it displayed was full of the kind of closely spaced text I associated with lawyers.

Damon tapped the desk just above the screen. "Before we go any further, I need you to sign this."

"What is it?"

"Standard non-disclosure agreement."

I touched the screen and began to scroll. The agreement was at least thirty pages long. Longer than any other confidentiality agreement I'd ever been asked to sign. Which meant I was going to read every word before I did. I moved my chair closer, determined to take my time.

Once I'd waded through the legalese, I'd figured out that Riley Arts took its confidentiality seriously. *Very* seriously. Basically, the agreement said they'd hunt me down and make me very sorry if I blabbed anything to anyone. Ever. It made me glad I didn't talk in my sleep.

But I didn't make a habit of discussing my clients' business with anyone—a consultant who was indiscreet was a broke consultant—so I didn't see that I was giving up anything I couldn't afford to give up.

"Before I sign, I assume you will be happy to provide me a reference if you're satisfied with my work, despite this?" I did my own imitation of his little screen tap trick. The agreement allowed me to mention I was or had been contracted by Riley Arts, but nothing more than that. And while that name would look good on my client list, a personal recommendation from someone like Damon Riley could open a lot of doors.

"If I'm satisfied, of course." He slid a stylus across the desk and it rolled to a stop right by my hand.

Show-off.

"Good." I signed the papers, added a palm scan when the screen demanded one, and rolled the stylus back across to him. The data screen disappeared as the desk section slid back into place.

"There will be a copy of that in your inbox," he said.

I nodded. "Now are you going to tell me why you brought me here?"

He nodded, not looking entirely happy with the prospect.

"It's about my new game."

My, not *our*. He took things personally. This time he was telling the truth. And he definitely had a problem if something was wrong with his latest and greatest.

A new Righteous game was an event that gamers anticipated, speculated, and debated endlessly. I lived each release through Nat and her teammates and had absorbed a healthy amount of industry gossip over the years despite my lack of real interest.

Said lack of interest in playing the games didn't mean I didn't find the thought of helping hunt down a problem with one intriguing.

"Go on," I prompted.

His eyes dropped to the place on the desk where the screen was hidden, then flicked back to me.

"I get it. Confidential. I signed, so unless I get hauled into court, this is between you and me."

Nat was going to give me hell. In Nat world, best friends told each other everything. Little things like professionalism and client confidentiality didn't matter. She'd nearly had kittens when I'd finally told her I had a meeting at Righteous, and had already started pestering for details. I was going to have to chain her in the basement or something for however long the job lasted to avoid being interrogated every night.

If I took the job, of course.

Damon picked up the stylus, twirling it back and forth between his fingers. "We're just starting the final testing phase. We send versions out to gamers we trust and let them do their worst."

I nodded again. That much I understood. Nat had done some beta testing a couple of times. Never for a Riley game—that was the holy grail for pro-gamers—but for other companies. It had been kind of entertaining watching her tie herself in knots trying to find bugs and make the games crash.

"There have been a couple of incidents with the testers." The stylus stilled suddenly.

The back of my neck prickled. "Incidents?"

Blue eyes went flat. "One nervous breakdown. One tester quit and vanished. Now another tester has gone missing."

Frustration rang in his voice. That was the problem with being the master-of-the-universe type—sometimes the universe staged a revolution. Damon Riley, it seemed, wasn't happy with disorder in his empire.

"Three out of how many?" I had no idea how many testers they would use.

The stylus began to twirl again, but his gaze stayed on mine. "A hundred or so."

Okay, not such a big sample. "That could just be coincidence. Gamers aren't always the most stable people." I'd met a few odd gamers over the years through Nat. Then again, I'd met plenty of people who had nothing to do with gaming who had mental health issues too. Medical science had come a long way, but fixing brain chemistry when it went rogue remained a challenge. I'd had my own struggles after the Big One.

"We vet our testers very carefully. We need reliability. We've never had these kinds of issues before." Frustration and regret thrummed under the words.

I couldn't imagine the pressure he must be under. I didn't know him well, but the research I'd done had revealed a man who took his responsibilities seriously. Righteous was very good to its employees, and Damon gave away huge chunks of cash to charities. He'd pushed to rebuild in San Francisco because he'd wanted to bring some life back to the city. Wanted to provide much needed jobs. And of course his testers were vetted. A Righteous beta version would be gold on the black market, so anyone given access to a copy had to be trustworthy. No doubt the legal agreements they signed would be several times longer than the one I'd just autographed.

Which made a missing tester a serious problem. Though why Damon had come to me was still a mystery. I wasn't an investigator. Not of people, anyway.

"Sounds like you need the police. Or a—" I cut myself off, remembering the hint of relief when I'd told him TechWitch was a name only. Some witches did this sort of thing, located missing people or property. But they tended toward high profile, not really discreet. Damon could afford to hire a whole coven of witches if he wanted magical assistance, but I doubted he'd welcome the publicity at this stage.

He shot me a look. "The police are involved. They have, so far, been unable to help."

That surprised me. Usually our charming city's police commissioner bent over backward to help those she thought could help her. A mega corporation like Righteous should've been afforded all the assistance they'd need. I wondered what Damon had done to piss Commissioner Cruz off.

"Apparently a few missing gamers rank somewhat lower than drug runners, black marketeers, and murderers," Damon continued.

"Imagine that," I said. "And this an election year."

He held up a hand. "Don't get me wrong, they *are* looking into it. Just not terribly . . . quickly."

And you like things fast. He didn't strike me as a sit-back-and-wait type.

"So you came looking for me?"

The stylus resumed its restless twirling. "The police or my investigators will find them. In the meantime, I need to know if the game had anything to do with their behavior. See if there's something wrong with the code. Testers plug in for hours at a time. I need my games to be safe."

"Like I said at Decker's, I would've thought you could do that in-house."

"So far my people have come up blank. They say everything is clean."

"Maybe it is. Maybe it is just coincidence."

The stylus clattered to the desk. "I don't really believe in coincidence. We didn't have any issues with the previous round of testing, but we've made substantial changes to several parts of our game engine since then. And I'm not prepared to launch the game until I know for sure. Which brings me to you. To TechWitch."

There was that frustration again. Like he still couldn't quite believe he was turning to someone who didn't have a four-page job description and a string of degrees from CalTech or MIT or—possibly—a past life as a world-class hacker. His expression was carefully neutral, but it was hard to miss the tension riding him.

"You want me to see if there's a problem in the code? In the game or in the operating system?"

He nodded. "Either. Both. Whatever it takes." His eyes dropped to my hands. "You don't have a chip."

My thumb skimmed my knuckles as my neck prickled again. I'd been so busy chasing the lowdown on Riley that I hadn't had much time to think about the tech he was using. "No. I've never needed one."

"You'll need one for this. We would, of course, foot the bill for the surgery. On top of your fee."

"My fee?" He was awfully sure of himself. But talking about money was easier than contemplating an interface chip.

He named a figure, and I was glad he hadn't offered me refreshments or I would've been spitting mine across the room.

Like I said, I made a good living at what I did—when the assignments came. But the amount he'd just offered came under the category of "no need to worry about the next client for quite some time." Like a year or two. It would go a long way to helping me rebuild my grandparents' house. My house, now. Which made me wonder whether there was more to the situation than he was letting on. The market would wait for a Righteous game, so it wasn't as if he was racing a ticking clock.

"That's a . . . generous offer." Too generous. And I had learned early on to be suspicious of things that seemed too good to be true.

He shrugged. "If you're as good as they say, then you're not charging enough for your services."

There was the arrogance again. I didn't need a critique of my business practices.

I took a deep breath, trying to stop being thirteen and think. Big client. Rich client. Big opportunity, and I had to admit—once I'd sent my inner teenager to her room—that given the man was six years older than me and could buy half the planet if he wanted to, whereas I'd thought I'd been doing pretty well to own my own business and support myself at twenty-nine, maybe I should listen to him.

But the offer still seemed a little too good to be true. "And if your missing gamer turns up and I don't find anything wrong with your code?"

"You still get paid."

Okay, now he was definitely making me nervous.

I opened my mouth to ask another question, but he held up a hand. "Before you make up your mind, why don't I show you around, let you see the systems you'll be dealing with?"

The knots in my stomach eased a little. Maybe he wasn't trying to distract me with cash after all. "I'd like to know more about the chip too."

He nodded. "Do you have concerns?"

I hesitated. How did you say "I don't like the idea of fusing a virtual remote control to my nervous system" to the man who'd helped pioneer the tech? Nat kept telling me chips were perfectly safe and I had control issues. She was right, but I couldn't conquer my fears completely. "I don't like first-gen tech."

Damon grinned. "Don't worry. You won't be getting first-gen. Not that the public chips *are* first-gen. But you'll be getting the same chip as me. It's not publicly available yet."

Oh perfect. Experimental next-gen was no better than first-gen.

As if sensing my nerves, Damon came around the desk, rested his butt against the edge, and proffered his wrist for my inspection. I squelched the wimpy voice of protest in my head and instead looked at his forearm.

His nicely tanned, even more nicely muscled, faintly spicy-smelling forearm.

Damn.

I blinked a few times while blood rushed to my head, then sucked in a breath and focused on the chip instead.

It looked almost natural, as though someone had drawn the circuit on his skin.

But skin wasn't supposed to be silver and gold, glinting and gleaming in thin lines between the more natural olive tones. It wasn't supposed to be traced with an intricate dance of circuitry. And a drawing wouldn't shimmer ever so faintly with every beat of his pulse. I wanted to run my finger over the lines, but that would just be weird.

"You'll even get the same surgeon as me. He's the best in the field."

I bit my lip. "I'm sure he's great."

"Touch it if you want."

My hands clenched. Even with permission, touching him didn't sound like a good idea.

"I promise I don't bite." He sounded amused.

The only thing worse than having an inappropriate reaction to someone is having the object of that reaction realize it. I stomped on my objections, wiped my palms on my trousers, and gingerly touched a finger to his wrist.

His skin warmed mine. To my cautious touch, the threads of gold and silver were slightly warmer than the surrounding skin. And beneath them, the flesh felt strange. Not smooth muscle like there was on either side of the circuit but rather nearly imperceptible ridges and crevices, reminding me that thousands of nanofilaments threaded from the chip into the surrounding nerves, giving whatever plugged into that chip direct access to his brain.

I jerked my hand back.

"It's not so bad. I'll even hold your hand if you like," Damon said, grin widening.

Heat crawled over my face as I imagined those long fingers wrapped around mine. Nice picture until you put him in a surgical gown and mask and included a bunch of medical types milling around with scalpels. "Won't I be asleep?"

"No, they just nerve block the arm. You can watch the whole thing."

Blood. I wasn't good with blood.

I swallowed, hard.

"Or not," he added hastily. "They can plug you into an entertainment system and you can watch a movie or read or whatever. You won't notice a thing, I promise."

Somehow I doubted that.

"Can I get you a glass of water or something? You look pale."

"I'm fine."

He ignored me and crossed the room, waving a hand at the wall. A panel slid back, revealing a small fridge. Fancy, as was the bottle of water he brought back to me. The label was written in French. *Water is water, I guess.* I cracked the lid with a twist and swallowed. The chilled fluid seemed to help.

Damon watched me, a slight frown wrinkling his forehead.

I straightened. "I'm fine, I swear." I just didn't like hospitals. Given that my main experience with them had been to get patched up after the few times when Sara's temper got the better of her, visiting the mass morgues to identify Grandad's body after the quake, and then sitting with my Gran as she slowly wasted away from her injuries over months, my feelings were justified. But I was going to have to suck it up.

"Why don't you give me that tour you mentioned?" I said, trying to sound casual. "I can't make up my mind until I know more about what I'm dealing with."

Anything was better than discussing imminent chip surgery. Plus, I had to admit I was curious to see what the inner workings of a place like Righteous were like. All I got to see at most of my clients were the standard gray cubicle tech dungeon IT departments and climate-controlled server and mainframe rooms.

Given most of Righteous was effectively an IT department and people seemed to fight to work there, I was hoping for something a bit more interesting.

Kind of Willy Wonka's Geek Factory.

Though Damon was a lot cuter than any of the actors I'd seen play Willy in Nat's classic movie collection, and definitely cuter than the latest VR version. As good as graphics had gotten, there was still something slightly off about the human figures. Something that creeped me out.

Unlike Damon, who had the opposite effect, much to my chagrin. I seemed to be developing an alarming urge to grin goofily whenever he smiled at me.

No dating the paycheck.

And with that rejoinder fixed firmly in my head, I stood. "So, show me the funhouse."

Chapter Three

To my relief, Damon didn't question my subject change, just rose and led the way back to the elevator.

His palm on the scanner prompted a cool female voice to ask, "Which floor would you like, Damon?"

"S2, Madge."

There was no S2 on the panel of numbers beside the door, but that didn't seem to matter. The doors slid shut and we began to whizz downward.

"Secret passages?" I quipped.

"Not secret. And floors, not passages. Though we do have passages for the lower levels connecting all the buildings. They're the next level down."

"Who's Madge?"

"She's a computer. One of the bits of tech around here that helps make life easier."

I hid my surprise. The voice had sounded completely natural. Voice tech kept getting better and better, but to my ear, usually the voices still sounded just faintly synthetic. Something off about their pronunciation. But Madge had sounded real. A reminder that I definitely wasn't in Kansas anymore.

Our descent ended and the doors slid silently apart, delivering us into a sterile white room. Damon immediately headed for another set of doors on the far side of the room and I followed. The skin on the back of my neck prickled slightly, like I was being watched. I scanned the room discreetly, but I couldn't spot any security cameras.

They had to be there. If this was the heart of Riley Arts R&D, then the security would probably put the Pentagon to shame. Which meant I probably had zero chance of spotting anything.

"You haven't worked with virtual reality systems before, have you?" Damon asked as he put his palm against the scan. The door didn't slide back immediately; instead, he had to submit to an iris scan and speak into the lock before it opened.

Definitely tight security.

I wasn't sure why he was asking. I had no doubts whoever he'd had investigating me had filled him in on every tiny detail of my career. "No. But I don't necessarily have to be familiar with the industry to understand the programming," I pointed out.

Code was code was code.

Sure, function and language varied. And every house that produced its own software had its own quirks and idiosyncrasies. But I'd never met a system I couldn't get along with.

"You've played our games though?"

"Yes. On a CX50 deck, mostly." Nat's home system. Formerly her pride and joy, but she was saving now for the latest generation chip system. I had no desire to try gaming on a chip interface. Good old sensor headsets were fine with me.

"You'll like this, then."

I made a noncommittal noise as we moved down a blank white corridor. I'd never played a game that could entice me to spend the kind of time serious gamers did immersed in an electronic world. But Damon didn't have to know that.

So I held my tongue as we walked. The light was bright,

coming from banks set into the ceiling and high on the walls, and the air didn't have the sterile air-conditioned smell that a lot of office buildings had, but I still knew I was somewhere below the earth. Quite a way.

Since the Big One, I'd never been entirely comfortable with being underground. Intellectually I knew I was probably in more danger out in the open than in a basement, but underground made me feel cornered. Made me think of my granddad and all the other people trapped by the bridges or the countless building collapses.

Made me determined to be cremated and have my ashes scattered to the winds rather than spend all time buried deep in earth.

Here, where I had no doubt no expense had been spared in making the buildings as quake-proof as possible, I still didn't like it.

Or maybe the churn in my stomach was just nerves about what I was getting myself into taking this job.

Damon did the palm/scan/speak combo again when we came to the end of the corridor, and this time the doors slid back to reveal a very different room.

It kind of looked like there'd been a three-way collision between a wizard's cave, a robot factory, and a VR club.

The right-hand wall was a series of huge screens, each fronted by a number of what looked like very expensive recliners but what were in fact very expensive game chairs. I recognized them from all the times Nat had spent drooling over them online.

They had the familiar ports for headset jacks, but also the wrist ports jutting up near the end of the arms for chip connections. I'd never liked wrist ports—they looked too much like expensive manacles, trapping the gamer to the chair—but they didn't seem to bother most people. And I didn't have a chip, so I didn't have to use them.

Three of the chairs were occupied, the screens in front of

them showing what the occupants were seeing. The other screens held static images. None of them seemed much like a game to me. Some of them had no background and figures that looked more like wire skeletons than anything resembling a person. Some had a single element like a rock or a flower or, in one case, a bright blue tabby cat.

"Scenes in development," Damon said. He squinted at one of the screens, where a pink furry blob was bouncing around a forest that looked as though the trees were made of different kinds of candy. "Or they're just goofing around."

I smiled. The detail on the pink furry thing was impressive. Individual tufts of fur waved in different directions with each bounce, and the gleeful expression on its little pink face was seriously cute. I didn't know much about VR and game animation, but the little critter had obviously taken some serious effort. Hardly goofing off.

"Do you want to try a game? See what you're here to help with?"

"One of those?" I nodded at the pink thing.

"No, the game in question."

My brows shot up. "The one that's maybe sending people crazy?"

"Ah, no. A slightly earlier version. One these folks have been working on for months with no side effects." He stopped as a guy wearing fishing waders and a green-and-yellow plaid shirt zoomed by on hoverblades. "Well, none outside the usual game designer nuttiness, at least."

He looked almost indulgent.

Which I definitely preferred to the whole I'm-in-charge vibe he'd been projecting at the club. Damon Riley on his home turf was far more likeable.

And he was offering me a sneak peek at the latest Righteous game. I might not be a total gamefreak like Nat, but I'd have to be a complete Luddite to turn down that chance.

"Okay, I'm game," I said, then winced. "No pun intended."

"I figured," he said with another smile. He waved at a group of guys huddled over a bank of monitors in the middle of the room.

One of them, short and thin with nuclear orange hair that clashed with the purple face paint he wore, bounded over.

"Can we set Maggie here up to look at Archangel?" Damon asked.

"Sure thing."

Before I had a chance to change my mind, he and Damon bundled me over to one of the vacant recliners and made me sit.

"You know how to use this?" Purple boy passed me the headset after a quick glance at my chipless wrist. He pressed a button and the wrist port sank into the arm of the chair, out of sight.

I nodded. "I think I've got it."

"Let me," Damon said and lifted the headset out of my hands. "Lie back."

I obeyed, and he smoothed the contact filaments across my forehead and onto my temples before lowering the lenses over my eyes.

I tried to ignore the fact that his touch made my pulse bump.

"Thanks," I managed as he smoothed another set of filaments over the backs of each of my hands.

"Put your left hand on the armrest," Damon instructed. "Standard button config. The big one's your quick release."

The virtual reality equivalent of a safe word. I nodded, letting my vision adjust to the soothing swirling patterns projected on the lenses.

"Otherwise, move—or think of moving—and the avatar moves with you."

"I have done this before," I said.

"Not quite like this." He sounded smug. "Ready?"

I nodded and the swirling patterns vanished, leaving me standing on the banks of a river in fading light. The rapid transition made me jump. The other games I'd played had eased in more slowly.

The river was high and flowing fast. The far side of the bank was lined with impenetrable trees, dark and somehow menacing.

I turned slowly, getting my bearings. Behind me stood a sparser row of smaller trees, not nearly as intimidating. I could even see a faint path, as though I'd broken my way through the undergrowth to reach the river rather than following the banks.

I finished my circle. River. River banks. Trees. That was it. I hadn't spotted anything living. Or rather, anything living and big enough to be a game opponent. Birds flitted above, darting in and out of branches, and the odd bug hummed through the air around me, doing whatever bugs did.

It felt completely real. Apart from the lack of smell.

Smell was the one thing they couldn't do with a headset. Nat had told me the chips gave you scent, but I found it hard to believe.

A breeze rippled the leaves, the air cool against my face. I moved closer to the river, curious to see what body I wore.

The path to the river grew convincingly slick under my feet, and I had to catch my balance once or twice as I almost lost my footing. My avatar wore heavy boots and dark pants made of something thick and ever-so-slightly slippery. Hardly natural. My legs and arms were well muscled but still seemed female.

Archangel, Damon had said. I didn't know whether that was actually the name of the game or whether it was a project code.

The light grew dimmer still, turning purplish gray twilight shades. The birds and bugs were getting quieter, and all around me there was a sense of calm. I started to feel relaxed for the first time all day.

Too relaxed. I took a careless step and suddenly lost my balance completely, windmilling my arms futilely as I tumbled forward in an inelegant sprawl that left me smeared in mud and slightly winded at the water's edge.

I thought of everyone watching me in the outside world and rolled my eyes, biting my tongue to keep from swearing a blue streak in front of my prospective employer.

The embarrassment lasted until I levered myself back onto all fours and leaned toward the water, catching sight of my reflection.

The avatar wore a replica of Avery Bannon.

The perfectly manicured platinum hair, shocking against the dark skin, and extravagant makeup looked so out of place against my surroundings that I started laughing, unable to stop myself.

I sat in the mud and howled helplessly until I started to gasp for breath.

When I finally regained control, I crawled closer to the water and stretched one hand out, curious as to whether virtual water could feel real.

The sudden icy wetness against my fingers shocked me. I jerked my hand back, felt the water run down my palm, then dipped it back in, unable to resist.

Again, the sensation was uncannily real. This was better than any VR I'd ever tried. If this was the next generation in games, Righteous had made a breakthrough that was going to make Damon Riley whatever the next level up from gazillionaire was.

Fascinated, I kept swirling my hand, chasing the sparkles of light caused by the combination of sinking sun and rising moon—no, *moons*—skittering across the surface of the water.

The night hummed around me and I smiled lazily to

myself, watching the deep red curve of Avery's lips mirroring my expression.

"Maaaaaagieeeeee."

The voice broke the stillness. Sibilant. Deep. Disturbing. The hairs on the back of my neck prickled.

I blinked, then swished my hand through the water again to try and slow my body's fight-or-flight response. This was just a game. I knew how to deal with a game opponent.

The water sparkled. I breathed in. Out. In again.

"Maaaaaagieeeeeeeeeee." The voice changed a little. It sounded surprised. Surprised and somehow satisfied. Creepily satisfied.

Around me, the night noises of the game faded, replaced by a muttering sort of droning sound that set my teeth on edge, a noise like something inhuman whispering just out of reach.

This part of the game I didn't like so much.

I started to rise but found myself frozen.

That wasn't right. You should always be able to move in a game, even if it was defying gravity to do so.

I tried to move my left hand, aiming for the dead man switch.

Nothing.

Fear snaked down my spine. Even if the game had glitched somehow, it shouldn't stop me moving in the real world.

Had Damon been wrong about this version of the game?

Was I about to go crazy?

"Maaaaaagieeeeeeeeeeee. Maaaaaagieeeeeeee miiiiiiii-innnnnnnne." It was louder now. Louder and darker and edged with the drone I'd heard earlier. Like a swarm of metallic bees, all humming at exactly the wrong frequency.

I tried to stand again, but my reflection stayed frozen, lips parted, eyes wide.

As I watched, willing myself to move, the reflection began to morph. Turned darker, wider. Inhuman somehow.

Glowing eyes—some color beyond red, beyond flames, beyond any human shade—widened and then focused on me.

"I see you, Maggie." The mouth moved in a horribly fleshy way, as though it wasn't designed for speaking English. "Where is this place?" The head swiveled from side to side, the movement almost mechanical, like it was scanning rather than seeing.

"Ah. Now I see. A human thing."

The eyes snapped back to me and pain seared in my head, like they were burning into me.

Wrong. All wrong.

I needed to move. To run.

To get away before those eyes consumed me utterly.

My muscles stayed motionless, so I did the only thing I could. I screamed as the reflection seemed to rise from the water and swoop toward me.

Everything turned black.

Then almost immediately went white as someone pulled the headset free, yanking out several hairs with it. Pain ripped through my skull—not like in the game, but enough to make me gasp.

"Maggie."

Damon's voice. I couldn't help a reflexive shudder at the sound of my name, as if I could still hear the weird buzzing.

"Maggie, open your eyes."

I obeyed, though my head responded with another throb of fire and I immediately squeezed them shut again.

"Get the doctor," Damon ordered. "Fast."

The last word was too loud and I winced.

"What happened?" I asked, keeping my voice soft.

"Your vitals spiked above the safety level, so we yanked you out of there. You tell me."

"There was . . ." I paused, trying to remember. But it was

all blurring in my head. Water? Then pain and a strange noise and . . . it slipped away, fading like mist. "There was a noise. Buzzing maybe? Then I couldn't move."

"Sounds like VR disorientation." A different voice.

I cracked my eyes open again. It was the purple-haired guy who'd helped hook me up. "VR what?"

"Wait until the doctor gets here," Damon told me. He was crouched by the chair. "Don't talk."

"Doc's here now," Purple Hair said, jerking his head at something behind me.

I wanted to turn to look but didn't want to risk setting off another round of hot pokers in my head. "That was fast."

"We have a clinic here," Damon replied. He rose as a woman with short dark hair came up beside him. "Ellen. Thanks for coming."

"What happened?" Cool fingers grasped my wrist, checking my pulse. The woman's brown eyes were focused but calm.

"She got the wobbles," Purple Hair offered.

"I what?" I asked.

"The wobbles. VR disorientation, that's what we call it."

The doctor turned her head to look at him briefly, brows lifting. "Benji, how about you let me do the diagnosis?" She turned back to me. "Can you open your eyes, Ms. . . .?"

"Lachlan," Damon filled the gap.

"Ms. Lachlan. How do you feel?"

"A bit queasy," I admitted. "My head hurts." I winced as the doctor pulled out a small torch and directed the light into my eyes.

"You felt all right before entering the game?" She pulled out a medical scanner and skimmed me.

"Yes."

"No recent illnesses?"

"No."

The scanner beeped and she glanced at the screen, then

nodded once. "Everything checks out as normal. I think Benji was right. You got the wobbles."

"Can someone explain what that is?"

"VR disorientation," Benji said.

"I got that much. What does that mean? I've gamed before but I've never heard of it."

Damon blew out a breath. "Doesn't matter if you've played before. Sometimes the wobbles just kick in. Basically, with some people, or even just some scenarios, the brain doesn't want to accept the illusion, so it kicks in a reaction to break the spell, usually by flooding your system with adrenaline. People hear strange things or see strange things and generally hit the panic button. But you didn't do that."

"I—I don't remember."

The doctor made a soothing noise. "It's okay, Ms. Lachlan. It's normal to feel, well, disoriented. It's kind of like fainting."

"I never faint," I said.

"I'm going to give you a dose of vitamins and something to counteract the adrenaline surge. And a painkiller for the headache. You need to make sure you drink lots of water today, and eat something soon."

"Thank you." Taking the headache away sounded like a wonderful idea. The doctor pressed a hypo against my wrist, the icy kiss of the spray almost shocking.

"There."

"Thank you," I repeated. "Doctor . . .?"

"Chen. Ellen Chen."

The cool sensation traveled up my arm, and my headache started to back off almost immediately. I rubbed my wrist lightly to chase away the chill, then froze as something occurred to me. "Will this happen again? Does it affect my ability to have a chip?"

Dr. Chen pursed her lips. "You say you've gamed before, yes?"

I nodded.

"No side effects previously?"

"Other than eating way too much junk during an all-night session, no."

Her lips curved. "Then you should be fine. The chip surgeon will do a full work-up anyway. They'll pick up any contraindications."

"And you'll be working in the code mainly, not playing the games," Damon added.

"Plus some people only get the wobbles the first time," Benji chimed in. "It's like getting your sea legs."

I hoped he was right, because wobbles aside, after seeing that game—no, make that *experiencing* that game-even such a tiny snippet, my geek side was salivating at the thought of working with the code that made it all happen.

I wanted in.

No matter what the risks were.

"Does this mean you're taking the job?" Damon asked.

I nodded and was happy that the movement didn't hurt my head at all. "Yes. Yes, I am."

"In that case, we'd better go back to my office," he said. "There are a couple more conditions I need to discuss with you."

Chapter Four

Cat was waiting for us outside Damon's office. "The food is inside. And your messages are on your screen."

"Thanks, Cat." He held the door open.

"Food?" I asked.

He nodded and ushered me in. "Ellen said you should eat something."

So she had. But I doubt she'd envisioned the small mountain of food that waited for us inside. Nor did I know when exactly Damon had the time to request it, because he hadn't left my side since the doctor had examined me. Maybe Dr. Chen had contacted Cat?

I eyed the groaning table. Platters of sandwiches, sushi, cold cuts, fruit, and a cheese board were crowded in with donuts and pastries and bowls of chips and pretzels. Aligned along one end were several bottles of water, a pitcher of orange juice, and one of what looked like iced tea. On the other end there was an actual teapot—china, the kind Gran used. The steam wafting up from it had a familiar scent.

I hadn't pictured Damon Riley as an Earl Grey enthusiast.

"How many people are you expecting?"

"I didn't know what you'd feel like. The leftovers can go

back to the kitchens. They'll use them in one of the cafeterias."

"One of? How many are there?"

"Four," he said. "Plus snacks-only kiosks in each building."

"The Riley army marches on its stomach, I gather."

I took a seat, gazing at the food. Despite the good doctor's recommendation, I wasn't sure I could actually stomach eating anything. In fact, now that whatever she had given me was really kicking in, what I mostly felt was sleepy.

I reached for the jug of orange juice, figuring if I could keep that down, I could risk eating something.

Damon waited until I'd poured myself a glass, then poured himself iced tea.

I sipped cautiously. Luckily my stomach didn't rebel. In fact, the tart flavor and sugar had the opposite effect and I suddenly wanted to devour everything on the table.

"You said something about conditions?" I reached for half a Reuben.

"After you eat." He pointed at my plate.

I waved the sandwich. "I'm not going to faint or anything. I'm a big girl."

"Tough talk from someone who passed out less than an hour ago. Eat. You still look pale."

"I'm always pale. Blame my Irish ancestors." At least the ancestors I knew about were Irish. Sara had the full package: red hair, milky skin, and green eyes. I got her eyes, but my skin was just pale rather than glowing cream, and my hair was medium brown and half-assed wavy. Sara had always been amused by the fact that she looked like a fairy-tale version of a witch disguised to lure men to their doom. Truth in advertising, she'd called it.

I was normal. So maybe it was just as well I looked it.

"Maybe so. You still need to eat. I'm not going to be the one who has to explain to Ellen why you didn't follow orders." He grabbed a donut, studied it, then shrugged and took a bite.

Setting a good example perhaps. Or just making it clear that I wouldn't be getting anything else out of him until I'd obeyed orders and eaten something.

Either way, it would be quicker not to argue. I turned my attention to my plate and obediently worked my way through the sandwich. It wasn't difficult. The food was wonderful. I stopped after the other half of the Reuben and a handful of potato chips. No point pushing it.

"Satisfied?" I asked, pushing my plate away.

Damon nodded, blue eyes steady on my face. He hadn't said a word while I ate. "You look better."

I felt better. Less shaky. I smoothed a hand over my hair, trying to see if the headset had mussed it, then wondered why I cared how I looked in front of him. "Good. Then let's talk business. What are your conditions?"

"You've seen the game now. Or part of it."

"Yes." Tension fluttered through my stomach. I didn't remember exactly what had happened in the game, but my body knew the ending hadn't been good. Before that though, it had been astonishing.

"What did you think?"

No point lying. "It was amazing. I've never seen—or felt—anything that realistic before."

Satisfaction warmed his expression. "Yes. This is the future for gaming. I need it to work. I need you to help find out if there's a problem. And I need for there to be no leaks."

Maybe the drugs were making me fuzzy. None of this was exactly news. "I already signed your confidentiality agreement. I'm not in the habit of revealing information about my clients." I wouldn't have many clients if I did.

"Yes. But I need more than that," he said.

"Like what?"

"I need you to stay here."

"Excuse me?"

"While you're working on this, I want you to stay at Riley

Arts. I don't want you going anywhere without me knowing about it."

I blinked. "Stay here?" I repeated blankly. "Stay where, exactly?"

"We have accommodation for visitors or staff who need to work crazy hours occasionally. The rooms are very comfortable."

Sure they were. And probably monitored to the eyeballs. The thought of Damon knowing everything I did was not appealing.

I toyed with my napkin, stalling so I could figure out how to say "not going to happen" without losing the job. "I have a roommate. I have a life. I can't just drop off the face of the earth for a few weeks."

"I'm not asking you to. I'm just asking you to tell them that you have an assignment out of the city." He smiled suddenly. "Tell them New Zealand, even."

"Won't they get suspicious if I don't come back with pictures of . . . ." I paused, trying to remember anything about the country. I knew it was a hub for the special effects industry and had earthquakes, but anything else was coming up blank. "You know, New Zealand stuff?"

"I can provide pictures. And souvenirs, if necessary. And we can fool any comm systems into thinking you're in New Zealand too."

"Isn't this a little extreme?" Extreme was diplomatic. It was completely paranoid.

"We have a lot riding on this."

"I understand that, believe me, but you can trust me. If you hire me, then I'll comply with whatever security measures you want, but I'm not going to give up my entire life for a job."

"It wouldn't be for that long."

"How do you know?" I countered. I could only imagine how many miles of code were involved in producing an illusion as realistic as the one I'd just been shown. This wasn't your standard assignment.

"It'll be more convenient if you're working long hours."

"Maybe. And I'll be happy to accept a room for any nights where that's the reality, but I'm not going to agree to live here. You either trust me or you don't. If you don't, then I'm sorry, but you've wasted your time today."

His mouth twisted. "I—"

I held up a hand. "Take it or leave it. I'll sign in and out. You can scan me. I won't take anything off the premises. Whatever you like. But I'm not going to sign my life over to you."

I could almost see him ticking off mental pros and cons as he watched me. Or maybe he was trying to come up with another angle. If he was, he was wasting his time. I wasn't going to let him virtually lock me away. I'd spent my childhood under my mother's control. Since I'd been free of her, I'd made sure I did things on my own terms.

Even when sticking to my own terms sometimes meant shooting myself in the foot professionally or personally.

Fortunately Damon decided not to push it. "You'd better be worth the money," he muttered eventually.

"I'll do my best," I said. " I'm told that's pretty good."

His eyes went a deeper shade of blue for a second. "Confidence. I like that in an employee—"

"Contractor," I corrected.

"Consultant," he amended smoothly. "A consultant who needs a chip to do her job. Let's take care of that first, and then we can discuss the security requirements in more detail."

By the time I left Righteous—after several hours of wrangling with Damon about how to do my job, the completion of my aborted tour of the facilities, and my introduction to most of the programmers I'd be working with—my brain was overstuffed with new information.

I had an appointment for chip surgery on Friday morning and a lingering feeling that I was going to have to either kiss or kill Damon Riley before the assignment was over. The man was bad for my peace of mind.

But maybe that effect would lessen with prolonged exposure.

My trip back to SoMa didn't take too long. It wasn't really a long way from the edges of the former Financial District where Righteous had built their campus. But Damon had insisted on calling a driver to take me home anyway.

The luxurious ride didn't distract me from the day. It just gave me time to think. And, apparently, time to get hungry all over again. Food. Then sleep. That was about all I could deal with tonight. I'd worry about rearranging my life for this new assignment in the morning.

Luckily, Nat was cooking. She almost always did when we were both home. I didn't mind doing the dishes, and she got sick of my variations on chicken in a wok with veggies. It was about the one decent dish I knew how to cook from scratch. Sara never bothered to teach me anything beyond nuking or pouring boiling water in packets, and I guess Gran figured I was a lost cause by the time I got to her.

I'd learned the wok thing in a Chinese cooking class Nat had dragged me to once. Once was enough. So she cooked, I cleaned up. It worked for us.

When I opened the front door to the apartment, the air was already fragrant with garlic and herbs and other good things. Nat had her favorite vintage Sinatra playing full blast. For a techno geek, she had distinctly low-tech tastes in music. Her heart belonged way back in the twentieth century.

I hit the volume button on the house comp panel near the door and the blare dimmed to a pleasant level. It took about five seconds for Nat to emerge from the kitchen, drying her hands on a blue-and-white checked dishcloth.

"Hey, you're home early. How were the salt mines today?" She flapped the cloth in my direction with a grin.

"Good." I dumped my bag on my favorite chair, hiding a smile. I hadn't told Nat about meeting Riley at Decker's yet—trying to avoid the inevitable "are you crazy?" I'd have received if I'd turn down the job. But now that I'd taken it, I was bursting to tell someone the small amount I was allowed to tell. And Nat, more than anyone else in my life, would appreciate what a coup this job was. "Got a new client."

"Anyone interesting?" She dropped the cloth on a side table, picked up the bottle of wine—a nice Napa red—sitting on the dining table, and poured a glass.

"Nah, just Damon Riley." I had timed it perfectly. She spat the mouthful of wine back into her glass as her eyes went huge.

"Damon Riley? Seriously? Shit, how did that happen?" she managed when she'd stopped gaping at me.

I rescued the wineglass, which was tilting at a dangerous angle. "It seems squillionaires can use search engines just like mere mortals." Given I had no idea who had actually recommended me to Damon, it was as good a story as any.

Nat's eyes were still wide and shocked. Then she suddenly grinned. "This is too great." She grabbed the cloth and mopped the few drops of wine that hadn't quite made it back into her glass off her tee shirt. It was old and black and advertised a band long consigned to history. "What did he want?"

"I could tell you, but you'd just tell everyone you know, and then I'd have to beat you up."

She looked hurt. "What, you think I can't keep a secret?"

"I know you can't, so don't bother arguing." I loved her, but Nat was never going to land a job at a Swiss bank or the FBI or really anywhere that required discretion and confidentiality. Lucky for her she had a trust fund that meant she didn't have to worry about earning a salary from the kind of company where that mattered. I'd chosen to tell her about Riley because she was my best friend, but I wasn't going to breach the agreement I'd signed.

She pouted some more, sipping wine in silence. I headed to my room to change into jeans and a college tee almost as elderly as Nat's. When I reemerged, she had finished the wine and was pouring another.

"Want some?" she asked. I took that to mean she'd decided to stop sulking, for now at least. There was no doubt she would try to pump me for information about her idol at some point.

I shook my head. "It's been a long day." I wasn't sure whether alcohol was a good idea on top of whatever it was that Dr. Chen had dosed me with. Aiming for a subject change, I sniffed the air. "What smells so good?"

"Dinner. Shit." She jumped up from the couch and rushed for the kitchen. Various clatters and thuds made me hopeful that she'd rescued whatever it was from a near-death experience. I should've saved the news about Riley until after our food was safely on the table.

I walked into the kitchen and grabbed a soda from the fridge. "Can I help with anything?"

Nat eyed the can in my hand with distaste. "You can set the table. And stop drinking that crap."

"Stop being the food police. I like it, and I need the syncaf. Like I said, long day." I popped the top and took a long swig, just to annoy her. Sometimes I wondered how I managed to end up living with the only health-freak geek on the planet. All Nat's friends seemed to live on soda and chips. Throw in some chocolate and I could relate to that as a dietary plan.

But not Nat. The sight of her munching on carrot sticks and tofu spread, plugged into her console in the middle of a sea of junk food–eating gamer buddies, had to be seen to be believed.

"Don't blame me when you can't sleep tonight. Or whine when we work out in the morning."

I stuck out my tongue and saluted. With Nat nagging me, I actually managed to stay mostly in shape despite what she regarded as horrendous eating habits.

Nat menaced me with a wooden spoon. "Can the attitude and make with the silverware. Dinner will only be a couple more minutes."

I obeyed. I was hungry.

An hour later, I lay on the sofa, stuffed with pasta and cake and happy in the knowledge that it had all been relatively good for me. Nat could've earned a fortune as a chef at one of the many spas that operated around town to cater to the rich and weak-willed. Of course, she would have to work regular hours and give up some precious gaming time, which explained why I was still the main beneficiary of her culinary skills.

"So can you at least tell me what he's like?" Nat said from her perch on the arm of the chair nearest me.

I smiled. I'd been about right in my estimation of how long Nat would be able to contain her curiosity—which was not that long at all. I scooted up on the sofa until I was semi-upright, propped on a pile of cushions.

"He looks like he does in photos." I half closed my eyes, trying to pull together my jumbled impressions of Damon Riley.

"That tells me nothing. What else?"

"He's . . . ." I searched for the right word. "Kind of intense. Focused." Drop-dead sexy was what I wanted to say. But I'd never hear the end of that. "A take-no-prisoners type. Focused on what he wants. I don't know what else to say."

"And you're not going to tell me what this is about?"

I shook my head, suddenly glad of Damon's draconian security arrangements, insisting I only work at the Righteous campus. Nat was a tech-head, after all. And I wouldn't totally put it past her to succumb to temptation and snoop a little if she thought I had info about Riley Arts on our home system.

She flashed her best "I'm cute and your best friend" smile at me "Not even—"

"No. Think of it this way. Suppose I told you what was going on. Suppose you, for some unimaginable reason, happened to tell someone else. And then Riley finds out. What do you think would happen?"

Nat opened her mouth to protest, but I continued. "I'd get fired, that's what. And we'd be lucky if firing was all he did. Believe me, the NDA I signed was not messing around."

Nat looked mutinous. Obviously I hadn't made the consequences dire enough. I permitted myself some poetic license. "Now, also suppose that he worked out exactly who I told and who had spread the information. And you end up banned from Righteous games."

I grinned as her expression turned thoughtful. "Or"—my mind was working overtime now—"Riley is beyond seriously pissed off and develops the next console and all the other consoles after it so it recognizes Natalia Marcos brain waves or whatever and they just won't work for you. No more gaming. *Ever.*"

"He couldn't do that," Nat said with a frown.

"Couldn't he?" I shrugged one shoulder, tried to look serious. "I guess you would know better than me. But think about it. Do you want to take that risk?"

She slid backward into the chair, legs dangling over the arm, looking more alarmed than thoughtful.

Good. She believed me. Or at least a part of her did. Enough to worry her. Hopefully the specter of a life ban from gaming would be enough to keep her off my back.

"Noooo," she said at last.

"Then we have an understanding?"

"Yes. Fine. I'll leave you alone. Doesn't mean I have to like it though."

"No telling your friends who my client is either," I warned.

Her head slumped against the chair. "Man, you really are no fun."

"So you keep telling me. I can tell you one thing."

Nat straightened, face eager. "Yes?"

"He's springing for chip surgery." The thought made my stomach twist, and I suddenly regretted the second piece of cake.

"Really? About time."

Nat had been trying to talk me into a chip ever since she got hers. "I haven't needed one until now," I said a little defensively.

"Everybody needs one. They're going to drive everything soon. We'll just have to think at things and they'll turn on or off or whatever."

"Yeah, there's no way that can go wrong. And it's not like saying 'TV on' takes very long."

In response to my command, the wall screen turned on in the background. It was, as usual, showing a game-streaming channel. One of Nat's favorites. She swung her legs down, leaning forward to watch. "Oooh, this should be good."

Apparently the chip discussion was shelved for now. Good.

I pushed myself off the sofa. "I'm going to get a glass of water and turn in. Do you want anything?"

Nat slanted her eyes at me but quickly focused back on the screen. "Don't forget the dishes."

I groaned.

"Make sure you load them—"

"I know, I know." I didn't want a lecture. The other side of Nat the health geek was Nat the enviro-conscious geek. Most of the world had wised up and tightened their environmental regulations after the bad years where temperature spikes and quakes and rising seas rewrote landscapes and most people did their bit to help halt the damage but Nat took it to the next level. Maybe she was making up for the industrial rape and pillage her family had indulged in for the last century or so. Didn't stop her enjoying the family fortunes earned from said pillaging though.

At least I didn't have to wash dishes by hand. The latest appliances were all so energy efficient and water efficient that they beat the old-school way by a mile. But I still had to scrape every last scrap into the recycler and stack the dishes according to Nat's overly strict system.

"Hey," she said as I headed for the kitchen.

I turned back. "Yes."

"Do you think you can find out if Righteous needs any beta testers?"

My heart sank. I should've anticipated this. It was inevitable that Nat would want to use any hint of an inside connection she had if it meant getting her hands on a Righteous game early.

And I couldn't explain to her why being a tester for them might not be such a good idea right now without giving away what I was working on. "I did mention the huge scary confidentiality agreement, right? You sure you want to sign up for something like that?"

"Are you kidding? I'd get to play the games before anyone else."

"I'm only a contractor. It's not like I have any pull."

"Please, Mags. Please. Just ask."

"We'll see," I said, knowing she'd nag for hours if I didn't agree. "Let me settle in for a few days first."

Chapter Five

"Not big on hospitals, are you?"

The harsh bite of the antiseptic staining my arm stung my nose as I breathed deep, trying to slow my racing pulse. "What makes you say that?"

Damon looked concerned. "You're approximately the same color as that gown you're wearing. It'll be fine, Maggie."

"Easy for you to say."

"Want me to ask the doc to put you under?"

I shook my head, avoiding looking at the doctor swabbing my wrist. The thought of being unconscious while he implanted my chip was somehow worse than being awake for it.

"Want to hold my hand?" Damon wiggled long fingers in front of my face.

Yes. But I wasn't going to.

I took another breath and tried to think of anything but hospitals. It would all be over soon. The doctor had promised chip surgery was fast.

Apparently not fast enough for my dumb nerves. The temptation to reach out for Damon's hand rose with each heavy thump of my pulse. Me and my stupid business ethics.

"Why are you here again?" I asked. On my own, I could've been a sniveling wimp about the whole thing.

One side of his mouth quirked. "Protecting my investment."

"Don't you have lackeys for that?" I gritted my teeth as the doctor pressed a hypospray to my left shoulder, pretending it was the cold of the local hitting my skin making me shiver.

"Just two more," the doctor said. The hypospray took up a new position at my elbow and I shivered again.

"Maggie, look at me," Damon said.

His voice was strong and soothing. I let myself look into his eyes as the chill from my elbow radiated up to meet the chill spreading down from my shoulder and then spread down toward my hand. I imagined the flesh turning blue. Blue like Damon's eyes. Only that was a warm blue.

"If you're not going to hold my hand, then I'm going to have to do something drastic," Damon continued.

My teeth chattered a little as the hypo hit again at my wrist. "Like what?"

"Shadow puppets," he deadpanned, making bunny ears with his fingers.

My heart thumped. Damon Riley making shadow puppets on the wall to distract me from chip surgery. It would be nice to lean on all that strength, but standing on my own two feet was pretty deeply ingrained. "Is that the best you can do?"

His dimples flashed. "Tough audience, huh? Well, I'm just getting started. Watch this."

True to the doctor's word, the surgery went smoothly.

Damon made truly terrible shadow puppets until I relaxed, then distracted me with tech talk while the surgeon did his thing. Somewhere along the line, Damon's fingers closed around my other hand, and I pretended not to notice.

"All done," Dr. Barnard said sooner than I'd expected.

I turned my head to the left as the nurse lifted the drape they'd placed between me and my arm so I couldn't see the actual operation. There it was. A chip. My own little gold and silver spider web spread over my wrist, looking like it had always been there. Weird. Even weirder when I couldn't feel a thing in my arm, so none of it seemed to belong to me at all.

They reversed the nerve blocks, ran some tests, and pronounced me free to go when everything seemed to be working as it should.

"You need to rest the arm," Dr. Barnard said, carefully smoothing the edges of a clear surgical shield over the chip with cool fingers. "No using the chip. The nerves need to adjust. So take the meds and take it easy. The shield will last at least five days, so I expect to see it intact when you come back on Monday for your final diagnostics."

Obviously he was used to eager game-heads who couldn't wait to try out their new toy. Not me. For once, I was more than happy to follow instructions.

"I told you it wasn't so bad," Damon said once we were tucked into the back of his limo and gliding through the streets to SoMa. He had an actual driver. Interesting. Self-driving cars had lost popularity here after the quake—due to a number of them not reacting to quake damage fast enough and plunging their occupants to their deaths down fissures and off bridges —but they were slowly making a comeback. I used them occasionally but stuck to the cab and ride companies that included a driver in the front seat to override in an emergency. I wondered if Damon shared my doubts or whether the driver was some sort of status symbol.

Not the kind of question I felt comfortable asking.

"I guess we'll find out on Monday," I said, determined not

to say, "Yes, Damon, you were right." My new theory was that the only way to deal with him and his unsettling effect on my nerves was to try and keep him a little off-balance. Not play into the whole lord-of-all-he-surveyed thing he had going on.

How the theory would work in practice remained, like the success of my surgery, to be seen.

I stared down at the chip, wondering if it was the slightly blurry view through the shield or mental whiplash that made it seem not quite real. Or the fact that whatever drugs the doc had given me were first-class. Apart from the odd sensation that my wrist didn't quite belong to me, I wouldn't have known I'd had surgery. I was strangely energized, like the chip was sending an extra current of electricity through my nerves. None of the drowsiness I'd been warned to expect. It seemed I wouldn't be catching up on my sleep after all.

"It will be fine," he said, pulling out his datapad. "We've never had a chip implantation go wrong." He started scrolling through messages and typing his responses. His hands looked strong and capable as his fingers danced.

I curled my right hand into a ball, remembering the warmth of those fingers on mine, and made myself look away. Time to admire the scenery out the window before my brain placed him permanently into the role of the all-too-appealing white knight.

"You don't need to get out," I said when the driver slid the limo effortlessly into a parking stack near my building. "I can make it up the stairs." In fact, I felt like I could run up them. Maybe I could convince Nat that we needed a workout. Then I remembered the doctor's orders to take it easy and blew out a breath. I was going to have to spend the next few days camped out at home, being sensible. Not a pleasing prospect if I was going to feel like this the whole time.

"It's no trouble," Damon said. His tone had a strong hint of "don't argue."

I rolled my eyes at him as the driver opened my door. "It's

two o'clock on a Friday afternoon, and this neighborhood is perfectly safe. Don't you have, you know, business to attend to?" A guy like him didn't just have a spare few hours in his schedule with short notice. He had to have canceled important stuff to accompany me to surgery. And there had to be a pile of work waiting for him. As the messages that had kept him busy during the drive here proved.

He shook his head. "Finding out if there's anything wrong with my game is my priority. And right now, that means making sure nothing happens to you. So I'll see you to your door."

I frowned. He just stared back calmly. Then the penny dropped. "You want to check out my security systems or something, don't you?"

He didn't bat an eyelid. "Like I said, I need to be sure nothing is going to happen to you."

"I'm assuming you're not going to leave until I agree?"

"Correct."

I climbed out with an exasperated sigh. "My roommate is home. She's a huge Righteous fan."

He came around the car with a grin. "I'm always happy to meet fans."

"*Huge* fan," I repeated. "Maximum geek. Don't say I didn't warn you."

From the look on Nat's face when I walked into the apartment with Damon in tow I thought she might pass out.

Instead she was just rendered speechless.

"Damon Riley, Natalia Marcos," I said as Nat made fish-face.

"Nice to meet you, Natalia," Damon said with a smile.

"You're . . . you're . . . you're Damon Riley," Nat sputtered.

"He's just here for a minute, Nat. Breathe." I turned to

Damon and pointed to the house comp panel. "If you want to check things out, the system is there."

I crossed the room to where Nat still stood, jaw open, and snapped my fingers in front of her face. "Nat. *Breathe*."

She blinked, blushing, then looked down at the sweaty gym slicks gracing her body and turned pale. "Argh! You could've at least warned me." She bolted from the room.

I turned back to Damon. "If you work quick, you can probably make it out of here before she gets back."

He shrugged, not lifting his eyes from the comp screen. "It's fine. What's the password?"

I crossed over and put my palm on the scanner, then punched in the code. "There. And I'll be resetting that once you've gone."

He nodded. "Of course." His fingers did their dance over the screen, calling up our security specs.

From the bathroom came the sounds of the shower. Obviously Nat had decided just changing wasn't enough. So we had a few minutes.

"I meant it when I said work fast. She'll probably try and hit you up for a testing role."

One blue eye slanted in my direction. "She's been doing well lately. Plays for the Raiders, right?"

I nodded. Of course he'd know her stats. After all, he'd tracked me down at Decker's. "Right."

He shrugged one shoulder. "They're good. So's she."

"Keeping secrets isn't her strong point." I felt obliged to be honest. The last thing I needed was Nat's inability to keep her mouth zipped losing me this job.

"There are different kinds of testers. We can keep things under wraps."

Maybe he'd lock Nat up on the Righteous campus. Which meant I'd probably starve. "I'm just saying, don't do her any favors on my account."

The comp beeped happily as he tapped in another sequence. "I'm not. We've been watching her."

"I'm not sure I want her involved in any of this. Not while there's a problem."

His head snapped up, eyes suddenly laser bright and narrowed straight at me. "You think I'd deliberately put someone at risk?"

"No."

"Then perhaps you'll just need to put the same trust in me that you want me to put in you."

Touché. And crap. I couldn't argue with that one.

Another series of beeps issued from the comp panel, one I'd never heard before. "What did you just do?" I asked, squinting at the screen. Nothing looked different.

"A minor upgrade. Nothing to worry about. I'll send you the documentation."

To quote Nat, "argh."

"Ever heard of asking for permission?"

He grinned. "I prefer asking for forgiveness after the event."

Why didn't that surprise me? "Does anyone ever not give it to you?" I snapped.

"You'd be surprised."

"I'd be shocked." I waved my hand irritably, then sucked in a breath when my arm throbbed. Apparently the doc's excellent drugs were wearing off.

Damon frowned. "You should sit down."

Back to white knight mode. I knew I should resist, but he made it difficult. It couldn't hurt, could it? Just to let someone take care of things for a few minutes?

My arm throbbed in agreement, and I stopped fighting and let him herd me over to the sofa. I still felt wide awake, but the ache in my arm was growing stronger. "Are you almost done?" I asked as he tucked a pillow behind my back and slid another one onto my lap beneath my arm.

"Almost. Take one of these." He fished a tube of pills out of his pocket.

"What are they?"

"Your prescription."

He held the tube closer to my nose and, sure enough, my name was printed on the label in nice neat letters.

I recognized the name of the drug. It was a painkiller but one that came with a side helping of sedatives. Wonderful. Even through the worst of my insomnia, I hated taking sedatives or sleepers. They just made the dreams worse.

"I'll need a glass of water," I said, stalling. Maybe I could palm the pill.

"I'll get it." He looked around, then nodded toward the door that led to the kitchen. "That way?"

Really, he was annoyingly competent and annoyingly nice when he wasn't being annoyingly highhanded. "Yes. Glasses in the cabinet next to the sink."

He disappeared and I leaned back against the cushions, rubbing my arm and hoping he'd get back fast and then leave.

"Is he still here?"

Nat. I opened my eyes reluctantly. "Yes. He's in the kitchen."

She looked like she didn't know whether to be relieved or upset. Her short blonde hair was damp, but otherwise she'd worked a major clothing upgrade in a very short time. "You could've warned me," she said in a softer voice.

"I didn't know he was coming up until we got here," I pointed out in the same low tone. "And yes, surgery went fine, thanks for asking."

She blushed again. "Sorry. It's just . . . he's Damon *Riley*."

"I know. But he's just a guy, Nat. And right now he's my client, so can you pull it together?"

"Pull what together?" Damon asked from the door. He had a glass of water in one hand.

"Dinner," I lied. "Nat was just asking what I felt like eating."

He leaned against the doorframe and did the dimple flash. "Is that an invitation?"

"Can I have my water, please? And no, you can't stay for dinner." I glared at Nat when she nudged my ankle in protest. "It's hours away. Go do tycoon things. I need to rest, remember?"

"Maybe some other time," Nat chimed in. "When Maggie's feeling better."

I doubted there was ever going to be a time when I felt like a nice casual dinner with Damon. At least not with a third wheel along.

"That would be great," Damon said, crossing the room and depositing himself on the arm of my sofa.

Nat's expression went a little star-struck when he smiled at her.

"You play for the Raiders, right?" Damon continued.

I fought the urge to smother myself with a cushion. He was going to offer her a testing job.

"Yes." Nat's voice squeaked. Her cheeks were bright pink. "Yes, we're in Division C, top eight."

"Impressive. What's your preference?"

"Quests, usually."

"Me too. More interesting than just blowing things up."

"Blowing things up sounds strangely appealing right now," I muttered.

Damon passed me the glass. "You can't use the chip for a few days, remember?" he said with an evil grin.

"You're assuming I'd need a chip," I retorted. His smile just widened, and I narrowed my eyes at him.

"That's why I like Righteous's games," Nat said. "They're just . . . more."

Suck up. I grimaced in her direction, hoping she'd cool it.

"Thanks. We try." He reached into his jacket again and

handed Nat a business card. "Maggie said you're interested in being a tester. Call this number and they'll organize for you to take our screening tests. If you pass those, you get an interview. I don't know if we have openings right now, but you can get on the wait list."

"Really?" Nat stared at the card like it was the holy grail. "That would be . . . ."

"Righteous?" I suggested sarcastically.

"*Chill*," Nat breathed, not noticing. "Thank you."

"You still have to pass all our evaluations," Damon said.

I relaxed a little. If Nat still had to earn her way in, then there was some time.

"Of course," Nat said. "But I'm thrilled to have the chance. Thank you."

"You're welcome. Maggie, I'll send a car to pick you up Monday to take you to the clinic for your follow-up. And I'll see you at work after that."

He didn't wait for me to say goodbye, just left. I reached for the pills. I figured between surgery, Damon, and Nat, I'd earned a painkiller or two.

The weekend crawled past. I alternated between sleepy from the painkillers and too alert from the same weird sense that the chip was feeding me additional energy. Nat, despite the fact that she spent most of her time in a Damon-induced daze, wandering around the apartment with a goofy grin, wouldn't hear of me actually doing anything. No, I was to rest and get better so I could do whatever her hero had hired me to do.

So I stayed on the sofa, watching bad movies and trying not to climb the walls. Nat did let me have my datapad but wouldn't let me use it for too long.

"It's the chip I'm supposed to avoid using," I protested after she'd confiscated it for the fourth time. "Not my brain."

"You're supposed to be resting. If you keep this, you'll work."

"I have rested," I said. It was true. I'd slept more over the last few days than I had for weeks, and the nightmares had mostly stayed away. Whatever the pills the doc had provided were, they seemed to work. "Besides, I don't have anything to work *on*. Riley's my only client at the moment, and I haven't started there." Couldn't start until my chip was good to go. I stared down at the surgical shield in frustration. If I hadn't been sure that Nat, Damon, and the surgeon would collectively kick my butt, I would've torn it off by now.

"All the more reason to relax now." Nat grinned at me as she coated her nails with iridescent polish.

"Forgive me if I don't find being held hostage on my couch relaxing," I grumbled.

"Be good, or no chocolate cake for dessert."

"You made cake?" The notion was cheering.

"I will. If you behave yourself."

"Blackmail."

"Absolutely. Now what do you want to watch next?"

She waved at the screen, but instead of neat squares of the program guide, the screen filled with a hissing fuzz of jumbled colors.

Nat swore. "What is up with everything?"

It had been one of those weekends. The lamp in my bedroom had blown not one but two bulbs in a row, our ancient syncaf machine had given up the ghost, and our net link had been temperamental all weekend. Now the screen.

Sara would've said the place needed cleansing. I figured it was just Murphy's law that everything would conspire against me when I was confined to quarters.

"Try rebooting," I suggested.

Nat nodded and picked up her datapad. Luckily, after an initial minute or so of irritated flickering, the screen came back to life. I settled back, hoping for something to distract me.

Monday morning, as advertised, there was a limo waiting out front to take me to my appointment. Less as advertised, Damon was inside.

"What are you doing here?" I asked. The car was already pulling away, so there was no chance to retreat to the safety of the sidewalk.

"Good morning." Damon held out an actual coffee mug. "Latte?"

I took the mug, unable to resist the rich smell wafting from it. Real coffee. "That didn't answer my question." I took another happy sniff, then sipped, trying not to moan as caffeine and sugar flowed over my tongue.

"I'm taking you to the clinic."

"Has anyone ever mentioned you're a control freak?" I muttered as I put the coffee down on the little tray table thingy in front of me and fastened my seat belt.

"I prefer to think of it as concerned for employee welfare."

I picked up the mug again and took another appreciative sip, trying to ignore how well he pulled off the suit jacket, T-shirt, and jeans look. "You escort all your employees to the doctor?"

"No. Just the annoying ones with pretty green eyes."

I choked on my coffee.

Pretty?

He thought my eyes were pretty?

What was I supposed to say to that? And how was I going to ignore him when he was complimenting me? I chose discretion as the better part of valor, pulling out my datapad and pretending to be absorbed by my newslink. The articles might as well have been written in Swahili; the only thing registering with my brain was the fact that this man, the one I was trying desperately not to let my hormones register as hot, thought I had pretty eyes.

It made me even more nervous than the imminent clinic visit.

Like I said, my mother liked her men tall and pretty. And in some ways, I was definitely my mother's daughter. Though I'd had years of carefully controlling that side of my nature, of only letting my libido loose on my terms. Damon Riley wasn't going to be the one to change that. Not if I had anything to say about it.

Dr. Barnard scanned my vitals and proceeded to gently prod my arm. "Any unusual pain?"

"No, I've been fine. My wrist has been sore but less each day."

He clucked his tongue. "Good. That sounds like everything is healing well. Let's test the chip, then."

I held out my arm and he sprayed the shield with something that made it peel away like shed skin. Thin, cool fingers closed around my forearm as he probed my wrist then scanned both the wrist and the chip with two separate scanners. He studied the read-outs in silence, then smiled at me. "That all looks good. You know how to engage it?" He gestured toward the armrest of the chair where the chip dock waited.

"I think so." I laid my arm gingerly against the dock. It connected with a soft click. I bit my lip.

"It'll be fine," Damon said calmly from the other side of the chair. For a moment I wished he'd hold my hand again. Instead, I curled the fingers of my free hand against my sweaty palm.

"Now," Dr. Barnard said, "when I start the simulation, you'll see a yellow door. I want you to think about walking to the door and opening it. Don't move at all. Just think. Your avatar should respond immediately."

I nodded, trying to breathe deeply as my pulse kicked up a notch or two. The hospital smells that immediately filled my nose didn't help.

I closed my eyes and leaned back. *It's all going to be fine. It's all going to be fine.* The voice in my head sounded convincing, but I couldn't stop the nervous hum in my stomach. What if I got the wobbles again? Would I lose the job? Would Damon think I was an idiot?

All you have to do is walk forward and open a damn door, I told myself firmly as the circling thoughts started to sound slightly hysterical.

"Ready?"

I focused on the colors playing inside my eyelids. "Yes." Between one heartbeat and the next, the colors blinked out.

:CONTACT:

A sensation like a cool breeze flowed over me, and then I stood in a small bare room with pale blue walls. The door, just as promised, glowed yellow about fifteen feet away from me. I hoped the color scheme didn't reflect a real room somewhere. The blue I could live with, but the yellow was more radioactive than soothing.

Sun-warmed air brushed my face, carrying the scents of spring and growing things rather than air-conditioning and antiseptic.

Smell. I was smelling something that wasn't real. Damon had said I was getting next-gen, and he'd apparently delivered. I sniffed deeply, but I couldn't smell anything like the hospital no matter how hard I tried.

Impressive.

But I didn't have time to think about how much code went

into fooling your brain into smelling something that wasn't there. I had to complete the test.

The door. Radioactive yellow or not, I had to walk across to it.

Not sure exactly what to do other than what I'd usually do in a game, I imagined myself walking across the room. My avatar moved forward smoothly—or smoothly except for the small stumble when the hyper realistic sensation of walking registered. As far as my brain was concerned, I was walking across the room, carpet squishing gently under my feet.

Doubly impressive.

The quality of the illusion was even better than the game I'd tried. I reached the door and opened it. Just as I stepped through, I thought I heard someone call my name. Faintly, almost on the edge of hearing. But despite the softness, the tone sent a shiver down my back.

:OVERRIDE:

"Maggie."

This time the voice was completely normal, and with that one word, the room vanished and I was staring at the insides of my eyelids again.

"Everything okay?" Damon asked.

I opened my eyes and smiled through a lingering chill. "Yes. That was cool. Everything is so real."

"No wobbles? We called your name twice—"

Relief blew through me. It had been Damon talking to me. And probably just some weird transitional effect that made his voice sound strange. "I feel fine."

"Great." Damon nodded. "Do what you need to, Doc."

Dr. Barnard repeated his tests, told me I could stop taking the painkillers whenever I was ready, told me he'd send me more aftercare instructions, then pronounced me free to go. Damon whisked me back to Riley Arts, and before I had too much time to think, I was down in a cubicle with a couple of the Archangel programmers, getting set up to go code-trawling.

Things started well when I turned on the screen at my desk and it flickered and died.

"Fuck," I muttered under my breath. Jiggling the switch didn't restore the stupid thing to life. Way to make a first impression. Blowing up the equipment always went down well.

I stuck my head out of the cubicle. "My screen's dead," I said to Eli, the youngest of the programmers.

"That's weird. We got new gear a few weeks ago." He came around the low partition separating us and peered at the stubborn blackness of the glass, blond dreads falling across his face. "Let me try."

He did the same jiggle-and-flick routine I'd tried, then fiddled around with some of the buttons on the control panel. No response.

"Must be my magnetic personality," I joked.

Eli grinned, then pushed up the sleeve of his shirt to lay his wrist against the chip link on the desk. "Let me log a job. Then we'll move you to a new station." His face went curiously blank for a few seconds, but then he blinked and the personality was back behind his puppy brown eyes. "There, all done."

We gathered my things and I moved one desk down, holding my breath as I turned the system on. This time everything behaved itself.

Eli flipped open a panel in the cubicle wall and pulled out a lead that ended in a flexible cuff with the familiar chip dock. "You use the desk dock and I'll use this. Then I'll show you how to call up the code."

I nodded and laid my arm against the dock, nerves rising all over again.

"This is a clean copy of the code," Eli said, strapping the

cuff around his wrist. "Dedicated server bank, isolated from the main systems. So we can't screw anything up."

I hadn't intended to screw anything up, but it was nice to know I couldn't. "You guys have been working on this for how long?"

"Couple of weeks. We haven't found anything though. Ready? I'll talk you through it. Close your eyes."

I did as instructed. "What happens if I keep them open?" I asked, suddenly curious.

"You'll see the data like an overlay of whatever you're looking at. It's kind of weird. And it gives most people a mother of a headache pretty fast. Plus it's almost guaranteed you'll fall over if you're standing."

"Eyes closed. Check."

"Okay, I'm starting the log-on sequence."

:CONTACT:

Multicolored flames danced across my vision, coalescing slowly into the Riley Arts logo floating above a keypad.

:GOOD MORNING, MAGGIE DIANA LACHLAN:
:CODE VERIFICATION REQUIRED:

"The system recognizes your chip, but we use our passwords as well. Punch it in."

Eli's real-life voice sounded too loud somehow. My hand flexed involuntarily, but I managed not to reach for the keypad physically. Instead I imagined typing in the sequence I'd been given. Evidently I got it right, because the Riley logo vanished, replaced by a clean white room with a giant screen covering the wall facing us. Neat rows of icons marched across the middle of the space.

Eli kept up a running commentary as he demonstrated each function and started explaining the various parts of the code. So much code. All the code. I'd never really appreciated just how much work went into these games. But the sheer volume was hard to ignore when you knew you were going to have to comb through it line by line.

"Any questions?" Eli shut down the last program and the screen cleared.

"Lots, but I think I've got the basics. Let me poke around a bit, and then I'll have more."

His avatar—pretty much him in real life, except his virtual hair was shorter and a more violent blonde that made me think he hadn't updated the skin for a while—cocked its head. "How does this work exactly? What you do?"

"I see if I can find a problem."

"One a team of us working for weeks hasn't been able to spot?"

Ah, I knew this conversation. Egos. They bruised easily. "Maybe not. But then we have a bigger problem."

"Such as?"

"If it's not the program, then the game can't be released until we figure out what exactly happened to the testers."

His expression changed as my words hit home. "Oh. I see. I'll leave you to it. Good hunting." He made a funny little bow with his hands pressed together, and then the avatar vanished, leaving me staring at the big screen.

Chapter Six

MORE HOURS than I liked later, I arrived home, showered, took something for the headache threatening to devour my brain, and curled up on the sofa in blissful silence. Apparently, all it took to drain my excess energy was a long day of trying to get my head around game code. I felt like I'd been stampeded, dusted off, and then run over by a steamroller. Sleep was irresistible.

I jolted awake about an hour later when Nat charged through the front door, calling my name.

"You're asleep?" she asked, bouncing into the room.

"I was." I pushed myself upright, telling my pounding heart to stand down. It ignored me, and the combination of adrenaline and nap brain was disorienting. I rubbed my forehead with the heel of my hand, trying to reconnect to reality, then regretted it. The headache was still prowling my synapses, though better than it had been. Maybe I needed food.

"What time is it?" My stomach rumbled as though answering the question.

"Nine-ish," Nat chirped, all bounce and enthusiasm as she

circled the room, depositing her bag and checking the comp screen for messages.

Definitely past dinnertime. "You're home late." Late and dressed in what were, for Nat, very conservative clothes. Practically a suit. Where had she been?

"I had an interview. At Righteous."

That snapped me into focus. "For the tester position?" Dumb question. The smile on her face told me all I needed to know.

"Yes." She twirled into the middle of the room. "I find out in a couple of days, but I think it went really well."

My stomach sank. I'd been hoping it would take longer for her to go through the process. Nat working for Righteous could only complicate things. And, despite Damon's reassurances, I wasn't happy about her taking a job as a tester for a company whose testers were currently having bad things happen to them. But it was also a big deal for her, so I just had to ignore complicated for now. "Congrats."

She wrinkled her nose. "You don't sound very happy for me. You haven't sounded very happy about this from the start. What's wrong? Afraid I'll muscle in on you and Damon Cutie-pie Riley?"

Cutie-pie wasn't the term that sprang to mind when I thought of Damon. He was beyond cute. Another realm beyond. I might not want to do anything with that fact, but I couldn't ignore it. "Hardly." Though the thought of Nat batting her eyelids at him did make my teeth grind a little.

"Then what's wrong?"

I tried to unclench my jaw. I couldn't tell her, couldn't warn her about the other testers. I'd signed that damned agreement, and I had to trust that Damon wouldn't let anything happen to her. In fact, I'd make sure he looked out for her. In the meantime, I had to do something to ease the hurt in Nat's eyes. "I'm sorry. I'm just tired. Long day."

Her eyes went to my arm. "Your chip? It's working? Chill."

"Very. But tiring. You wouldn't believe the amount of code I looked at today." Acres of code. Or miles. My head hurt too much to figure out the correct measure.

"Anything interesting?"

"Nothing I can tell you if you want any chance of landing this job."

She pulled a face. "No chill, Mags."

"Tough." I yawned. "What do you say to pizza for dinner? Or did you already eat?"

"I ate. But there's leftovers in the fridge. You shouldn't be eating crap. You just had surgery. You need good food."

"My wrist's all healed." I held it up so she could see. "The doctor said so. So pizza isn't going to hurt."

The expression on Nat's face told me she wasn't convinced by my argument. She headed into the kitchen. "How do you want your tofu?" she yelled back at me.

"Wrapped inside a pizza?"

"Fat chance."

The next morning, I descended to the depths of my cubicle at Righteous only to find a message alert floating on my screen. Damon, requesting my presence in his office.

"I've been summoned," I said to Eli. "Back soon."

I allowed myself a short detour to one of the cafeterias for a syncaf fix. Despite my exhaustion last night, I hadn't slept well. Which was my fault for napping. Napping never helped. My headache had taken another two doses of painkillers to vanquish, and, despite the drugs, it was hard to find a position that didn't make my wrist uncomfortable. Worst of all, every time I'd started to drift off, I'd thought I'd heard someone calling my name and jolted awake again.

"Here I am," I said when Cat ushered me into Damon's office. "What's up?" I tried not to feel happy to see him but couldn't stop the silly teenage glow that warmed my stomach.

He leaned back in his chair and stretched, like he'd already been working for hours already. Maybe he had. His greenish-blue shirt was wrinkled. The rumpled look suited him.

"I wanted a status report," he said.

Irritation zapped my glow as a familiar tension squeezed the muscles up my back. "I sent you one last night. If you want another one, then you have to give me time to do some more work first."

One side of his mouth curled. "Actually, I meant on you. How are you feeling?" He eyed the takeout cup in my hand.

Whoops. Maybe I should have asked for a triple shot. Then I might not have jumped to conclusions. Still, something like the glow returned at his concern, though it was immediately chased by confusion. He'd been there when the doctor had cleared me, so why was he asking how I was? Maybe he wasn't happy with the report I'd sent him.

"All chill," I lied, then drained the last of the syncaf. I needed my wits about me. "No problems."

"Nat told you about her interview?"

She's Nat now? I nodded, pasting on a smile. "She's very excited."

"You're not? My HR manager says she's an excellent candidate."

I nailed him with a look. "That's not exactly what I meant. You have a game that's doing weird things. Why should I be happy that my best friend wants to volunteer to be potential cannon fodder?"

His shoulders squared and he gave me a look as annoyed as mine. "Nothing's going to happen to her. That's why I hired you."

If sheer force of will could guarantee her safety, then he'd be right. Unfortunately, I didn't believe the universe would organize everything so it turned out the way Damon Riley wanted.

"Can't you put off hiring her? Tell her you're all full up until the next game needs testing?" My grip tightened on my takeout cup, squishing it slightly. I hated myself for asking—Nat would kill me if she ever found out.

Damon shook his head. "Truth is we need testers. With things held up, once we sort this problem, we're going to need more of them than ever to complete everything in our usual timeframe."

Damn. I tried to think of another argument. Nothing. "So wait until we've fixed the problem, and then hire her."

"She has to complete our training before she can move onto testing, so she needs to start soon. Now. Don't worry, all the training is done on an earlier version. No one has had any problems after playing it."

Well, I'd tried. But his tone didn't exactly suggest there was any wriggle room. "Was there anything else?"

"Not at the moment. Keep me updated." He reached for a pile of datachips on his desk and slotted one into his screen.

"As soon as I know anything, you'll know," I promised as I stood.

He looked back up at me, eyes serious. "Don't push too hard. You're still healing from the surgery."

"You're not paying me to take it easy."

"No, but I'm not paying you to blow out your interface either."

Blow out my . . . ? I squinted at the tangle of gold and silver embedded in my wrist. "Can that even happen?"

One sharp nod. "So I'm told. We've never had it happen here. Don't be the first."

That was one order I was happy to follow. Now that I had the chip, even though I'd barely scratched the surface of what it could do, I didn't want to blow it up by being stupid.

"Yes, boss." I flicked him a salute and headed back to my cubicle.

"Hey, Maggie." Eli and Benji were hanging out by one of the testing chairs, scarfing bagels spread with something that smelled strongly of onions from a platter balanced on the chair's arm.

I joined them. "Mind if I have one of those?" I needed to line my stomach so I could keep up the caffeine today. And there was no way they could eat all the food still on the platter between them.

"Sure," Eli said.

I reached for a bagel and my chip glinted in the light.

Benji's face lit up. He hadn't seen me yesterday. "You got a chip? Chill." Today his hair was blue and the face paint orange and red. It clashed. "Less wobbles with a chip." He jerked his head toward the chair. "You wanna try it out?"

Tempting. The game had been pretty damn good without a chip, so it would have to be amazing with one. But then I remembered the wobbles, my head twinging in pained recollection. And I remembered Damon's warning not to overdo things. "I think I'd better leave it a few more days."

Benji shrugged. "Best to get back on the horse when you take a header."

"Only if you need to keep riding," I shot back. "I don't really game much."

Eli actually dropped his bagel. Both of them stared at me like I'd just uttered something blasphemous.

Benji recovered first, blue hair flying around his face as he shook his head sadly. "Snap, Eli. We gotta work on her. She needs to learn the ride."

Eli nodded. "True. But she's right. Fix the horse first. Then we can worry about her piloting. Slick her right down."

Gamer jargon. Just what I didn't need.

"Eli's right," I said, hoping to kill the conversation. "So if you'll excuse me, I have a bug to hunt."

"Gonna need a very small swat," Benji muttered. "We've been looking hard."

I gave him my best pacifying smile. "I know. You guys do good work. It might not be a bug, per se."

"Then what?"

"I'll know that when I see it." I picked up my bagel and carried it back to my work station. Once I was settled, I clicked my chip into place on the dock.

:CONTACT:

I tried not to feel too relieved as Eli and Benji went away and nice straightforward code flowed up to surround me.

By midmorning, my headache started to creep back, an ever-tightening band of iron clamping my head from temple to temple. I decided another hit of caffeine—particularly when Eli had mentioned that some of the bigger cafeterias had real coffee—couldn't hurt.

But when I found the place, I spotted Nat at one of the tables talking to a guy just as cute and blond as she was. *Damn.* If she was back so quickly, they must've already offered her a test slot.

I pasted a smile on my face as I reached their table. "Do you come here often?" I said, hoping a joke would cover my lack of enthusiasm.

Nat's answering beam made me feel like a rat—a bona fide plague-carrying rat.

"I will be from now on," she said proudly. "Maggie, this is Ajax. He heads one of the testing teams. *My* team." She beamed. "Ajax, this is Maggie. She's consulting here on some secret project for your boss."

I held out my hand. "Nice to meet you."

His handshake was strong. "You too. You're working on the wings issue?" He tilted his head at Nat slightly.

Wings. Right. Angels, as in Archangel. I guess as a head tester, he would know about the problems. But I wasn't going to confirm or deny without Damon's approval. "I could tell you, but then I'd have to kill you."

Nat snorted. "Sheesh. He works here, Mags."

I shrugged an apology.

Ajax smiled. "The D-man got your signature on one of those NDAs, huh?"

I nodded, then slanted a grin at Nat. "Have you signed one yet?"

"I'm doing paperwork with HR next," Nat said. "They wanted Ajax to give me a tour before I start my training."

"You survived the experience, I see. She didn't start drooling over the gear or anything, did she?" I eyed Ajax with consideration. Knowing Nat, the gaming rigs weren't the only things at risk of being drooled on.

Nat blushed. "Maggie!"

Aha. Score one for me. She definitely thought Ajax was cute. Nat was kickass in VR but tended toward stumbly around real-life guys she had the hots for. This could be entertaining.

"No more than usual for a newbie," Ajax said with a smile that suggested he thought Nat was pretty chill herself. "Only minor flooding."

I laughed. "I was headed to the coffee bar. Can I get you guys anything?"

Ajax looked at his watch. "I have a meeting. But, Nat, you have time to hang here with Maggie. You can find your way back to HR, right?"

I watched Nat look from me to him. Then she shook her head. "I'm not sure. Is it on your way?"

He looked pleased. "Sure."

"Rain check?" Nat said to me with a tiny smile. I got her "sorry, I'm going with the hottie" message pretty clearly. After sixteen years of friendship, we didn't need the words.

I tried not to smirk as I waved her after Ajax.

The coffee loosened my headache a bit. Enough that I could contemplate looking at a screen again without wincing at least. I returned to my cubicle, where I spent another frustrating day fruitlessly scanning through code, not seeing anything that made my spidey-sense tingle.

Even more frustrating was the fact that I had to keep taking breaks every few hours because of my head. The pain was beginning to bug me. I didn't know whether it was some strange adjustment process to using the chip or a bigger problem. The doctor's ream of instructions hadn't included anything about headaches. A sensible person would ask, of course but frankly, I didn't want to find out.

By the time I logged off for the day, I was just as exhausted as the day before. So, of course, I arrived home to find Nat wearing her favorite club gear and boiling over with excitement after her first day of training at Righteous. Apparently it had gone well.

"Get changed, we're going out," she said, doing a little boogie to one of her ancient tunes in the middle of the living room. Her silica-silk dress let off tiny firework bursts of light with each hip shake.

My head throbbed at the thought of going anywhere near a club. I needed quiet and sleep. "Nat, I really—"

"Rule One," she said before I could finish.

"But—"

"No buts. This is definitely a Rule One occasion."

I pulled a face. "When we made up Rule One, we were thirteen."

She did another shimmy. "And it's worked well since then. Go on, get changed."

Going out was the last thing I wanted to do, but I couldn't fight Rule One. It had gotten us through heartbreaks, car accidents, all-night cramming sessions, and numerous other disasters. Rule One meant "drop everything and be my best friend." Once it was invoked, there was no other choice but to go along with whatever the other person wanted.

Looked like I was heading out.

"No gaming," I said, watching Nat dance. "I'm still supposed to take it easy with the chip."

"Sure," she agreed. "I've played today anyway. They showed me Archangel." She raised her arms over her head like wings. "Talk about chill. Tonight I want to celebrate. Dancing. And Jammers."

Jammers were worse than Insomniacs. Perfect. The thought of booze made my head hurt even more. "I was a moron when I was thirteen," I muttered, but went to change.

I was wrong about the Jammers. Maybe it was the vodka, or the red lightning rum, but after Thai food and several cocktails strong enough to kill a horse, my head felt just fine.

"I told you this would be fun," Nat said to me as we pushed our way through to the bar at our third club of the evening.

I grinned. "Your round, I believe." Someone trod on my foot as we finally reached the bar, but in my current state, it didn't really hurt.

She nodded and pointed to the rear of the club. "Go look for a table."

The crowd didn't make it any easier to retreat than it had been to advance. As I dove through a gap between groups, I caught a whiff of incense and had to fight off an instinctive shudder, suddenly regretting that we hadn't chosen a game club. Part of the reason I hung out with Nat and her friends at places like Decker's was I rarely had to come across a witch.

No witches meant no reminders of Sara. Or magic.

The smell caught my throat, and my mother's face, intent over a glass bowl full of dark liquid, rose in my mind.

I shoved the memory back and moved away from the scent, heading for the back of the room where there were less people. With a bit of quick footwork, I nabbed the last open table.

Luckily, Nat appeared with the drinks almost as soon as I sat down.

I downed half of mine in a gulp. "It's packed here. Are you sure you don't want to go to Decker's?" I couldn't smell anything other than too many different perfumes and too many bodies close together in this part of the club, but I couldn't stop myself scanning the crowd, wondering where the witch might be. Of course, it might've just been a drunken clubgoer who liked incense, but that particular blend had been familiar. Not the sort of thing that was easy to find.

Nat shook her head, clinking glasses with me. "You said no gaming."

"Yeah, but Rule One, remember? Your pick."

"I'm good." She smiled as she looked around the room. "This will be fun."

I smiled weakly. "If that's what you want."

She peered at me over the glass. "You okay?"

"Just tired." I'd mostly kept my feelings about magic to myself. Nat knew I didn't talk about my mother, but like me, she lived her life with tech, so the subject of magic rarely came up.

"Dr. Nat prescribes more Jammers. Then you'll sleep like a baby." Her gaze grew more intense for a moment. "How is the sleep lately?"

"I'm doing okay."

"Nightmares?" Nat had schlepped with me through multiple rounds of sleep therapy, normal therapy, hypnosis, and anything else the doctors thought might help chase away the monsters that stalked my nights. She knew most of it hadn't worked. She just held my hand on the really bad nights and never complained if I spent half the night pacing the apartment or slept half the day. For some reason, the nightmares came less during the day.

"Nothing out of the ordinary." In fact, better than normal, but I wasn't banking on that lasting.

"Sure?" She reached across the table and squeezed my arm.

I put my hand over hers. "Sure. Now what were you saying about drinks?"

In the morning, I regretted the Jammers. But at least I had an excuse for taking painkillers.

Eli and Benji took one look at me when I arrived and left me alone. Benji came back briefly to silently put a couple of cans of Afterburn on my desk. It didn't help much.

Wednesday and Thursday passed in a blur of repetition. Read code. Get headache. Take drugs. Read more code. Go home. Listen to Nat chatter about testing and Ajax and plans for her team's next bout. Get some broken sleep. In between, I got to drag my butt up to Damon's office and give him status reports that boiled down to "I got nothing."

Fun times.

Friday morning started in much the same way. Cat called down to my desk before I'd even finished logging on to say that Damon wanted to see me.

I hated to admit it, but as annoying as it was to report that I didn't have anything to tell him, I did look forward to the time I spent with the man.

He was easy to talk to when he wasn't playing his big boss man role. He did interested and attentive well. And he was smart. His brain and the way it worked fascinated me. His success hadn't been luck; it had been talent and hard work. I'd always been a bit of a sucker for smart.

And, as my hormones kept reminding me, he was exceedingly easy on the eye.

Not that I was going to let him know I thought so.

Nope.

I still had some sense.

Maybe, I amended as he turned to me with one of those brain-melting grins when I walked into his office.

"Morning, Maggie," he said. His smile went down a couple of watts in voltage as he studied my face. "You look tired. I told you not to push yourself."

"I'm not, I promise." *Liar, liar.* "Some idiot called my apartment at five this morning. Wrong number. But I couldn't get back to sleep."

He didn't look convinced. "Take an hour or so in one of the nap pods if you need to catch up."

The thought of crawling back to bed was nearly irresistible. But just changing location wasn't necessarily going to help me sleep, and I had no desire to risk having one of my nightmares—toned down though they'd been recently—and waking screaming in the middle of Righteous. That was pretty much guaranteed to get back to Damon.

I was trying to prove I was fine, not weird. So no on-the-job naps for me. Just more of his excellent coffee. "I will if I need to." I nodded at the silver jug on the tray near his desk. "Is that coffee?"

He shook his head. "Juice. A blend Ellen told me about. Good for energy levels. Lots of veggies and vitamins. Want some?" His voice held a challenge.

Veggie juice? Even Nat had given up trying to make me drink veggie juice. Was Damon another health nut?

For a moment I hoped it might be true. It would make him far more resistible. Then I remembered him chowing down on a roast beef sandwich and a donut the day I'd had the wobbles. I was pretty sure he was squarely in the omnivore camp like me.

So this was some sort of test. "Thanks, but I already ate." My stomach rumbled in protest at the lie and my lack of breakfast.

"You should try it." He poured a glass. Dark greenish brown and sludgy, it looked like it was made from compost, not vegetables. Possibly rancid compost.

I tried not to shudder when he held it out. "Honestly, I couldn't deprive you."

"Oh, there's plenty for both of us." His arm didn't move.

I arched an eyebrow. "Then you first."

He lifted the glass and drained it without a flicker of expression, then poured a fresh one and passed it to me.

I tried not to look too appalled. "Can I get it to go?"

He perched on the edge of his desk, arms folded. "You have somewhere more important to be than your employer's office?"

I would have if I drank that stuff. Like the bathroom. Throwing up.

I looked down at the glass and sighed. "Really, I've eaten already."

"Drink or go visit Doc Chen."

That I definitely didn't want to do. Any test Ellen ran on me would show the painkillers I'd been downing, and then I'd have to admit why I was taking them. Not a pretty scenario. Uglier, in fact, than the green sludge.

He had me. And part of me couldn't help being impressed at just how easily he'd won. Smart. Sexy. Competent. Funny. Maybe it was just as well that he was trying to force-feed me green sludge; otherwise, I'd forget why I was trying so hard not to like him too much.

"This is harassment," I muttered, then started drinking.

After surviving the sludge and convincing Damon I really was fine, I made it back downstairs with a quick detour to a cafeteria for yet another caffeine fix and something to take the taste of the sludge away.

"Maggie D," Benji greeted me as I came through the doors juggling coffee and pastries. "You up for a run with the angel later?"

I smiled noncommittally and kept walking. I'd been avoiding the guys' attempts to get me hooked back into the game all week, but I was running out of excuses and willpower. As much as I reminded myself that curiosity killed the cat, I really wanted to try again.

"Yeah, Maggie." Eli blocked my path, with Trisha, the third programmer on our team, not far behind him. "You still haven't tried your chip on something that can really show you what it can do. Aren't you curious?"

I backed toward my cubicle, shaking my head. "Right now I'm more curious about what I'm being paid to do."

Eli pulled a face. "It's Friday. Friday afternoon, we usually try out new stuff with the testers anyway. It's kind of a tradition."

"But we don't have new stuff," I pointed out.

"You have a new chip," he countered. "And there are some new testers. Your friend Nat will be there, I'm sure." His cheeks reddened. I'd introduced him to Nat at lunch on Wednesday, and he seemed a bit smitten. Unfortunately, Nat seemed seriously smitten with Ajax.

"Let me see how things go this morning," I said with a shrug.

Behind Eli, Trista said, "Yeah, Eli, give her a break. She's probably worried about getting the wobbles in front of everyone again."

I ignored the dig. So far, Trista and I didn't exactly get along. She was small, slim, and redheaded in a delicately pretty way that made her look like she should be decorating the top of a Christmas tree or something. For some reason, she hadn't taken the news of what I'd been hired to do well. I tried to limit our interactions as much as possible and keep things professional. Hopefully she'd figure out that I wasn't after her job and back off eventually.

I smiled tightly at her. "I'm sure I'll be fine. But like I said, I have to work. So we'll see."

Eli shrugged. "Chill for now. But you're riding the angel soon."

:CONTACT:

I focused on the file icon as the now familiar sensation of the chip interface flowed over me. Cool. Clear somehow, like I'd taken a half step away from the emotional side of me. Not a bad thing at the moment.

:INITIATE FILE EXTRACTION:

The icon shimmered and blurred away, and code filled my vision. I set it to scrolling with a gesture, letting the lines flicker past, trying to absorb the meaning without reading, without consciousness.

Trying to *feel* if anything was wrong.

Line after line. Page after page. All too soon, my head started to throb. I steeled myself against the sensation, determined not to give up so easily, trying to lose myself in the flow of information.

It worked for a while, but the headache grew more determined until I felt like someone was pounding against my brain with a spiked fist with each breath.

Nausea rose.

I was going to have to disengage.

Again.

Frustration dug the fingers of my right hand into the arm of the game chair. That hurt too, as if the headache was making a move to take over my entire nervous system.

It was too much. Heat swept through me, and I started to mouth the words to stop the sequence when something in the code caught my attention.

:PAUSE:

The page froze, black text floating in the air. I tried to make sense of the words and symbols, but I couldn't see anything unusual. Nothing but the feeling that there was something strange about them. I'd learned to trust that feeling, but I needed help. Which gave me the excuse I needed to disconnect before the flares of pain nailing my eyeballs to the wall melted my brain entirely.

:ENGAGE:

:SELECT SECTION:

:TAG:

:CLOSE FILE:

:DISENGAGE:

I took a shuddering breath as the interface vanished. The pain throbbed once, even more viciously, then subsided a little.

I risked opening my eyes.

Bad move.

The light made me want to retch. I clenched my teeth against the sensation. I was *not* going to barf. I wasn't going to let anyone know I was still having trouble with the interface. Not when I might finally be getting somewhere.

I sucked air through my nose and waited for a minute or so before cracking my eyes just a fraction.

This time the pain was bearable. I leaned forward slowly, fumbling for the bottle of painkillers stashed in my purse.

The lid went flying in my haste, and I didn't bother with

water, just choked down two tabs and put my head down on the desk, praying no one would wander past until the drugs kicked in.

As they spread through my system, the headache retreated to a manageable level, and I managed to sit up and chug half a bottle of water.

The liquid helped. I sipped more, fighting a running battle with my conscience as to when I was going to fess up to Damon or Doc Ellen about my little problem.

Part of me voted for never.

The rest of me wasn't so sure.

Damon wasn't going to react well if I kept hiding this from him and he eventually found out. It might just cost me this job.

Then again, so might honesty at this point.

By the time I'd drained the bottle completely, I decided to file the conversation in the "too hard" basket for now.

Because finally, after days of chasing my tail, I had the tiniest hint of a lead.

I pulled up the file fragment I'd saved. Projected on the perfectly normal screen in front of me, it didn't make any more sense than it had in the interface.

I pushed to my feet, ignoring the distinctly wobbly feeling in my knees, and went to visit Eli.

He wasn't at his cubicle, but I tracked him down near his favorite testing chair. Trista was hooked into the system, and images from the game—mostly of a female angel flying over the forest, endless trees below, and a blinding blue sky above—filled the huge screen.

Eli was tapping notes into a datapad with a look of focused determination, but he raised his head as I approached. "Hey, Maggie."

"Eli. I need some help with something."

His gaze sharpened. For once he didn't look like a seventeen-year-old game-freak but more like the twenty-something-year-old programming machine he was. "You found something?"

"I'm not sure. I need to know what some code I found does."

"Sure thing." He pressed a button on the back of the chair. "Trista, hang on. I have to go, but I'll send Benji over."

The angel paused midflight, then started doing lazy loop-the-loops in the sky. Watching the motion didn't make my stomach feel any easier.

"Are you okay? You look pale," Eli asked as we reached my cubicle.

"Just tired," I lied. *Time for distraction.* "This piece of code." I called up the snippet and increased the screen resolution. "What does it do?"

Eli frowned at the screen for a moment, but then his face cleared. "That's just part of the static."

"Static?" I had no idea what he was talking about.

"Nobody told you?"

I shook my head. "No. What is it?"

"Something Damon figured out back in the first game. It's kind of a distraction for the brain. For the logic centers that might not accept the VR."

Clear as mud. "How does it work?"

"This code produces a thread of junk. Well, not quite junk. Deliberate gibberish sort of. We use long sequences of numbers or letters, kind of like a DNA sequence or Pi. It's projected with the game, below conscious level—"

"Subliminal? Isn't that kind of dicey?" There'd been a whole hoo-ha about subliminals in the last election campaign when it came out that a candidate was using the tech to solicit contributions. The regulations had tightened considerably since then. All publicly broadcast subliminals had to be blockable, and most people screened them routinely. I wondered if gamers did the same. And how you might be able to use the code to influence someone if not.

"We got approval. There's no actual information in there. It's not going to make you crave a Superburger or give all your money to Riley Arts or anything. It just seems to deepen the experience. We haven't figured out why exactly yet. But we refine the filter with every new game."

It sounded harmless enough, but my gut told me I had something. "Okay. Does this static interact with anything else?"

"Everything, in a way. It feeds into the overall simulation, with the graphics and sound and sensory stuff. But it's not new. We've used static from the beginning. It's one of the things that makes our games more immersive."

"Have any of the other elements changed?"

Eli nodded. "Of course. All the generating engines get refined with every new game."

"Even the static generator?"

"Only minor changes. It's pretty simple code."

Simple at Righteous didn't necessarily fit anyone else's definition. "Can you show me how it talks to the other systems? And find me the code from a previous game as well?"

He shrugged. "Sure. Give me twenty minutes or so to finish with Trista, and then I'll get what you need."

Chapter Seven

"THE STATIC GENERATOR? ARE YOU SURE?" Damon asked after I finished explaining my theory.

I shook my head. "No, not at this stage. But it's worth looking at."

He frowned, his eyes darkening to something near the shade of his slate-blue tie. The tie and the sleek suit he wore suggested he'd been doing something serious before I interrupted him.

I stood. "If this isn't a good time . . ."

He waved me back down. "The analysts can wait. In fact . . ." He yelled for Cat and she appeared in the doorway. "Reschedule the briefing to Monday. Tell them . . . hell, I don't care what you tell them. You know the drill."

She nodded and disappeared.

"Blowing off the stock analysts. That's bold."

He grinned, and the familiar glow of warmth swept over me. "They love it when I'm unpredictable. Adds to the mystique."

I snorted. "You have mystique?"

"Sure. I buy it the same place as these suits."

"Oh? Is it overpriced too?" I heard the flirt in my voice and told myself to can it. But I got another glow as his grin widened and something purely male flickered in his eyes. He'd heard it too.

"You don't like the suit?" he asked with a rumble that hadn't been there before.

"It's perfectly fine," I said tightly, maligning the brilliant work of whoever had designed the damn suit. It was way more than fine, showcasing every inch of his body beautifully and drawing my eyes to all the places I didn't want to look.

I looked down at my hands. I really needed to find a way to convince myself he was off-limits. Too complicated. Too risky.

I kept things simple with men. Sex. No strings. Rarely any repeat performances. I had the feeling that if I ever got a taste of Damon, I'd want more.

And more wasn't something I could do.

Which meant I needed to lock down the hormones. Or take them out for a run with someone who fit my criteria. Getting all sweaty and boneless with a willing body would drive Damon from my mind.

If I hadn't been so tired the night I'd gone clubbing with Nat, I could've done just that. But now, looking at him, the thought of another one-night stand with a relative stranger didn't seem appealing at all.

So maybe it had to be plan B—bury myself in work and rely on sheer exhaustion to trump lust.

I looked back up to find him studying me with that unsettling something still lurking in his gaze.

"Enough about your fashion choices. Let's talk about this code," I said, tapping my datapad to send the snippet to his screen.

His gaze lingered on me just a second too long before moving to the code. "This stuff is random. It's not going to be the easiest thing to test. The algorithm just generates junk. How do you analyze junk?"

"I haven't figured that out yet."

"I'll get more programmers on it to help you. What do you need to be able brief them?"

"A few more hours poking around."

He frowned. "Then it'll have to be tomorrow morning."

"But it's only lunchtime. We could do it tonight."

"No can do. Didn't the guys tell you? Friday afternoon is playtime."

"Even when you're facing a time crunch and a crisis?" I'd never met a boss who wasn't willing to crack the whip when the chips were down.

"You don't even know if you're right yet. Everyone will work better after they blow off a little steam. Including you."

"Me?" Did he really expect me to play? I wasn't sure I was ready for that. "I told you, I'm not much of a gamer. I'll just watch."

"You've got to try it with the chip. Trust me, you'll be a convert." He looked like a little boy holding up his prized puppy for approval. An irresistible combination of charm and something I hadn't seen in him before—vulnerability.

Damn. I really should get back to nice, safe code.

"C'mon, Maggie," he coaxed. "Haven't you always wanted to fly?"

Not particularly. But something about the way he said it made me wonder exactly what I might've been missing.

It was hard to act relaxed lying in a game chair with fifty or sixty people watching me.

"It's chill, Maggie D," Benji said from where he stood beside Nat, right next to the chair. "You're going to love the wings."

Yeah, sure. Just like the last time.

Deep breaths. I closed my eyes as the chip clicked home. When my heart rate slowed a little, I started the game.

:CONTACT:

This time I was confronted with a menu rather than being dumped straight into the game. I chose an avatar—glad to see there was a range of body types available as options, not just the stupendously endowed Amazons many games still defaulted to for women—and selected an easy level.

"Chicken," I heard Nat say from a distance as music slid through my head.

:WELCOME ARCHANGEL:

I stood in the forest again, in bright sunlight, warmth beating down on my shoulders. The rapid transition made me blink. The game world felt solid. Real. *Completely* real. A tiny bug zipped past my face, buzzing and darting, and a bead of sweat rolled down my cheek.

Sweat I could *smell*. Along with the old-leaves-and-green-dampness smell of a forest, and something warmer and dustier.

I turned in a circle, taking it slowly. From the clearing where I stood, four paths threaded compass points through the forest, disappearing into the dappled light between the tall trees. Nothing marked the trails to indicate which way I should go.

Then I realized I had another option.

Up.

Even as I thought it, unfamiliar muscles flexed along my back and air fanned my face with a soft rustle.

Wings.

Chill to the max.

Or it would've been if I had any idea at all how to use them. Surely you couldn't just leap into the air and fly?

I beat the wings again slowly. Flexed my knees in preparation for a jump.

Then chickened out and decided to walk. I was so not going to crash and burn with an audience. No wings until there was no one to witness any potential wipeouts.

I considered my options. Maybe I could find the river again, prove to myself there was nothing there but water. The only question was which direction to take. I tried to remember the landscape from the first time I'd been in the game, the position of the river and the trees and the light. The memory was still blurry, but I had a feeling the sun had been setting directly behind me as I'd knelt by the water.

East, then. Assuming the sun in this world followed the same path as in the real one. With no way to know if that were true or not yet, it seemed as good a choice as any.

:SHOW COMPASS:

A display floated in the air in front of my eyes. East was the path to my right, slightly wider than the rest, but it also seemed a little darker, as though the trees crowded closer together in that direction.

Almost as though they didn't want me to go that way. The hairs on the back of my neck prickled as I stood and studied the path.

Stop being dumb. It's just a game.

I turned off the display and headed east.

The air cooled as I crossed the tree line and stepped onto the path. I walked slowly, scanning my surroundings with each cautious step. Who knew exactly what was lurking in the bushes? There would be enemies to defeat. Cunning and unexpected enemies. It was, after all, a Righteous game.

I hadn't taken the time to read the player's guide. Nat had given me the basic premise: something about winged humans —descendants of angels—trying to explore and colonize a planet inhabited by dark creatures.

Your standard quest narrative.

A holster rode my right thigh over the black suit, the slick black handle of a high-tech gun protruding from it. A leather sheath held a knife on the other hip. So I should be able to deal with any surprises lurking on the path. And surely "dark" creatures were more likely to attack at night?

I picked my way along the trail, winding around rocks and over small streams, each step taking me deeper into the forest. The light grew dimmer, the air cooler, the dense leaves of the unfamiliar trees creating a thick canopy that provided a constant background song of whispering leaves. The knife came in handy where the undergrowth tangled into barriers of vines and thorns, and the wings gave me a boost as I clambered over dead tree trunks almost as tall as me. It was kind of fun.

And thank God, there was no sign of the wobbles.

After a few minutes, the wind picked up and the sound of the leaves seemed to take on a different pitch. My spine prickled at the eerie rustle. I picked up the pace, telling myself I would be at the river soon.

"Maaaaaaaagieeeeeeeee."

The name was a whisper among the trees. I froze. Spun around.

Nothing. But my pulse pounded and my skin crawled. Every instinct told me I wasn't alone.

Nothing I could see, then. Maybe Damon's dark creatures liked catching some rays after all.

I flicked the top of the holster open and curled my fingers over the gun before starting forward again.

Each crackle of a twig beneath my boot made me flinch, ratcheting up my pulse.

Then the wind called my name again.

My heart leapt into my throat. This was why I didn't game much. I was a big old scaredy-cat when it came to the shoot 'em, hunt 'em, fight 'em types of adventures. Risk-averse in a big way.

Nat and her friends delighted in telling stories of the

stupid ways they'd bought it in games. I didn't find it entertaining. Something in my brain was fooled too well by the illusions. I always felt like something was really hunting me. Trying to kill me.

"Not real," I muttered.

Then a nightmare stepped out onto the path in front of me.

"Maggie," it snarled. "I've been looking for you."

My fingers yanked the gun from its holster before I had time to think. My arms trembled as I pointed it at the creature.

It laughed, and the sound sliced at my ears like breaking glass. "Imaginary guns. Do you think that will save you?" It flowed forward a little, dark skin shining greasily in the dappled light.

I took a step back as the breeze carried its odor to me. Despite its appearance, it smelled good. Like baking bread and jasmine perfume and all my favorite scents. Except, as I sucked in a breath through my nose, I caught the faintest hint of something fouler.

I backed up again and fired.

There was an arc of light from the gun, and I expected the creature to burst into flames or fall to the ground smoking.

Instead, it looked completely unharmed. It laughed again, revealing more jagged teeth than should've been possible to fit in its head. Something black and oily dripped from its mouth. "You're mine, Maggie."

"I don't think so." I moved backward faster, trying to replay the path in my head. Shit. There was one of those monster trunks not far back. My retreat was blocked.

"Mine," it repeated. "Or you will be. Again." Its face twisted with something like frustration. The result wasn't pretty. "How did you do it, human?"

"Do what?" I fired again with the same lack of result.

It closed the gap between us with one lightning-fast leap. Fingers wrapped around my throat, my skin burning where it touched me. "You know very well," it said. "Who broke the bond?"

Its breath stank up close. Like rot and mold and something dead left too long in the sun. The fingers squeezed tighter on my throat, and stars of light wheeled in front of my eyes.

I really didn't like this game. "I don't know anything about bonds, but I'm out of here." My mind groped for the correct command as I struggled to breathe.

The creature roared, and I felt myself losing the struggle, stars wheeling before my eyes.

"I will find you," it snarled. The pressure on my throat eased a little and I gasped. "You will not escape me."

:DISENGAGE: I thought frantically as I saw it draw back its hand. Too slow. Claws raked the side of my face and I flew backward, hitting the dirt with a thump that knocked the breath from me. Warm dampness covered my face, and I tasted the coppery tang of blood as pain suddenly bloomed like fire along my jaw.

The creature came toward me again, claws extended.

"Disengage," I screamed as it drew closer and darkness took me.

I woke up with no sensation in my left arm and a mouth that felt like I'd been sucking on cotton wool for a week.

"Welcome back."

Damon.

I turned my head toward his voice. Dr. Barnard stood beside him with another woman I didn't recognize. Her dark hair was piled high on her head, and her clear gray eyes looked concerned. She wore a white coat like Barnard, but no other medical paraphernalia hung from her pockets or neck.

I tried to remember what was going on.

Nothing. I remembered going to work. Then . . . nothing.

There was a dead spot in my memory. Why? And why was my arm numb? I glanced down and froze as I registered the neat strip of pale green surgical seal running down my wrist. Right over my chip. Fear gripped my throat. "Where am I? What happened?"

"Back at the hospital," Dr. Barnard said. "I'm sorry, Maggie, but we had to remove your chip."

My chip? I choked back a flare of panic. Without the chip, I couldn't work for Damon. "Can I get another one?"

Damon and Dr. Barnard looked at each other, avoiding eye contact with me. Bad sign.

"We're not recommending it at this point," Dr. Barnard said in I've-got-bad-news tone.

"Damon?" I asked, searching his face as the fear sank deeper into my gut.

"You need to listen to the doctor," he said, moving closer. His hand closed over mine.

I pulled free. "What happened? Did I have an accident?"

"You don't remember?" Damon asked. He looked back at Barnard. "Is this normal?"

The doctor shrugged. "Nothing about this is normal." He moved closer, pointing a scanner at me. "There's nothing to indicate she suffered any lasting damage. Memory loss could just be the anesthesia."

Lasting damage? I struggled to sit up. "Someone tell me what the fuck happened!"

Damon captured my hand again. This time I didn't fight him. If I didn't hold on to something, I might just start screaming.

"You were playing Archangel," Damon said. "We were all watching. Nat was betting you were going to try to fly."

None of it triggered anything at all in my head, but I

could worry about that later. I swallowed, desperately wanting water. "And then?"

"You were walking through the forest in the game, and the picture started getting messed up. Your feedback readings went through the roof. You started shooting at something, and we couldn't see what. Then you—"

"You went into a convulsion, Maggie," Dr. Barnard interrupted. "Your nervous system seems to have had an abnormal reaction to the chip. We couldn't control the seizures with medication. That's why we had to remove it."

They'd taken the chip.

My fingers curled reflexively. "I don't understand. Was the chip faulty?"

"We're testing it," Dr. Barnard replied. "But we tested it before installation. It was perfect then. I've never seen anything like this."

Oh lucky me, I was unique. "So you don't know what caused this?" I looked at Damon. "What if it was the game?"

His grip tightened. "It was the clean version. It's been played hundreds of times with no incidents."

I tasted bile. There was something wrong with me. There had to be. Why else would I be the only one to react like this? And why couldn't I remember?

"Will I get my memory back?" I asked.

Dr. Barnard looked down at his scanner for a moment. "I'm going to introduce you to my colleague, Dr. Dempsey. She can tell you more."

The dark-haired woman stepped closer, and I suddenly smelled her. Green somehow, with a hint of smoke. Eerily familiar. A smell I'd grown up with.

She smelled like Sara.

My stomach tightened.

"You're a witch," I blurted, yanking my hand free from Damon's.

She nodded. "Call me Meredith."

My stomach flipped, and for a moment, the room swam. I was going to throw up.

I sucked in a breath. "Get her out of here. I don't need a witch."

Meredith reached out and laid her hand over mine. The nausea flowed away.

A healer, then. That made me a little easier. Healers didn't do any of the stuff Sara was into. They took oaths.

Or at least that's what they told everyone.

A shiver racked me. "I don't need a witch," I repeated. I twitched my hand away.

She drew back calmly. "Maggie, I'm sorry to be the one to tell you this, but you do. I think your reaction may be due to something magical."

Magical? I stared at her, not understanding. "How can something magical interfere with an interface chip?"

"I'm not sure. But I think someone put a binding on you."

I laughed. I couldn't help it. "Don't be ridiculous. Bindings don't work without consent."

Damon's eyebrows shot up. But I didn't have time—or the inclination—to explain how I knew about bindings. I wanted the explanation of why Meredith thought I could be under one.

She looked grave. "You have the signs. I can feel it on you."

I just stared at her. Then pinched myself. None of them vanished, and I didn't wake up safe in my own bed. I was really here. Really having this conversation.

I tried to remember anything Sara had ever told me about binding. There wasn't much, but I knew you had to agree to be bound. "How could I be bound? I've never even seen a binding ritual, let alone consented to participate in one."

"That's what we need to find out."

I curled my hands into the blanket covering me. "That's why you're here?"

She shook her head and a long tendril of hair came loose from the pile, snaking down her face. She brushed it away. "I just made the initial diagnosis. This is not my area of expertise."

"Is it anyone's?" Were there really that many cases of involuntary binding—which, if I was remembering right, could be anything from a suggestion to outright magical possession of another's will—that people could specialize in assisting the victims?

I shivered again as I realized that was a big assumption on my part. What if no one *could* help me? I had no idea what had actually been done to me. Or what the effects might be if it were undone. Collapse and convulsions weren't promising symptoms.

"There's one person in town I can send you to," Meredith said. "Her name's Cassandra. Cassandra Tallant."

I sank back into the pillows. Cassandra Tallant. Even I knew that name, and I knew next to nothing about the magical community. Cassandra was a power. I could even remember Sara talking about her.

If I needed Cassandra's help, then I really was in trouble.

Tears prickled my eyes and I closed them, suddenly exhausted. "I want to sleep."

Meredith cleared her throat. "The sooner you do this, the better."

"She just had surgery." Damon's voice. Good. He could use his master-of-the-universe powers to get everyone to just leave me the hell alone for a while.

Like forever.

"The chip surgery isn't a big thing," Dr. Barnard said. "Her scans are clear. If she feels well enough, she could go home."

"She needs to see Cassandra," Meredith repeated.

"Yes, I'm sure she'll be impressed if I toss my cookies all over her," I muttered, not opening my eyes.

A hand pressed against my forehead, soft and cool. Meredith, then. "I can help you with the nausea and do something about the soreness from the convulsions. But until you see Cassandra, you're vulnerable."

That made me look at her as fear rose again. "Vulnerable to what?"

"All sorts of things. Your aura is half-shredded. You're wide open."

Whatever that meant. I didn't want to know. I wound my hands into the cotton blanket covering me.

"Nothing's going to get to her here," Damon said. "You can stay and watch over her."

Like I wanted a witch watching over me when I slept. Especially one who thought I was vulnerable. Oath or no oath, the thought made me want to scream. The look on Damon's face told me he wasn't overly happy with the idea either.

"Can't I just go home?" I said, hating the whine in my voice.

"It's here or Cassandra." Meredith's tone suggested resistance might just be futile.

The thought of climbing out of bed, getting dressed, and going to talk to another witch made me feel drained. "I need to sleep."

"Then sleep. But then you're going to see Cassandra, or else we won't discharge you."

"I'll come with you," Damon said.

Oh no, he wouldn't. If I was mixed up in something magical, then I wanted it fixed pronto, but I didn't need anyone else knowing the details. Especially not Damon. His world was tech, like mine. He'd been relieved when I'd told him Tech-Witch was just a name. I didn't want him thinking I was mixed up with magic.

"I don't think so."

He stared down at me, mouth thinning. "Doctors, can I have a word with Maggie alone please?"

They looked at me, then at him. Apparently he won, because they both filed from the room.

"You're not coming," I said before he could get started.

"This happened to you because of me." Anger crackled in his tone. Master of the universe didn't like what was happening. Well, he could join the club on that one. But as I was the founding member, I got to call the shots.

"Maybe. Maybe not. Either way, it still happened to me. And I'm the only one who needs all the gory details."

"What if it's—"

I hiked up my chin. "If I hear anything that I think affects you or Righteous, I'll tell you. But I'm doing this alone." I stared at him, ready to fight.

His eyes were that laser-bright shade again, but he eventually looked away. "I'll organize a car for you."

"Thank you."

"You need to rest."

"That's what I said. And yet all of you keep talking to me." I folded my arms across my chest, trying to look tough. Hard in a hospital gown. And when I had to fight not to wince because I felt like I'd gone several rounds with a bulldozer.

"We're worried about you. If you'd seen yourself today—" He broke off for a moment, and I caught my breath at the edge of concern in his voice and the fleeting look of fear on his face.

Was he really worried about me?

Because worried implied caring.

And caring implied possibilities that I really wasn't prepared to think about right now.

My mouth went dry again. "You going to finish that sentence?" I managed.

He hesitated. "Let's just say you'd be worried too."

"Believe me, I'm plenty worried. But right now, I'm even

more tired." I let my eyes drift closed, hoping he'd take the hint and leave.

He did.

But not before I thought I felt a hand brush ever so softly across my head.

Chapter Eight

THE NO-NONSENSE BLACK lettering on the window read CASSANDRA'S CAULDRON.

Not the most inspiring name, but I guess it made clear what waited beyond the door.

I stood, shifting from foot to foot in the late afternoon sun. I'd slept for maybe an hour at the hospital—unsettled, twitchy sleep. I'd woken to find Meredith by my bed, bearing the news that a car was waiting for me if I chose to see Cassandra and get her verdict on what was happening to me.

Faced with another night or two in the hospital, being poked and prodded and examined at regular intervals, I'd given in, signing the discharge papers as fast as possible just to get out of there. But now that I was standing outside Cassandra's door, I wasn't enthusiastic about the idea. And the cutesy name wasn't changing my mind. With a name like that, how much help could I possibly find here?

The voice inside my head replied, *Maggie, if Meredith is right, you need all the help you can get.*

I hated it when that voice was right.

With a sigh, I turned the door handle and stepped over the threshold. A shrill buzz announced my presence, and I jumped. I'd been expecting wind chimes or bells or something a lot more woo-woo than your standard buzz and scan. When my heart stopped pounding quite so hard, I took a few more steps and peered into the depths of the store.

The store smelled familiar, even though it had been many, many years since I'd set foot anywhere selling magic supplies. My nose tickled with fresh and dried herbs, spiced oils, and old paper. Beneath it all ran a thread of something indefinable. Every magic supply store my mother had ever dragged me into had the same smell. I'd never known what it was.

But I knew it made my heart skitter nervously and tightened each individual muscle down my spine.

I had to forcibly unclench my hands, my palms stinging where my nails had pressed too deep. To stop my fingers curling back into fists, I lifted a stoppered clear glass bottle off the nearest shelf and sniffed cautiously. Lavender and clary sage and something woodier. Basil, maybe?

"Can I help you?"

When I saw the woman asking the question, I almost dropped the bottle. "You're Cassandra?"

She laughed, the sound a deep, joyful chuckle. "Yes, I am. Don't sound so surprised."

I put the bottle down carefully while I shrugged an apology. "Sorry, you don't look—" I broke off, not wanting to insult her. She might be a witch, and I trusted her about as far as I could throw this whole building, but apparently I needed her help. Best I not make an idiot of myself straightaway.

The laugh came again. "It's okay. I know I look more like Mrs. Claus than a witch."

At that I had to laugh. Her description was perfect. Cassandra was short and round, with silver gray hair pulled back in a utilitarian knot. She wore black trousers and sensible shoes and a linen tunic in a deep, rich red that lit her pale skin.

The only things that made it clear she wasn't someone's

grandmother who had wandered into the wrong store on her way to the mall were her eyes. Huge, glowing gold-brown with deep green flecks, they drew attention. But the color wasn't the startling thing. It was the wisdom in them, the sense that she was old with a knowledge beyond even the years evidenced by the lines on her face.

I knew that look.

She was the real thing. Powerful.

The hairs on my arms stood on end. I hugged myself, rubbing skin gone suddenly cold. "Sorry," I said as I gained control of myself. "I'm—"

"Maggie Lachlan," Cassandra finished for me.

I hesitated, the hairs on the back of my neck standing on end.

She cocked her head. "It's all right, Meredith described you to me. She said I'd know the eyes. She was right."

Know my eyes? What did that mean? That she'd recognized my green eyes? That my eyes said something else about me? That she knew—please, no—my mother?

I decided I didn't want to know. "She said you could help me."

Those wise eyes studied me, growing sad somehow. "We'll see. Come upstairs, child."

She walked past me and pressed a button on the comp panel by the door. "Now we won't be disturbed. Come on in back."

I followed her down the length of the store, breathing in her amber and spice perfume as she led me past the counter and through the heavy black velvet curtain that hung behind it.

"I usually see people in there." She waved her left hand at a red door in the far end of the hallway. "But this could take some time, so we might as well be comfortable." She set off again, up a staircase made of worn wood. Wood, not hypercrete. The stairs creaked under Cassandra's feet, forcing me to wonder how they had survived the Big One. Nothing that rickety would pass the post-quake building codes the city had enacted so it must have been built before. Which meant it had to be safe enough.

"Do you live up here?" The store was on the edge of the Tenderloin. Parts of the neighborhood had started to be restored, but there were still plenty of broken buildings reclaimed by dealers and pimps and worse. Definitely a no-go zone at night. I wouldn't have wanted to live here.

"No," she said, unlocking the door at the top of the stairs and ushering me in. "I live in Berkeley."

I couldn't help feeling relieved, which was dumb. If Cassandra was anywhere near as strong as Meredith's respect suggested, then she could take care of herself. She'd probably be amused to know I'd even had any doubt.

The room was light and airy. The late afternoon sun lending a golden sheen to a couple of comfortable-looking chairs and a sofa covered in the same fading pale teal velvet. A low table painted lavender stood between them. Plants lined the window ledges, and framed photos marched along a small mantelpiece above what I had to assume was a nonworking fireplace. Through an archway, I caught a glimpse of a tiny kitchen with aqua and white tiles on the floor and deep green cabinets.

"My grandparents lived in Berkeley," I offered when the silence seemed to stretch. One day I might live there again. If I could find out what the hell was going on so I could finish this damn job. Damon's fee would be enough to get me a long way toward rebuilding the house.

"We can do small talk later. Sit down." She shooed me toward the sofa. "Would you like some tea?"

"Do you have syncaf," I needed more caffeine than tea could give me. I didn't know what drugs they'd pumped me full of at the hospital, but whatever they were, I still had the edges of a headache and a healthy dose of I-need-a-nap.

"Tea," she said firmly. "You'll like it. I blend it myself. Sit." She disappeared through the archway. The sound of water running and cabinets opening ensued, leaving me with nothing to do but follow her instructions. Maybe I should have snooped a little, but my mother had taught me that snooping around magic wasn't smart.

The sofa faced the mantelpiece, so I studied the photos. There were several of Cassandra at various ages looking happy with a man I could only assume was Mr. Witch, and more of two boys—dark-haired twins—doing everything from Cub Scouts to graduating college.

Cassandra reappeared with a tray that held two steaming mugs decorated with the store's logo, a plate of chocolate chip cookies, and a battered red silk pouch. She handed me a mug, put the other one down on the table with the cookie plate, picked up the pouch, and sank into one of the chairs with a faint pleased sigh.

"Thank you," I said, sniffing cautiously. My nose filled with spearmint and chamomile, nothing alarming. But I reserved judgment. I'd shared an apartment with Nat too long not to know that things that were supposedly good for you didn't always taste like they smelled.

"Drink it before it gets cold."

I glanced up guiltily. Cassandra had a look just like my Gran's favorite "I'm older than you so don't argue" face. I drank automatically. It wasn't too bad if you liked mint-flavored hot water, but it wasn't exactly the caffeine boost I needed.

"Good," she said when I put the mug down after several more sips. She drew a deck of well-used cards out of the pouch, shuffling them idly.

Each hissing snick of the cards as they slid over and between each other wound my nerves tighter. *Time to get down to business.*

"Meredith said I'd been bound," I said. "Is she right?"

"That's what we're here to find out." Cassandra put down the cards and studied my face. "You're sure you know nothing about this?"

I had no trouble meeting her gaze. "Nothing at all, I swear."

She held out a wrinkled hand, palm up. "Then give me your hand and we'll start solving the mystery."

"You don't want to ask me some questions, first?" In her place, I'd want to know something about me.

"I prefer to start with this. Hand, please."

I sighed and rested my hand on hers.

Her skin was warm and soft, her grip surprisingly strong. She closed her eyes, and then there was no sound in the room but the steady rhythm of her breath in and out and the pounding of my pulse in my ears.

I had to keep reminding myself to breathe as well.

After five minutes or so, Cassandra opened her eyes. "Well." She reached for her tea and drank deeply. "Meredith was right and wrong."

A chill swept through me. I picked up my tea, clinging to the warmth. "What does that mean?"

"You were bound. But not by a witch."

Suddenly not even the tea was enough to warm me. "What then?"

"A demon. You were bound to a demon."

A demon? I almost dropped the tea. Demons were very nasty magic. The kind that got you locked away for life if you were caught. Nothing I wanted anything to do with.

A thousand denials rose as my skin crawled, but only one made it into words. "How is that possible? I don't know anything about demons. I've certainly never seen one. How could one bind me?" The knowledge part wasn't entirely true, but the seeing part was. I was pretty sure meeting a demon was the kind of thing that would stick in your mind.

Cassandra's expression was stern. "You're telling the truth

about this? Because such things generally require consent. And this binding—what's left of it—feels old. You never did anything foolish in high school?"

I shook my head. Sara had died not long after I'd started junior high. I'd been sent to my grandparents after that, and I'd done my best to forget I'd ever known anything about witches. Dabbling held no appeal for me. After all, I already knew I had no power. Sara had told me so. Repeatedly.

"You said what's left of it. It's not there anymore?" The thought made it a little easier to breathe, but the crawling sensation didn't ease. I desperately wanted a bath or a shower or a bucket of bleach. Anything to wash even the mere thought of a demon away.

Even Sara hadn't messed with demons. I wouldn't have put it past her to try an imp or a small elemental, but not a demon. From the small amount I did remember her telling me, binding a demon was risky. And nine times out of ten, the demon won and the person doing the binding became slave, not master. Or dead.

"No. There are traces but they're fading. Something has broken the binding." The creases in her forehead deepened. "Usually that only happens when the demon dies or the bound one does. And demons don't die very often."

That didn't make me feel any better. My grip on the ratty velvet cushion tightened. To deal with this, I had to stay calm. Stay detached. Deal with the facts. With logic. I could work with logic. Stick with that and I could freak out later. "Explain this to me. How does a binding work?"

"It's a contract of sorts. Or a deception. The demon feeds off the energy of whoever it's bound to. In return, the bound one gets something."

"Like what?"

"Power, usually, if the contract is with a witch. Otherwise more material things. Money. Or maybe influence or charisma."

I wanted to believe that people weren't that dumb, but there was ample evidence to the contrary. "I'm not sure having a demon feeding on me is a price I'd be willing to pay to have people like me."

"Not everyone is like you," she said. "Some people think a few years of life is worth—"

"Years of life?" I choked.

"The demon feeding shortens your life span."

White noise roared in my ears for a second. "Are you saying I'm going to die young because of this?"

She shrugged. "Hard to say in your case. If you didn't consent to the binding—"

"Damn straight I didn't."

Cassandra shook her head. "If that's true, then I'm not sure there's any way of telling what the effect might be. But the demon's ability to use you must've been limited. After all, you're still sane."

I wasn't sure she was right about that. After all, I was sitting drinking tea with a witch and discussing whether a demon had been nibbling on my life force for years. Icebergs were either floating down the Styx or my life had taken a severe left turn into crazy town. "Should I be crazy?"

"It's not an uncommon side effect of being around demons."

"It's not like I have one hiding in my closet at home," I said.

"I would hope not," Cassandra said. "A demon strong enough to come through to this world is not a good thing. You'd probably be dead."

The noise in my ears came roaring back, accompanied by dancing sparkles of light whirling in front of my eyes. I bent over the couch and concentrated on remembering how to breathe for a few minutes.

When the urge to barf finally receded, I straightened and

glared at Cassandra. "You know, your bedside manner leaves a bit to be desired."

"I believe in the truth," she said with another shrug. "Keeping people in the dark never helps them. You'd rather be a person than a mushroom, wouldn't you?"

Mushroom? It took my brain a few seconds to catch up. *Mushroom. Right. Kept in the dark and fed shit. Not my style.*

I gritted my teeth and straightened my spine. "So let me get this straight. I've been bound to a demon that may or may not have been feeding off me. That's how demons get power? Feeding off people?"

Cassandra nodded. "They use our energy, yes. Feeding is as good an analogy as any."

My head was spinning. "I think we need to go back to the beginning. Demon 101."

"How much do you know?"

"I know they exist. And now I know they feed off people. Assume that's it."

Cassandra picked up her cards again, cradling them between her hands. "Demons live on another plane. From the little we know, they're creatures largely of energy in their world."

"Go on."

"Like I said, we don't know a lot. No one has ever been to their world, and not many, thank the powers, come through to ours, but demons seem to focus on gaining energy. Whether they use it for politics or breeding or something else entirely is anyone's guess."

"So humans are an energy source?" I pressed my fingers to my temples, trying to concentrate.

"A very attractive one, we think. Almost as though they can do more with human energy than their own sources."

"Like we're a better grade of fuel? High octane or something?"

Cassandra nodded. "I guess. But also one that burns faster. The demons use up the bound ones and they die. Usually."

"So this bond may or may not have sucked years off my life?"

Another nod.

I looked at the ceiling for a moment. "Well, at least I don't have to worry about another Social Security collapse." As jokes went, it was pretty lame, but I cut myself some slack. I wasn't exactly on top of my game right now.

Cassandra gave me a small smile. "Don't invite trouble. Like I said, a lot depends on the nature of the binding. And we can get Meredith and the healers to examine you eventually. They can tell if any damage was done. But that brings us back to the question of how exactly you were bound."

It was my turn to shrug. "Like *I* said, I have no idea."

That earned me a look. She clearly still hadn't decided if she believed me or not.

"Then we need to go back to the beginning. Let's start with your mother. You're Sara Lachlan's daughter, yes?"

I flinched automatically. *Crap, crap, crap.* "You knew my mother?"

"My dear, I know—or know of—most of the true witches in the country. Especially those like your mother."

I didn't think there was much point playing innocent. "The bad ones, you mean." I couldn't keep the bitterness from my voice.

"The ones who operate from, shall we say, self-interest."

That sounded like Sara all right. "It's okay. You can say bad. I figured out pretty young that my mother wasn't Glinda the Good."

Cassandra nodded. "All right. Bad, then. Though believe me, there are those who are much worse than your mother. Some we cannot control. Some who escape us."

"Us?"

She waved dismissively. "Don't worry about that. We were discussing your mother."

Curiosity burned. Did the witches have some sort of ruling body? Or a police force, tracking down witches who did the wrong thing? I tried to imagine Cassandra as some sort of witchy detective. It didn't gel. And the more I thought about it, the more my initial curiosity was burned away by a torrent of anger.

If such a group did exist, why hadn't they ever come to stop my mother? I'd spent too many of my teenage years trying to imagine what I might've been like if I'd grown up solely with my grandparents rather than Sara not to hate the thought that somewhere out there was a group of people who could've made that dream a reality. Who could've rescued me. But didn't.

"You probably know more about her than I do," I said, the words sharp, not hiding the sudden bitterness in my heart.

Cassandra shook her head. "No. Your mother was clever. She stayed under the radar most of the time. And she never quite crossed the line that would mean we would have to act to stop her if we could."

There was that "we" again. And if "they" had a line my mother hadn't crossed, then that line was much further out than I'd draw it. As far as I knew, she'd never killed anyone, but some of the requests those who came looking for her had whispered were nasty enough. But maybe she worked things both ways—promised to do what they asked, took the money, and then worked a spell that didn't deliver.

That would explain the frequent midnight creeping out of town.

"Then again," Cassandra said, "perhaps she did."

I froze halfway in my stretch to put my now-cold mug of tea down. "What do you mean?"

"How old were you when your mother died?"

"Thirteen. And a few months."

"And you've never done anything magical since?"

"I don't have power. Sara told me that."

Cassandra pursed her lips. "In which case, the binding must've happened when you were a child. But why on earth would a child be of interest to a demon? And why don't you remember? Maybe . . . ." She leaned forward and put a hand against my forehead, closing her eyes again.

I stayed still, caught in my awkward pose, hoping like hell that Cassandra couldn't read my racing thoughts.

"Damn." Her eyes opened. "Nothing."

"Nothing of what?" I had no idea what was going on.

"I thought maybe you'd been made to forget. But there's no trace of such a thing."

"You think Sara did this to me? Bound me to a demon? My own mother?" I heard my voice go high and thin. Sure, I'd never thought that Sara was mother of the year, but I'd always thought she cared about me—as much as she was capable of, anyway. Most of the time. Or at least before she informed me that I was powerless and seemed to lose interest in me altogether. But then she'd died, so I never knew how that change might've played out.

Probably just as well. I couldn't hide the shiver that ran down my spine at the thought, throat burning with the complicated mix of regret and shame and anger and loss that always accompanied my memories of her.

Cassandra bit into a cookie and chewed thoughtfully. "It seems most likely. I'm just not sure how."

"Why? Why would she do that?" It hurt to talk, and I grabbed for my tea. It was cold but it was wet, chasing away some of the pain gripping my throat.

Surely Cassandra was wrong. My mother wouldn't sell me to a demon. Nobody's mother would do that.

Another head shake. "I can't tell you that. I can only think that she'd gotten into some sort of trouble."

"What sort of trouble warrants binding your child to a demon?" My hand shook a little as I sipped.

"The worst kind." She leaned across and put a hand on my knee. "I'm sorry, Maggie. I know this must be a shock. But the important thing right now is to work out how the binding was broken."

"Why does it matter?" I looked down at my lap, determined not to cry. My mother hadn't bound me to a demon. I wouldn't believe it.

"It matters if you don't want the demon to suddenly try to reform the bond. Now that you're older and aware, they may be able to use you differently. Take more. This binding must've been limited somehow, or I'd feel stronger traces on you. Demons leave their mark." She narrowed her eyes. "I take it you've never had the urge to kill chickens at midnight or anything like that?"

I tried to smile. "Not unless you count a fondness for Korean fried chicken."

She laughed, a warm soothing sound that made me feel—just for a moment—like everything might be okay. Until the sound died down and reality flooded back.

"Junk food isn't quite a demonic act," she said. "But really? Nothing strange at all?"

"Nothing. I—" I started to speak, then paused.

"What?"

"I have nightmares. Bad ones."

"For how long?" Cassandra's eyes were intent.

"Since my mother died," I admitted, trying to ignore the feeling she could somehow see inside me. "No one's ever been able to help much with them." I bit my lip, the pain a familiar sting as I pressed too hard. "Do you think they might be because of the bond? Could a demon affect me that way?"

"It's possible. If it were trying to influence you and couldn't, perhaps. Or it could just be coincidence. Have the nightmares been different lately? Better or worse?"

I tried to think. The past few days were a blur of exhaustion and headaches and work. "Maybe a little better. I'm not sure."

"Then we'll have to wait and see. And in the meantime, you'll want to take care of this." She put down the cards and poured herself more tea.

I didn't need convincing. If I needed to protect myself from a demon, then it was a no-brainer that I would. "What do I need to do?" I reached for a cookie, in dire need of something simple and comforting like sugar and fat.

"We need to get your aura back into good shape. I can give you some cleansing and grounding rituals. You need to replenish your energy levels. Sex would be good too."

I almost choked on a mouthful of cookie. "Sex is good for your aura?"

"Sexual energy is one of the most potent forms we have, dear. Do you have a partner?"

I shook my head, swallowing cautiously.

"A vibrator?"

This time I did choke.

Cassandra smirked at me. "I'm surprised that Sara's daughter is shocked at the idea of a sex toy. You did say you grew up in Berkeley, didn't you?"

I doubted my mother had owned a vibrator. She preferred her pleasures to come attached to a real live male. And I didn't need to add talking about my sexual habits with someone who could be my grandmother and who I'd just met to the disaster zone my life seemed to have become in the last twenty-four hours.

"Can we change the subject, please? You said something about a cleansing ritual?"

"I need to understand what broke the binding first." She picked up her cards again, shuffling them with a familiarity that spoke of long practice. I got the feeling that they were almost her equivalent of worry beads. "What have you been doing, Maggie? I've never heard of anyone breaking a binding involuntarily." She looked fascinated.

"Nothing. I've been working for Riley Arts for the last week or so."

"There must be something that's changed." Her eyes swept over me, paused at my wrist with its neat surgical shield. "Meredith said you'd been in surgery. She didn't say what for."

I didn't want to talk about the chip. "They took out my interface chip. Said it was giving me convulsions."

The cards stilled. "How long have you had the chip?"

"Not long. A week."

Cassandra put the deck down and reached for my hand, fingers skimming over the shield ever so gently. "And the convulsions started after the implantation?"

"They only happened once. But yes, I've never had a seizure before."

"Anything else unusual happen since you've had the chip? Any symptoms?" She released my hand, but her eyes were still fastened on my wrist.

"I've had some headaches. I don't understand. How can the chip break a magical binding?" I stared down at the seal for a moment, then pulled my sleeve down to cover it.

"How does it work, the chip? I know what it does, kind of, but tell me how. Explain it to me exactly."

I had to think about it. About how to break down the concept. I mean, I understood it at a high level, but it wasn't like I knew all the technical details. If she wanted that, she'd have to talk to Damon. Or Dr. Barnard. "The chip interfaces with my nervous system, so a computer that links to the chip can talk directly to my brain."

"The signals travel via the nerves? Piggybacking on the electrical impulses they send?"

I nodded. "That's right."

Cassandra grinned. "Then maybe it's that simple."

"You've lost me."

"I'm not sure if this will make sense to you, but everyone has an energy pattern—a signature, if you will. It's part of you, like a fingerprint. Your aura, your thoughts and feelings, the very pulse of your brain through your body. It's unique. Witches work with energy. And a binding, to put it very simply, chains one energy signature to another in a very specific way. I think the chip may have altered your energy pattern slightly. The extra impulses it sent would be small but possibly enough to make a difference."

I stared at her. "So the spell didn't work anymore? Just because this energy pattern was different?"

"Obviously it took a while for the change to actually break through. That's probably why you had the seizures—some sort of energy backlash." She looked thoughtful. "I wonder if that could be prevented."

"Can we worry about that later and focus on me right now? You're saying that I had a demon somehow joined to me for years, and then because I stuck a chip in my wrist, the whole thing blew up."

"Yes. It's simple. So simple no one has thought of it before. Most witches don't get chips, of course. The effect would be minute. Like I said, it seems to have taken a few days for the changes to be big enough to weaken the spell. The small changes would amplify over time."

"Like a sine wave resonating? Setting up a vibration that can tear things apart?"

"Exactly." She smiled in approval. "You'd have to be using the chip a lot."

"I was."

"And when you had the convulsions?"

"I was playing a game. Full immersion."

She nodded. "What happened exactly?"

I tried to remember. Damon had mentioned me firing at something they couldn't see on the screen. I struggled with the wisps of sensation I could recall. Danger. Panic. My hand drifted to my cheek as it twinged with a phantom of pain. I caught a flash of claws then . . . nothing.

"I don't really remember," I said slowly. "But I think there was a creature. It attacked me."

"A game creature?"

I rubbed my forehead but couldn't bring back anything more. "I'm not sure."

"You need to find out."

"Why?"

"Because if it wasn't a game creature, then it might have been the demon."

"How does a demon get into a game?"

"Demons feed from energy. They *are* energy in our world. That's why they work through others. A computer game is largely electricity. Energy. It could have piggybacked off your bond somehow. "

"I thought you said the bond was broken."

"After you got your chip. Had you played the game before?"

I nodded, feeling sick, remembering my reaction the first time I'd played Archangel. Had that been the demon too?

"Then that could be the answer. Though it worries me that a demon can figure out how to manipulate one. It would have to be clever. And very powerful."

I remembered what she'd said about a demon getting powerful enough to come through, and my stomach twisted. "How powerful?"

"Let's worry about that later on. You need to find out about the game." She stood and beckoned me to follow her. "In the meantime, I'll put together some things for you to start cleansing."

I followed her downstairs on slightly wobbly legs, leaning against the counter for support, thoughts racing as I watched her bustle around, gathering herbs and oils, pouring and grinding. She added white candles and several different crystals to the pile assembled on the counter.

Demons and witches and spells. Energy signatures. Danger. My thoughts bounced around like hail on a hot roof, making no sense.

I doubted there were enough herbs in the world to ground me at this point. I felt like I might just fall over or float away, like I wasn't quite in my body.

Cassandra peered at me as she passed by, then reached out and handed me a chunk of something. "Hang on to this."

I closed my fingers around it automatically, feeling it smooth and cool before it started to warm. "What is it?"

"Smoky quartz. Keep hold of it while I finish."

I did as she told me and slowly started to feel a little more together. Cassandra nodded as she poured oil into a bottle. "That's better. Put it in your pocket and keep it close for a few days."

I opened my hand and stared down at the translucent stone. "You're going to tell me crystals can affect energy patterns or something, aren't you?"

"Smart girl."

My mother's daughter. The thought rose unwanted, and I almost dropped the crystal.

As I slipped it into my jacket pocket, another even less pleasant thought struck me. "What's to stop the demon from fixing the binding now that the chip is gone?"

"If I'm right about your energy signature changing, then the spell would have to be redone. Refocused on who you are now. Your energy field won't be quite the same, even without the chip. And this time you would have to consent."

Okay. That made me feel fractionally better. Because consenting to a demon didn't sound like anything I was likely to do any time soon. Still, my fingers played with the stone in my pocket.

"Which doesn't mean it won't try," Cassandra added. "It won't like having lost a healthy power source."

"You really do need to work on that bedside thing," I told her, wondering why I didn't feel more shocked. Maybe my nerves had just had all they could take for one day. "Sometimes being a mushroom is just what the doctor ordered."

"Be a mushroom on your own time," she said with a shake of her head as she started bundling things into a carrier bag.

I gripped the crystal tighter. "You mean a demon could be coming after me?"

Cassandra nodded. "But it's okay. We'll be watching your back."

"That's the 'we' you haven't exactly explained? Isn't that kind of making me a mushroom?" I protested.

"Even people don't need to know what they don't need to know." She handed me the carrier bag. "Start with this. We'll talk more tomorrow."

"I can't wait," I muttered as I headed for the door.

Damon's car was parked outside the store. Not the one that had brought me here but the big black one that I'd ridden in with him all those other times.

Fuck. I should've known he wouldn't leave me alone. He had to do things his way.

I scowled at the dark windows, turned on my heel, and started walking in the opposite direction, in no mood for company after the revelations I'd just been through.

I had a vague idea where the nearest Muni station was. I'd get home under my own steam.

Where I'd have a very long hot bath in Cassandra's oil, drink her herbal gunk, and then hopefully fall asleep for a week or two.

Behind me a car door slammed, then came the sound of rapid footsteps.

"Where are you going?" Damon asked.

"Home," I snarled. "I'm tired."

"You're in no fit state to walk."

What did he know? If what Cassandra had said was true, I was going to be feeling healthier than I ever had in my life now that a demon wasn't sucking my energy away.

I didn't want to think about anything else she'd said.

"I'm in no fit state to keep anyone company, Damon. Go away." I kept walking, speeding up even though my legs felt like I was wearing concrete boots.

"No." He overtook me in two long steps, turned, and blocked my path. "What did she say to you?"

Where would I start? With the part where I'd been bound to a demon? Or the part where Cassandra thought my mother may have been the one to do it? Or, better yet, the part where the demon might just be coming for me again to turn me back into its personal snack bar?

I had no intention of telling him any of it. I tried to go around him. "It doesn't matter."

He moved with me. "Yes, it does. Tell me."

"Back off. This is my shit." I waved my wrist in his face. "And seeing as I don't have a chip, I'm no use to you. So you don't get to tell me what to do anymore." And I could kiss my paycheck and my hopes for the house goodbye. Not to mention any tech that needed a chip.

"You think I'm firing you?" he asked incredulously.

I stared at him. "Aren't you?"

"No. You have to figure out this static generator issue."

"How? No chip, remember?"

"We'll do it the old-fashioned way. You can still search the code with a headset. I still need your help, Maggie." He put a hand on my arm, and I wanted to let myself move closer and just rest against him for a moment.

God. I couldn't even think about code right now.

"I need a drink," I muttered.

He dropped his hand with a wink. "That I can arrange. Dinner even," he added. "It's been a long time since breakfast, and you've been through a lot."

Understatement of the century.

Despite myself, my stomach rumbled at the thought of food. And Damon could definitely afford better-quality alcohol than me. Plus he had that very nice car to drive me home afterward.

It couldn't hurt to let him take charge, just for one dinner. To let him take care of me and wrap me in his nice safe world where I could pretend witches and demons didn't exist. Just this once . . .

"I want steak," I said. "And scotch. Single malt. Very, very old single malt."

The grin that spread across his face was very "master of the universe gets his way."

"Is there any other kind?"

Chapter Nine

TURNED out my instincts were right. Two hours, a steak as big as my head, and one and a half scotches later, my mood had lifted to comfortably numb rather than totally freaked out.

"Ready to talk about it yet?" Damon asked, reaching for his half-empty glass. The light from the candles on the table sent shards of red reflections from his pinot noir dancing across the table.

What remained of the ice in my scotch clinked softly as I considered the question. I'd been waiting for him to steer the conversation in this direction. I hadn't expected it to take several hours for him to get around to it. Hours that had slid by very easily with us just talking about anything other than chips and games and witches.

Maybe too easily. Talking to him was like talking to an old friend. But I'd had a little too much scotch to decide how I felt about that. It might take even more before I was ready to deal with all the shocks of the last day or so. "Not really."

His eyes narrowed, but then he seemed to decide to let it slide. He took a couple of swallows of wine and eased his chair back from the table.

Wise man.

We were the only two left in the tiny Nob Hill restaurant. The antique analog clock on the wall told me it was close to midnight.

The witching hour.

I slapped the thought away, swigged whiskey, and tried to think about a bath and Cassandra's herbs. Tried *not* to think about how good Damon looked right now. Or how Cassandra had said sex would be good for me. The warm glow of scotch was making it hard to remember why I shouldn't just follow her advice, especially while Damon's eyes held a glinting light that even slightly tipsy me couldn't pretend was strictly professional.

"We should get going," I said, holding on to my sense of self-preservation with an increasingly slippery grasp.

"Okay."

His easy agreement stung. And those instincts of mine that I kept such a tight rein on muttered low in my belly, everything female and interested and in need of some . . . grounding, rebelling. I wasn't quite ready to let him disappear into the night yet. Apparently scotch and surgery and unpleasant revelations didn't exactly enhance my ability to be logical. "Can we stop at my office?"

"At this hour?"

I held out my shielded wrist. "If I have to do the rest of your job the old-fashioned way, then there's some stuff I need. It won't take long." Just long enough for me to grab things and check in with my service.

Now that I was chipless and likely to remain so, I needed to think about my next client. Even if Damon was serious about wanting to keep me on for now, I wasn't going to be much use to him in the future with no chip.

So I needed to start planning. No rest for the wicked after all.

Damon paid the check with a minimum of fuss, and twenty minutes later, I let myself into my tiny office, waving the lights into half-life. Any brighter would just wake me up, and I was enjoying the nice floaty feeling I had going on.

It stopped me from thinking too hard.

Damon stood near the door, watching me as I powered up my system. Light and shadow from the adscreens on the opposite building played across his face and my breath caught.

Damn. The man was hot.

He caught me looking. "What?"

I ducked my head. "Nothing. I won't be much longer."

"Maggie." His voice was a low rumble in the darkness. "You're avoiding."

"Discretion is the better part of valor." I looked up and found him right next to me. Warm. Solid. Smelling like man and strength and spice and, ever so faintly, of wine. In other words, yummy.

Heat scorched over my face. I looked back at the screen, but the letters and images made no sense at all.

"Maggie," he repeated. "You can talk to me."

His voice rolled through me like heavy bass, sinking through my skin and lighting fires as it did. Talking so wasn't what I wanted. And I was worried that I might just be dumb enough to reach out for what I'd been trying to deny all week.

He moved closer still, and his arm brushed mine.

"Oh, what the hell," I said, making my mind up for once. Sex with Damon Riley had to be better than ceremonial baths with stinky herbs. I grabbed his tie and pulled his head down to me, seeking oblivion.

Our lips touched and I tasted him. Then his tongue moved against mine, and things got a little blurry in a way that had nothing at all to do with scotch. I pulled back when they finally cleared and stared up at him, breathing hard. "What was that?"

Damon grinned, seeming somewhat stunned. "I don't know. Let's do it again."

He kissed me again, and things got way beyond blurry as I

let myself let go. I wanted his hands on me, but at the same time felt like I might explode if he touched me. My nipples ached as I wrapped my arms around his neck and hung on for dear life, riding the heat.

His hand slid between us and flicked open the top two buttons of my shirt. He barely paused before his hand was inside the fabric and brushing the lace of my bra. Two fingers captured one nipple and rubbed it exactly right. I purred against his mouth, unable to stop myself.

"Like that, do you? Good," he muttered and did it again. At which point my Sara side took over and sanity fled the room.

I reached down and did some unbuttoning of my own, dispatching zippers and layers of cloth until I had him, hot and hard against my hand.

"Jesus, Maggie. Are you trying to kill me?"

"No, just fuck you." I tightened my grip.

He didn't need much encouragement. He lifted me in one swift movement and turned. The edge of the desk bit into the backs of my thighs, and several stacks of miscellaneous desk crap slipped and crashed to the floor as he swept the surface clean. He kissed me harder and we did the blurry thing again, though this time it didn't clear when he stopped. His hand slid under my skirt, and the other arm pulled my hips toward him. He pressed hard against the fabric of my panties even as his hand moved to shove the barrier aside.

He paused one last time as his cock slid against me. "Any last words?"

I looked at him and smiled. "Yes," I said, then arched to take him.

"You got it," he said and began to move.

Is this what grounded feels like?

The thought drifted across my mind sometime later as I lay on my back on the floor, breathing heavily and feeling no pain. I would've thought grounded meant solid and real, not boneless and floating.

But I couldn't bring myself to care too much about the definition. Not after what we'd just done.

Or *who* I'd just done. Damon Riley. Right here in my office. On my desk. And it had been *fabulous*.

A grin spread across my face and I stretched. Besides me, Damon stirred and rolled onto his side. The look on his face made me smile harder.

"Hi," he said.

"Hi, yourself," I replied and moved closer.

"I think we should do that again." I nodded before I could think. He sat up. "But not here." He laced his fingers into mine and pulled me to my feet.

"Where are we going?" I asked, not caring.

"My place," he said, releasing my hands and kissing me quickly before bending to pick up his clothes.

I followed suit, finding my jacket and shoes and skirt, fastening my bra and buttoning the shirt. Not the easiest task given several buttons had gone AWOL. I was still hunting for my panties and stacking things haphazardly on my desk when Damon came up behind me.

"You're taking too long," he growled into my ear. I forgot all about underwear and organization and turned into his embrace. This time the kiss was longer and hotter.

"Patience," he said, breaking for air. I made a sound in protest, but he just grabbed my hand and led me toward the door, snagging my bag from the chair as he passed.

The car was waiting at the curb, the driver standing by the open back door.

"Home, fast," Damon said as I stepped into the car and slid along the smooth leather of the seat. A few seconds later he followed, touching a button that blacked the screen between us and the driver as he pulled the door shut behind him with his other hand.

"What are you doing?" I whispered.

Damon grinned, teeth very white in the dim light. "Don't worry, he can't hear us. Now come here. I'm not wasting half an hour." He slid partway toward me on the seat.

My brain reeled and my cheeks flamed. The driver was approximately two feet away, screen or no screen. "We can't do that here. We're in a *car*."

He laughed. "As opposed to an office? This is softer, for one thing." He reached out and ran a hand up my leg, sending shivers of pleasure along my nerve endings.

My resolve wavered. "Well, I guess we could fool around a little."

"Good." He pulled me toward him and kissed me, hot and sweet and hungry all at once.

That much I could handle. I let myself flow into it, reveling in the play of lips and tongues and skin.

After a long moment, his hands began to roam over my body, and I decided I could handle that too. In fact, I could return the favor. It was when his fingers moved to my few remaining buttons that my brain took over again.

"What are you doing?" I asked against his mouth. His hand had reached my breast, and I arched into him despite myself.

"Hopefully you," he said. "Stop thinking, Maggie."

I pulled away, jerking my head toward the front of the car. "Your driver is right *there*."

"And I told you, he can't hear anything. Or see anything." His voice was thick with the heat circling us. It did interesting things to my stomach.

He took advantage of the space between us to kneel on the seat. There was plenty of room—the limo was huge. I made a mental note to talk to him about environmental responsibility before his hands were on me again, and somehow I ended up on my back, leather soft underneath me and Damon hard above me.

He found my mouth before I could say anything, and I went boneless and breathless and wanting again.

My mind hadn't completely gone though. He began to kiss his way down my body, circling and tracing my skin with his tongue. His right hand pushed my skirt up and I remembered the no underwear issue at the same moment his fingers slid into me. I tried to wriggle away, but that only made it feel better as he moved with me.

"What are you doing?" I managed to say before he moved again and I gasped.

His tongue circled my navel before he raised his head. "Stopping you thinking," he said. "Is it working?"

He bent his head again and moved even lower, skipping the roll of fabric that was my skirt and finding the skin of my upper thigh. He slid his fingers inside me again, and I moaned and twisted.

"I'll take that as a yes," he said softly, and then his mouth closed over me, hot and soft and *God*, so right. I forgot about the driver, forgot about where I was, forgot about everything but Damon and his touch and his tongue and the heat until I couldn't take it anymore and I came, screaming.

"We're here," Damon announced shortly after. I raised my head and looked at him blankly. "We're here," he repeated, and I realized the car had stopped.

"Shit." I scrambled into an upright position, trying to straighten my clothes for the second time. The driver would be opening that back door any minute and—

"Slow down," Damon said. "The driver's gone. He's very, um, understanding." He grinned at me, and I felt myself blushing at the thought of the guy—I really needed to learn his name—being discreet because he knew his boss was doing wonderful things to me in the back seat. The man didn't even look like he knew the meaning of discreet.

"Shit," I said again. "I guess he's had lots of practice." I glared at Damon, feeling stupid. Of course he had done this before. He was rich and sexy, and women would be dying to get into his goddamn stretch limousine. I shoved the top button of my shirt closed with enough force to make it fly off.

"No," Damon said. "I'm not that guy. Don't believe what you might have read in the press about me. And you're thinking too much again." He kissed me, lips soft as his voice, and I felt the anger and embarrassment melt away.

"Sorry, I'm not good at this."

His dimples leapt into life. "Oh, I think you're good at it," he said in his deadly purr.

I blushed as a goofy grin spread across my face.

"So can we get out of the car now?" he continued. "Fond as I suddenly am of desks and cars, I happen to have this great bed upstairs and a whole lot of ideas."

Despite the fact that I was already three orgasms in, heat stirred again. The man was a genius.

"Then what's taking you so long?" I said and pushed him toward the door.

When I finally woke, the room wasn't fully dark. Hints of daylight were escaping from behind the thick curtains. Morning, my brain decided, but very early. I shut my eyes again, settling back against the warmth of solid male behind me. His arm tightened around me and I smiled. My first impression had been right—he definitely knew all about sinning.

And whether due to great sex or sheer exhaustion or something else altogether, I'd slept. Slept like the dead. No dreams. Better yet, no nightmares.

It was vaguely unsettling, but I wanted more. I tried to slow my breathing and slip under again, but my bladder had other ideas. I wriggled out from under Damon's arm, watching as he rolled over and curled into the covers like a cat, and then sat up on the edge of the vast bed.

Where was the bathroom?

I studied the room in the dim morning light. It was big enough to make the bed seem small. Curtains covered the length of wall opposite the bed, possibly blue, though it was hard to tell. No bathroom there though. To my left was the door I could vaguely remember tumbling through after our mad dash through the house last night. I looked right, making out two faint outlines that could be doors. Closet and bathroom, I decided. I would just have to take a guess.

I padded across the thick carpet to the nearest door, then stopped, confused. No door handle. I put my hand on the smooth wood and the door swung open, revealing gleaming glass and mirrors. Good guess. I stepped inside and the door swung shut behind me, making no noise. Neat, but hopefully powered by something that had lots of backups.

I took care of my most pressing need and stood at the sink to wash my hands, gawking at the luxurious room. It was big, big enough to hold a huge tub, a separate shower that looked large enough for three people with multiple shower heads sprouting from the blue and white tile, cabinets, and the room-length vanity that held two sinks. Soft lights had sprung to life when I first walked in, and brighter ones had switched on as I approached the long counter and the massive pristine mirror hanging above it.

Despite the lipstick long lost to Damon's kisses, and the tousled hair, I looked good. Damon obviously agreed with me.

My hands slowed under the stream of water.

He agreed with me?

Oh no. *Bad* thought. This was supposed to be mindless sex to take my mind away from the mess of my life. Exactly what the witch doctor ordered.

There weren't supposed to be any warm and fuzzy feelings. I didn't do warm and fuzzy feelings with men. Especially not with clients.

Just sex. One night only.

The woman in the mirror looked skeptical. My body agreed with her. It wanted more.

My body and my reflection were idiots.

Idiots who were in charge, because even though the smart thing would've been to go back out there, gather up my clothes, call a cab, and leave, I found myself drawn to the bed like it was magnetized.

I slid under the covers carefully, keeping space between us, telling myself I'd just sleep for a few more hours. But as soon as my head hit the pillow, Damon rolled, catching his arm around me and pulling me back against his chest. He had done it several times during the night, each time filling me with a ridiculous glow of warmth and safety and contentment.

"Your feet are cold," he said sleepily into the top of my head, and the sound of his voice sent a shiver of pleasure through me. I snuggled closer. Apparently I wasn't ready to go anywhere just yet.

I sighed and relaxed against him. "Go back to sleep," I said, then listened to his breathing, feeling the rise and fall of his chest against my skin slow and deepen.

When I was sure he was asleep, I let myself do the same.

I was alone when I woke. I sat up, feeling small in the big empty space. Someone, Damon presumably, had half opened the curtains, and clear sunlight flooded in. At last I could see where I was. Apart from my bathroom excursion, last night's impressions had pretty much been limited to big room, soft mattress, and hot naked guy. Without said hot naked guy distracting me, I was curious to see what his bedroom looked like.

Simple. Simple but expensive, I amended. White walls, deep blue curtains, plain lamps made out of the same pale wood as the bed. In front of the window was a huge squishy chaise, currently draped with Damon's jacket. The walls were broken by several large pictures—no, movie posters. Old sci-fi and adventure stuff: *Star Wars* and *Indiana Jones* and *The Lord of the Rings*, even a *King Kong*. Worth a lot if they were originals. Damon obviously shared Nat's retro taste. A gamer thing, I guess.

Speaking of Damon, where was he? I wrestled with my conscience. Part of me knew I should get dressed and leave, but part of me wanted to stay. Without Damon himself to weaken my resolve, logic won.

Things would be better if I left. Hopefully I'd done my aura some good last night, but if I started spinning the scenario into something longer term, then more important things than my aura were at stake. Like my job.

And maybe, if I was completely honest with myself and listened to the tiny voice of protest as I stepped out of the bed, my heart.

My clothes had formed a small, wrinkled pile at the foot of the bed. I picked them up, pulling a face. The shirt had lost a button and my skirt resembled a rag. The combination of hospital and incense and sweat and sex covering everything made my nose wrinkle.

I couldn't wear any of it.

I headed for the other door near the bathroom. Bingo, a walk-in closet. I pulled a white shirt off a hanger at random and slipped into it, then found a pair of boxers and sweats that fit me once I cuffed them a few times.

My shoes were fine. The outfit wasn't going to win me any style points, but at least it was clean.

Now if only I knew where I was.

Walking back to the window, I pulled the curtains all the way back and looked out onto a vista of manicured garden.

Tall trees edged the expanse of perfect lawn and neat garden beds. Beyond them I caught glimpses of pale walls and big windows and tiled roofs that suggested other big houses, but nothing that gave me a landmark.

Apparently I'd paid no attention at all last night in the car.

My cheeks heated as I remembered exactly what I *had* been doing last night. The slight stiffness of my body as I stretched my arms reminded me as well.

"Now there's a pleasant view."

I spun to see Damon at the door, wearing a dark blue robe and carrying a tray that wafted good smells.

"Hi," he said. "Nice shirt." He walked over and put the tray down on the bed before joining me by the window.

"I hope you don't mind, but my things are kind of . . . ." I wrinkled my nose and waved at the pile.

Damon looked at me, then deliberately slid his gaze down my body and up again. I fought the urge to do up a few more buttons as heat rose in the wake of his eyes.

His eyes darkened to a shade close to his robe. "I don't mind. In fact, you can steal my clothes any time."

"Thanks." I turned away as he reached for me, unnerved by the strength of my attraction in the clear light of day. I couldn't blame alcohol or shock or stress now. And Damon didn't look any less appealing.

And then, to add to my confusion, there was the memory of the things we had done last night. "Is that breakfast?"

He nodded. "You were sleeping pretty hard. I didn't want to wake you."

I paused in my investigation of the tray, croissant in hand. I had slept well. All night. I hoped it was due to the fact that I no longer had a demon hanging on to me rather than being in Damon's bed. "That was nice of you."

I bit into the croissant, not knowing what else to say. I wasn't used to the morning-after process. I usually kicked the guy out before the sleeping part. Feeling awkward made me cranky. What exactly was the etiquette for waking up with your boss?

Damon passed me coffee in silence, and I wondered if he felt as weird as I did. Maybe he was just trying to work out the polite way to kick me out after all.

"You know, I can just get going . . . ."

"What's the rush?"

"Well, for one thing, I need to go home and change. I can't go into work dressed like this." I gestured at the shirt with the croissant.

"It's okay with the boss, if that makes you feel any better." He wiggled his eyebrows at me, swigging coffee.

"Not really."

"Then buy something online. They can deliver it here. Besides, it's the weekend. I know we're all hands on deck, but you need to take it easy. Are you registered anywhere?"

I shook my head, mouth full of flaky pastry that tasted almost as good as him. "No." Registration meant custom sizing, body scans, and tailoring. All in the comfort of your own computer. My budget was definitely off the shelf only.

"But you know your sizes, right?" He gave me another look that seemed to say he could make a pretty good guess at them himself.

I nodded, taking another bite. The memory of his hands sliding over my skin warmed my cheeks.

"Good." He crossed to me and took the non-croissant hand. "Come on."

As soon as his fingers tangled with mine, my resistance melted again and I followed obediently.

He only let go of my hand when we reached another room across the hallway, and then only long enough to lay his palm against the very expensive security scanner. I took one last bite and wiped my hands free of crumbs as I followed him through the door.

"It's me," he said, and lights sprang to life as a screen slid up from the big mahogany desk. "Access shopping channels." He steered me across the room and motioned for me to take the chair.

The room was clean and uncluttered. I assumed most of his work paraphernalia would be hidden away until needed, like the screen.

"Knock yourself out," Damon said, leaning on the desk next to me.

I tried to ignore the scent of him and the heat radiating off his body under the robe. Mostly I tried to ignore the very nice chest I was getting an eyeful of. I focused on the screen, looking for names I recognized. Luckily there were a few stores in my price range. I touched a logo and sorted swiftly through the choices.

"I'm paying for this," I said, risking a glance at Damon. No way was he paying for my clothes.

He shrugged. "Fine. This is all connected to my account, but I'll copy the bill to you and take it out of your fee."

"Good." I selected pants and a shirt and added underwear as quickly as possible.

"Finished?" Damon asked as I dropped my hands. At my nod, he touched a couple of keys to finalize the order. "Should be an hour or so. The gate guard will bring it up to Amy."

"Amy?"

"My housekeeper."

"You have a housekeeper?" And a gate guard? *Right. Rich.* I needed to remember that. *Rich. Rich. Rich. Out of my league. Off-limits.* Good reminder.

I blushed as another thought struck me. We hadn't exactly made it to the bedroom immediately last night. I had tackled him on the stairs and repaid the service he had done me in the car. Neither of us had been quiet. All the time with a housekeeper somewhere in the house?

"Yes. But she doesn't sleep here." He must have read my

mind. "And the security system doesn't record authorized guests."

Cameras? Authorized guests? I vaguely remembered a flash of red as we walked inside the front door. A body scan. I was an authorized person after one night? Hopefully he was telling the truth. I didn't relish the thought of being the star of some security drone's vidporn fantasy.

"Scout's honor."

I looked up at him, all gorgeous and reassuring. He smelled wonderful too. Why was I resisting again? After all, we had another hour to kill. "Kiss me and I'll believe you."

"A lady after my own heart," he said. He held out his hand and I took it as I stood. "And now that's done, we have this hour or so . . . ."

I batted my eyelashes at him. "Why, however are we going to fill the time?"

He pulled me close. "Well, I don't know about you but last night, while great, was very—"

"Very what?"

He began kissing my neck. "Very fast." Kiss. "And hot." Kiss. "And dark." Kiss. My legs started to tremble. "I wanna see what we can do when it's light."

I couldn't speak. The thought of him and me and a light-flooded room had dried my mouth.

He picked me up effortlessly, no mean feat. "And," he added, "I want to see what you look like when I take things slow. Very slow."

Me too.

I tightened my arms around his neck and let him sweep me away.

Chapter Ten

"You know, you have to let me go home sometime," I said. I'd kind of lost track of time but knew it was getting late from the color of the light through the windows. Apparently time passed quickly in Damon Riley's bed.

"Why?" Damon muttered sleepily, pulling me tighter against him.

I twisted in his arms, which only gave him the chance to hook his leg over mine and pull me closer still. Too close. I had to bite my lip not to gasp as our hips came into contact. "I'm serious. Nat will be wondering where I am."

Damon cracked open one blue eye. "You're a big girl, and so is she." His hand skimmed down my back.

I repressed a purr. *Nat. Worried. Me leaving.* That was the topic. Not sex. "Yes, and big girls check in with their best friends. They don't just drop off the face of the earth."

Guilt stabbed at my stomach, burning away some of the endorphin-overloaded fog of pleasure. I put a little distance between us, tucking as much of the sheet as I could around me. Stupidly expensive three-zillion-thread-count cotton wasn't much of a barrier, but it was the best I could do at this point. "Does she even know I'm okay?" Guilt twinged. I should have called Nat myself. But I hadn't touched my datapad since I'd left the hospital.

He yawned, showing gleaming white teeth, then frowned down at the sheet between us. "Yes. I called her when you left the hospital. Said you needed some time to yourself."

"And she accepted that?"

"No, but I don't think she wanted to yell at her new boss just yet." He propped himself up on one arm and studied me, a long, lazy grin spreading across his face.

I ignored my automatic instinct to move closer to the smile. "That won't last."

"I had a feeling." His hand drifted down my side, warming the cotton and my skin.

I shimmied backward. "Oh no, you don't."

"What?" He tried to look innocent.

"You know very well what."

"I do?" He rolled onto his back and stretched. Pure beautifully muscled temptation. The only part of the sheet I'd left him lay across his stomach and upper thighs, spoiling my view.

No. That wasn't right. I didn't care about the view. I needed to leave. After all, we had work to do. Work he was paying me for. And beyond that, I had stuff to think about. Stuff that needed serious alone time.

"You know exactly what I mean," I said, trying to convince myself to sit up and get out of the bed before I forgot all those good reasons to leave.

His head turned toward me, followed by the rest of him. The sheet slipped and my pulse hitched.

"I'm a little slow," he said. "Sleep deprived for some reason. You'll have to spell it out for me."

"No beguiling me with sex," I snapped.

"You're beguiled?" His expression turned smug. "Already? Hell, girl, you ain't seen nothing yet." He hitched forward and the sheet gave up the fight, revealing he was more than ready for round five. Or was it six?

I'd lost count? Triple hell.

This man was definitely dangerous. I didn't do beguiled. Too complicated. Especially when the one doing the beguiling was someone like Damon.

I wriggled backward until I was balanced precariously on the edge of the huge bed. "Down, boy."

"I just want to make the most of this opportunity. In case it's a onetime offer." The pleasure on his face vanished. "Is it?"

I froze. Was he asking if we could do this again? Or giving me an out? Did I want an out? I should have wanted an out, because this was still a terrible idea, no matter how good the sex was.

I looked at him, temptation wrapped in nothing at all, thought about never having his hands on me again, then sighed. I just couldn't do it. Not yet. "Somehow I doubt it."

His delighted smile nearly stole my resolve. And haunted me all through the steaming-hot shower that failed completely to wash the feel of him off my skin.

"She's not even home," Damon said from behind me when we finally walked into my very silent apartment.

"Maybe she's asleep. She probably went gaming last night." Hopefully I was right about that. The silence was unusual. Nat normally hung around Saturday afternoon, either cooking up a storm or relaxing in preparation for a big night of competition.

His arms came around my waist. "Maybe she's out, and we're wasting a perfectly good opportunity."

I wriggled free. "Is that all you can think about?" I stuck my head through the door to the hall and saw Nat's bedroom door standing open. That would be a no to her taking a nap, then.

Damon came up behind me and wrapped his arms

around me again. "Don't tell me you're not thinking about it too," he growled.

I tried to ignore the instant rush of heat. "I have other things on my mind." Like demons. And looking for the bug in the static.

"C'mon, Maggie," he coaxed. "There's a bed just down that hall, right? I showed you mine, you show me yours."

It was nearly irresistible. Damon's hands and mouth and body against mine. A place where I didn't have to think. Didn't have to deal with witches and demons or any of it.

Trouble was I'd been avoiding dealing for nearly a day. At some point, denial wasn't going to work anymore.

Damon's lips skimmed the edge of my ear and I melted. I wondered if I could justify giving in to him on the grounds of, um, grounding. But after the last twelve hours or so, I figured I was as grounded as I could stand. Bits of me that I hadn't felt in a while were aching—in a good way, but still aching.

Self-preservation won out.

I slipped out of his grip, shaking my head. "Nat could come home any moment."

"And she might not. Even if she does, what's the big deal? Surely you two have guys over now and then?"

I ducked my head. Right now wasn't the time to explain the rules of my sex life to him. Not when I'd already broken them as far as he was concerned. "You're not just a guy. You're my boss. And hers."

"I'm not just your boss."

I sat down on the nearest chair with a bump. What did that mean? And how did I feel about it? "You're not?"

"You have to ask that after last night?"

I nodded. "Because it was only *one* night. What are we supposed to be now?"

He shoved his hands into the front pockets of his jeans. "I hope, at least, that I'm now more than just the guy signing your paycheck."

Hopefully my cheeks weren't as hot as they felt. "We still need to find that out. And the fact that you *are* the guy signing my paycheck complicates matters."

"Are you saying you want this to be done? Or to quit?" His voice had turned a little chilly. It made me want to do something to get the sexy Damon back. That impulse was enough to make me even more confused about what was going on.

"No." I sighed, my thoughts spiraling around and getting me nowhere. Too much to think about. Too many changes. "But this is why we need to take things slowly."

"Isn't it a bit late for that?" he said, lifting one dark eyebrow.

I refused the bait. "I mean, we both need to think about this. Work out how we feel."

"What's to think about? We were fantastic."

I pushed to my feet. "Great sex isn't a relationship. And great sex with your boss tends to be career suicide."

"Who has to know?"

"Are you kidding me? You're the exact opposite of low-profile. We start doing this on a regular basis and it's going to get out, even if we try to be sneaky."

"Would it be so terrible if people knew?" He was sounding chilly again. Chilly and slightly confused.

"That depends. I have a professional reputation to protect. I need the people I work with to respect what I do, not think they can sleep with me or get to the guy I'm sleeping with. So in this case, no, just great sex isn't enough."

He rubbed a hand over the stubble lining his chin. "You want more?"

No. Yes. Who the hell knows? My neck muscles ached. Much more of this and I'd be back in serious headache territory. "What I want is time to think. I don't know more than that. I've only known you just over a week. And it hasn't exactly been a normal week." I stopped myself before I could add, "And you don't even know everything about what happened."

This was definitely not the moment to confess all. I needed time to get my head straight.

"Maybe you do this all the time, but I don't," I finished, hating the defensive tone in my voice.

"This? You mean sleep with people who work for me? No. I don't." He moved closer. "But you can't deny there's something between us." His finger traced my jaw and my breath caught. "Can you?"

"No," I said honestly, stepping back. "No. There's definitely something, but—"

His mouth twisted. "We fit. The way I see it, we can fight it or run with it. I think you know what I'm voting for."

I stared up at him in frustration. Easy for him to say. He ruled his world. There wasn't going to be any fallout for him if this went wrong. "Maybe this is why you're the big-shot billionaire and I'm not, but I just don't make up my mind that fast."

"You want a list of my pros and cons?" he teased. "Playing safe doesn't always get you what you need, Maggie."

Maybe not, but I'd fought hard for the safety and order in my life. I couldn't just be careless about this. "I don't need a list." Big lie. I was so going to drive myself nuts writing mental pluses and minuses in the next few days. It was a little scary that he saw that in me. "I just need some time. Alone."

The teasing light in his eyes faded as he held up his hands. "Okay. I get it. You need girl time. Call me when you're done thinking."

I blew out a breath as my stomach twisted. "Now you're mad. See, this is what I was talking about. You shouldn't be mad that I need some time after one night."

"I'm not mad. Just confused."

"Me too. And one thing last night proved is that neither of us is going to have an easy time thinking straight while we're together."

That earned me a small smile and my stomach eased.

"Maybe you're right." He looked down at his watch. "I should go downtown and check in with work anyway."

"I—"

"No," he said before I could finish. "You rest up. Your job will be easier if the other guys have had time to look at the filter first and see if anything looks weird. I'll see you Monday."

Monday? Why did that make my stomach sink? I'd gotten what I wanted, hadn't I?

Hearing the door close behind Damon, feeling my lips buzz where he'd dropped one last fierce kiss on me, I wasn't so sure.

"What stinks?" Nat said as she wandered into my bedroom around six.

I propped myself up on my elbows, glad she was finally home. I'd been driving myself crazy lying on my bed, bouncing between trying to figure out how I felt about Damon by myself and having mini freak-outs about demons. I'd tried doing some research, but the first few netfeeds on demon lore had made me feel even more freaked. I needed a distraction. Nat was always good for that.

"You're back," I said, a little too chirpily.

She looked at me for a moment, then wrinkled her nose. "Yes. And like I said, what stinks?"

"New bath oil. It's supposed to be relaxing." Now wasn't the time to go into demons and magical possession.

"Only if you've got no sense of smell," she grumbled, scrubbing at her eyes with one hand.

I sympathized. I'd had time to get used to the scent. Mostly. It was woody and green, but there were other stronger, less pleasant smells beneath those. I'd spent my prescribed hour in the bath seeing what I could identify in the mix. To my chagrin, I'd only managed four ingredients. Sara hadn't taught me much but she'd made sure I could identify common herbs and spices and oils. Mostly so she could put me to work mixing stuff up for her clients.

I almost hadn't gotten in when the smell first steamed up from the water. Sara used to make me oils to soak in when I was little. When we were having a good time. She told me they were to help me grow up strong and beautiful. God knows what was actually in them, but they'd made me feel special at the time.

Unlike Cassandra's scrub-the-demon-off-me mix. The heated rush of fragrance seemed to flow straight through me, leaving a choking mix of nostalgia and sheer dread at the thought of a demon riding me all these years in its wake. It had been the latter that had driven me to the bath.

Knowing why I was about to soak in this stuff finally brought it all home, and I'd spent a good five minutes crying and shaking before the feeling that I might never get clean again made me climb in.

I'd stayed in the bath until I'd turned pruney and the water was cold. Half an hour after I'd climbed out, I'd wanted to take another one.

Nat flopped down in the gel chair by my desk. "What happened to you last night? Damon was very mysterious. Are you okay?"

Argh. I put my head back down. What the hell should I tell Nat? "I slept with our boss"? Or "Hey, it's possible I've been under a spell as long as you've known me"?

"Damon took me out to dinner. Turns out scotch after surgery isn't a good idea. He let me crash at his place."

Her gaze flicked down to my wrist. "He said they removed your chip."

"Yes. But I'm okay, really." She looked unconvinced. "It's not a big deal, Nat. One good night's sleep and I'm good to go." I hoped she'd take the bait and focus on the fact I'd stayed at Damon's rather than ask me why they'd had to remove the chip. "Damon has excellent guest rooms."

Just the fact I'd stayed would hopefully distract her. I didn't want to get into the sex part.

Sure enough, Nat's expression turned curious. "Really? What's his house like? What's *he* like?"

Time to change the subject. "Standard mansion. You know. Nothing to tell, really." Nat couldn't argue with that. Her family had its share of mansions. "What about you? Where've you been? You look wiped."

"After you got taken away, I didn't want to go home. So I went gaming with some of the Righteous guys."

"All night?" It wasn't unusual for Nat to play into the wee hours, but it had been a long time since she'd crawled home the following *afternoon.*

She yawned and then nodded. "Yes." She waved a hand in front of her nose, frowning again. "That stuff really reeks."

"It's not that bad. Where did you play?"

"They took me to this new club down by the piers."

"Branching out, are we?" Nat usually stuck to the upmarket clubs in the Haight.

Her eyes narrowed. "What if I am?"

Her tone was a fraction too defensive. Which made me wonder exactly how sleazy this new club might be. Between quake damage and the water level changes, the area around the piers was no longer a tourist attraction. Well, at least, not for tourists looking for wholesome family entertainment. The businesses that had reestablished themselves there were...well, those that were legal were the minority. But I was too tired for another argument. "Just asking. I didn't mean anything by it."

Her shoulders relaxed. "Good. You should come with me. You'd like it."

Not likely. "I think I'll lay off the games for a while. Yesterday was enough for me."

She looked at my arm, frown deepening. "Are you getting another chip once that heals?"

I hesitated. Dr. Barnard had seemed pretty adamant, but I wasn't entirely reconciled to being locked out of the interface for good. After Archangel, I wasn't that keen to keep gaming, but searching code was a lot easier with a chip. An advantage I wasn't ready to entirely write off. But no way was I going to touch a chip until Cassandra could assure me there would be no demons involved—not that I could explain that to Nat. "I'm not sure."

Nat's eyes widened in horror. "You can still game with a headset though?"

"Maybe when I'm feeling better." Right now, the idea of any game was a scary proposition. Better to wait a while, see if my "plug in and let the weirdness begin" karma would disappear now that the bond to the demon was broken. If Cassandra was right about that. "I just need a day or so to rest. And you look like you should be in bed too."

"Yeah," she agreed. "Need to catch some sleep before tonight."

"You're going out again?" I was used to Nat pulling all-nighters, but I'd kind of expected her to stay with me like she'd done after my chip implantation. Or at least want to tone it down a little to be in top form for Righteous.

"You want me to stay here with you?"

Her expression was oddly intent. I didn't know whether it was me, or the aftermath of the surgery, or maybe that Nat was just tired, but there was definitely a weird vibe. Besides, if I was just going to crash all night, there was no point depriving Nat of her fun. "No, you go. I'm just going to sleep."

"Chill." She rose with another yawn. "I guess I'll see you tomorrow."

My stomach's protestations about the lack of dinner woke me at midnight. Staggering out of bed still half-asleep, I found Nat in the kitchen, downing syncaf soda, something she only drank when she was expecting a long night in the clubs.

"Feeling confident, are we?" I asked, rummaging in the fridge for sandwich makings.

Nat frowned. "Huh?"

I tapped her can of soda. "The caffeine? You expecting a big night?"

"I'm just tired." She drained the can and tossed it at the recycler. "Anyway, I'm not the one with the caffeine habit."

Her tone was tense. I paused in my sandwich construction. "Just asking. Chill."

She hitched a shoulder at me but didn't reply as she left the kitchen. A few minutes later, I heard the front door close.

"Goodbye to you too," I yelled at the door, annoyed at her attitude.

Sandwich assembled, I headed to the living room. Thanks to the nap, I didn't hold out any great hope of getting back to sleep any time soon. Channel surfing it would have to be.

Nothing grabbed my attention. Instead, my thoughts turned to Damon and how I could be wrapped around him right now rather than here by myself with only Oreos and chicken salad for company.

My hand crept toward my datapad several times, but I resisted temptation. I was the one who'd sent him away. It would be dumb to send mixed messages before I knew what I wanted. Much as my body protested, I needed time to sort out what happened last night.

And what I wanted to happen in the future.

Besides the obvious.

I killed another few minutes flicking through a couple of cycles of the available channels. Nothing.

Annoyed, I switched off the screen and curled up on the sofa, cocooning myself in my favorite throw.

The sudden silence wrapped around me, making the apartment feel too big somehow. As though the shadows had stretched the room so there were dark places lurking at the edges of my vision.

Perfect for something to hide and watch.

A shiver ran down my spine. "Don't be an idiot," I said firmly.

There was *nothing* in the apartment with me. There couldn't be. Still, I reached over to flick on another lamp and jumped out of my skin when the globe popped and died with a spark of light.

My heart sped into overdrive, banging in my chest like a bird startled into flight.

"Stupid," I muttered when I managed to remember how to breathe. Next time I saw Cassandra, I was going to have to ask her if there was such a thing as the electricity fairy and how one pissed her off. Because I was definitely having a banner week when it came to things blowing up in my face.

I switched out the bulb, then settled back on the couch, this time armed with one of my favorite comfort reads and real chocolate—one of my few expensive habits—rather than cookies. If I wasn't going to sleep, I might as well load up on caffeine and sugar too.

I got about a chapter in before the skin on the back of my neck started to crawl. I lifted my head, turning around slowly. Nothing behind me. There was no way there could be anything behind me. Our security system was the best we could afford, plus Damon had worked his computer—guru-fu on it. The building security was even better. I was just being an idiot.

But I couldn't settle back down to the book. Couldn't focus on the words. Something kept distracting me.

Eventually I got up and prowled around the apartment, opening doors and nervously peering into rooms and cabinets. And I found exactly nothing.

Despite that, when I'd returned to my nest on the sofa, I couldn't shake the nerves. My eyes fell on my datapad. One quick call and Damon would come running—I hoped. If anyone could keep the bedbugs from biting and the bogeyman at bay, it was him.

Of course, then I'd have to worry about what having him in my bed might mean instead of worrying about make-believe things that went bump in the night.

Plus, what if Nat came home? I could hardly call the man over in the middle of the night only to kick him out again after we'd had hot sex. Nor could I come up with a plausible explanation to give Nat if I wasn't here when she got home.

"Suck it up, Maggie," I muttered to myself. My voice seemed to echo weirdly in the apartment and I shivered, then flicked the screen back to life. Only to be rewarded with a blank screen and static.

I thumped the control in frustration, and the picture slowly came into focus.

"Maggie."

I whirled. Nothing. The voice had been soft. Edge-of-hearing soft. Or maybe it hadn't been there at all. Goose bumps blossomed along my arms, all the fine hairs standing to attention. I smoothed them down with slightly shaking fingers.

"Stop being an idiot," I said firmly into the empty room, then reached over to raise the volume on the screen, nibbling on the chocolate bar to soothe my frazzled nerves. The noise of the brainless vidmercial did nothing to dispel the weird atmosphere.

"Nobody here but us chickens," I said firmly into the empty air. "So go away and bug someone else."

It didn't help. I jumped at every creak and groan and whir of the building around me. Several times I dozed off only to jerk awake, heart pounding, the sound of my name ringing in my head.

After the third time, I made myself tea and took it back to

the couch, wrapping the throw tight around my body. The air in the apartment pressed in on me and I curled into a tighter ball, fighting to remind myself to breathe.

Nothing was here. I was alone. And safe.

Logically I knew it was true, but the rest of me wasn't buying it. I sat there for what felt like forever, until suddenly I relaxed as all the spooky sensations disappeared.

I stayed still for another few minutes, waiting for something to spook me again, but nothing did. Eventually I got brave enough to uncurl myself and do another round of the apartment.

Everything was perfectly normal.

"Okay," I said slowly when I reached my bedroom, exhausted. "Maybe it was just some sort of weird reaction to the meds they gave me. Or Cassandra's damn voodoo oil."

That sounded reasonable, but I wasn't really buying it. Instead, I grabbed my datapad and looked up Cassandra's hours. Lucky for me, she was open Sunday mornings.

"Think about it tomorrow," I told myself as I climbed into bed. It had been one of Sara's favorite sayings, stolen from her favorite ancient movie heroine. For once I found it comforting rather than annoying as I dropped off to sleep.

I didn't hear Nat come home, but a quick look into her bedroom when I forced myself to crawl out of bed after just a few hours of sleep revealed a mussed blonde head on the pillow.

At least one of us had a good night.

Now that the sun was up, I felt somewhat stupid that I'd let myself get so rattled. But I was also determined to talk to Cassandra.

Just to put my fears to rest once and for all.

I reached her store just after nine, feeling gritty-eyed and wrung out despite the two coffees I'd downed on the way.

The neighborhood around Cassandra's store still seemed sleepy. One lone café was open, though not exactly inviting with a security shield out front. Otherwise the streets were mostly deserted. Luckily Cassandra seemed to be an early riser.

Her door had an Open sign, and the buzz of her scanner brought her out from the back room in a flash.

Her eyebrows rose a little when she saw me. "Couldn't stay away?" she asked, settling herself on a stool behind the glass topped counter.

I shook my head. "I have a couple of questions."

"Looking at you, that doesn't surprise me. I thought I told you to ground yourself?"

"I did," I protested. "I used the herbs and everything."

She peered at me, an assessing expression on her face. "And maybe not just the herbs?" she asked with a grin.

I tried not to blush. "Does it matter?"

One shoulder hitched. "Maybe. Maybe not. Your aura looks a bit better, but your energy is all over the place. Did you rest at all?"

"I tried to."

Her eyes fastened on mine. It wasn't comforting. "Tried?"

"I woke up last night and couldn't get back to sleep. Maybe I'm just paranoid, but it felt like someone was watching me."

"Describe the sensation."

I crossed my arms, feeling cold again. "You know. Prickles at the back of my neck. Uneasiness. It's dumb, I know. I'm probably just tired."

Cassandra fingered the heavy silver pendant at her throat. "Did something specific wake you? A sound? Someone calling your name?"

"No . . . ."

"You don't sound terribly convinced."

"Nothing woke me the first time, but I kept thinking someone was talking just out of hearing."

"Do you often feel that way?" She pursed her lips, still twisting the pendant.

I shook my head. "No. No, I'm usually fine on my own. I'm not jumpy at all."

"But not last night?" She beckoned me closer and held out her hand. I took it and waited while she closed her eyes, humming softly to herself.

The sound was soothing, and the tension started flowing out of my body. By the time her eyes opened again, I was a lot calmer.

"Well? Could it be the demon? Or something like it?" I asked.

"There's nothing that makes me think something was trying to get to you. But it's possible. Something was speaking to your intuition, and that's not to be argued with. You're going to have to learn how to protect yourself."

"I'm good with a gun." I didn't own one, but I knew how to shoot one. Nat had made me go with her to the range a few times. She figured knowing how to fire the real thing might help her reflexes in the games. I'm not sure it worked, but both of us were decent shots.

She smiled and shook a finger at me. "Not that way. Psychically. Magically."

"But I don't have any power."

She tilted her head. "Perhaps, but you can still learn how to keep your mind closed."

It sounded good to me. I didn't want to turn into someone who jumped at shadows and couldn't sleep with the lights turned off, so if whatever it was Cassandra was talking about could help, then I'd try it. No matter how much I disliked it, I'd never doubted that magic worked. "How fast can you teach me?"

"It depends on how good a student you are. It's not the type of thing you can pick up in a day."

Of course not. That would be too easy. "But you can teach me?"

She nodded. "It's something we teach everyone who has power, and the technique works for those who don't too."

I bit my lip, the thought of coming anywhere near the edge of real magic making me queasy. But not as queasy as the thought of a demon trying to invade my mind. "Okay."

"Your mother never taught you any of this?"

"No. I guess when I was little, she figured she'd take care of it for me. And after . . ." I stared down at the rows of crystals and jewelry lying neatly on black velvet under the glass counter as my throat tightened.

"After you turned thirteen?"

I swallowed. "Yes. After that, I guess there was no point."

The words made me feel sick. Whether or not what Cassandra suggested was true—and part of me still wanted to believe it wasn't—Sara had still written me off after my thirteenth birthday. She hadn't wasted any time trying to teach me anything in those last few horrible months. She'd barely spoken to me at all except to snap out an order or tell me to go to my room. Like the sight of me infuriated her.

"And anyway, she died not too long after that." I figured Cassandra knew my mother was dead if she'd known who she was. "My grandparents raised me. Neither of them had any power." At least not that they'd ever shown any hint of around me. It did kind of beg the question of exactly where Sara had gotten hers from.

"Even so," Cassandra said, "no child of a witch should grow up without knowing this. So you've got some catching up to do."

Great. It wasn't like I had a lot of spare time in my schedule right now. "I'm kind of busy with work."

"For this you can make time. Or do you want to be demon food again?"

I sighed. "No."

Cassandra gave a short nod. "Good."

"What do I do in the meantime? If it takes time to learn this psychic stuff, is there anything I can do between now and then?"

"Well, I could give you a bit of an energy boost." She waggled her fingers at me.

"You mean a spell?" I shivered, I couldn't help it.

"Not a spell. Just a gift." She tilted her head. "Then again, maybe not. There's no need to turn pale, child. I'm not going to cast a spell on you against your will. Relax."

I fought to lower my shoulders, feeling awkward. "I know. Sorry. It's just the thought of it. After all of this—" I gestured vaguely, hoping Cassandra would understand—"it's too close to home." Magic had always held bad memories for me. Adding the knowledge I'd been bound against my knowledge hadn't exactly improved my comfort level.

"I understand."

"Isn't there anything else you can do?"

"Perhaps."

She pulled a key on a lanyard out of her pocket, inserted it on a lock on her side of the counter, and slid the tray of jewelry out. Her hand drifted gently over the pendants before pausing over a thick silver chain that had little purple stones glinting on either side of a thumb-sized chunk of something dark and shiny.

"Here." She held out the pendant. "This is black tourmaline and amethyst. For psychic protection. Also, ring your bed with salt."

I slipped the chain over my head. "A circle? Will that work if I'm not a witch?"

Cassandra locked the drawer. "It can't hurt."

Great. She was giving me the magical equivalent of a sugar pill. "Anything else?"

"More grounding. But not just sex. I'll give you more herbs. And you should go stand in a garden somewhere. Put your bare feet on the earth for a while."

"I live in an apartment." Though Damon had a lawn surrounding that great big house. Of course, getting my feet on that lawn would mean deciding I was ready to face Damon again, which I wasn't.

"Find a park," she said dryly. "I hear Golden Gate is starting to look good again."

Chapter Eleven

I STOOD in the park by the newly reopened Japanese Tea House, trying not to feel like an idiot for wriggling my bare toes against the grass. The air was heavy and sticky, backing up the storm warning my datapad had beeped at me earlier. Even barefoot, I was hot, so after thirty minutes or so, I headed home, stopping at the market to load up on sea salt.

I'd just made it to the apartment when the skies opened.

"The place still smells like that horrible oil," Nat said as I dumped my bags on the counter. "You need a different brand."

I sniffed the air. I could just faintly smell the oil, but it was hardly strong. "You could've opened the windows."

"It's hot," Nat grumbled.

"Not anymore." The temperature had dropped as the storm approached. I moved to the window, disengaged the weather screen, and pushed it open. The rain pelting down drowned out any noise from the streets below, and the air that flowed in smelled cool and clean.

"There." I turned back to Nat. "Did you win?" I asked to distract her. There were plenty more stinky herbs and oils where last night's had come from. She was just going to have to deal.

Nat's grumpy expression cleared. "It smoked. So good. You have to come to this club, Mags."

I grabbed a soda out of the fridge. "Maybe."

"How about tonight?" She looked like a little girl waiting to show off a new favorite toy.

I cracked the can open as thunder boomed. Going to a club in that part of town held zero appeal. Gaming in one even less. "Don't you have to work tomorrow?"

"Yes, but that's fine. I'm a big girl."

"I have to work too."

"They didn't give you any time off?"

"I'm fine," I said, then gave myself a mental head slap. Nat wasn't going to ease off her nagging to go out if she thought I was fully recovered. I pulled up the stool next to hers. "But I do have to be at work early."

"You're no fun," Nat said, but her tone was lighter than it had been.

"Gotta pay the bills. And hey, without my work, you wouldn't have had an in at Righteous." I closed my hand around the pendant Cassandra had given me. Talking about work made me think of Damon. My heart bumped up a notch or two as I tried to banish his face from my brain.

"What's that?" Nat leaned in, studying the necklace.

"This? Just something I saw in the market." I lifted out the chain so she could see the crystals.

She slanted her eyes up at me. "Not your usual style." Her hand stretched toward the pendant, then fell back before she touched it. "You turning hippy on me?"

"You can talk. You're the tofu queen."

"Yeah, but I don't *wear* tofu." She narrowed her eyes at the necklace as though she was planning to call the fashion police and have them forcibly remove it from the premises.

"Well, I like it," I said. I tucked the damn pendant underneath my shirt, out of sight.

Nat rolled her eyes. "So tonight? The club? What do you think?"

That I'd rather eat dirt than do anything but try and sleep alone in the apartment tonight. But I was supposed to be sensible. "Let me see how I feel."

"You said you were fine." She pouted at me. "C'mon, Mags. It'll do you good to get out. Or would you rather hang around and wait for Damon Riley to call?"

My cheeks flamed. "Why would I be waiting for Damon to call?" The lights flickered as another round of thunder boomed. Perfect. A blackout was all we needed. "Maybe I just don't want to get fried by the storm."

Nat ignored my lame attempt to change the subject. "Oh, I don't know. Maybe something to do with why your message queue on the hub has his name five times today?" She waggled her eyebrows questioningly. "What's going on? You said you just crashed."

"I did." I swigged soda to hide my embarrassment.

"Neg to that. Guys don't call five times after you crash in their guest room. You doing the nasty with the boss, Mags?" Lightning illuminated her face, angling strange shadows across it for an instant.

"No," I lied. Or half-lied. There was nothing nasty about what Damon and I had done in bed. Quite the opposite. "He's probably just calling to see how I am."

"O-kay. If you want to play it like that. But that's one concerned boss." She clearly didn't believe me.

"He's just protecting his investment. I'm working for him," I reminded her, not liking how this conversation was going. "And so are you. Tomorrow's Monday. We both have to work. That's the only reason I don't want to go out."

"Nice try. You can't change the subject quite that easily." She tapped a nail on the countertop. "You're hiding something. If it's not Damon, then what? Is it your chip? Something about why they had to jack it?"

I considered whether I should tell her the truth. She was my best friend. It wasn't like she was going to disown me if I told her I'd been under a spell, but the thought still made me uneasy. Particularly when she seemed to be in a strange mood. "I had a weird reaction. The doctor said he thought it would be safer to just remove it."

"Was the chip defective? Are they looking into it?"

"They don't know. And yes, I think so. What's with the third degree? You didn't think I was going to turn into a game-head just because I got a chip, did you?"

Her eyes seemed to flash in time with the lightning. Just for a moment. "No. But you have to admit it's weird. I don't know anyone who's had to have their chip removed."

I drained the rest of my soda and crushed the can. I fed it and the other waiting trash to the recycler. "Sometimes things just happen."

Nat shook her head as the unit rumbled to life. "You have the right to know. You should find out."

"I will, eventually."

Nat didn't look like she was ready to drop the subject, and I could only think of one thing that was likely to distract her, much as I disliked the idea. "So. This club. Where is it, and can we be home by midnight?"

Nat was preoccupied in the cab, staring out the window with a slightly dreamy expression, a half smile drifting over her face at intervals as we wound our way down through the city to the bay.

After the quake and the rising water levels, a lot of the former Fisherman's Wharf buildings had been abandoned as their owners decided higher ground was a better option. Even

Ghirardelli had decamped. Most of the piers farther up the Embarcadero had been repaired, revamped to suit the new shoreline, and reopened, but around Jefferson and the Marina, things had lain where they fell or succumbed to the waters.

The area had gone downhill until a few enterprising souls moved in and stabilized a few buildings here and there along the water, opening clubs of various degrees of legality. Dancing. Gambling. Gaming. Sex. You name it, you could get it down here—if you weren't overly concerned with personal safety and the company you kept.

Now it was generally just called Dockside. It was kind of notorious. Nat usually avoided Dockside gaming clubs like the plague, claiming they were full of tourists and wannabes.

"Tell me again why we're down here," I said as the driver held out his datapad and I tapped for the credit transfer.

Nat's smile looked even stranger in the weird light thrown by the neon and the reflections of the water. "It's a new club. The Righteous guys told me about it."

I couldn't picture either Eli or Benji down here. But there were some wild guys amongst the testers. "What's wrong with Decker's? Or Pandemonium?" Nat's other regular club. I didn't mind going there. Great coffee bar, plus quieter places to hang around and observe the games. And I knew a fair few people who played there. I doubted I'd be seeing any familiar faces tonight.

I should've done some checking up once Nat told me where we were going, but she'd been eager to get going and there hadn't been time. Pity. Feeling less like I was walking into the unknown might have dispelled the unease riding me.

"PD's okay. Same old, same old. Trust me, you'll like this. It's chill." Nat started down the street, weaving her way around the puddles left by the rain on the uneven paths. Thunder still rumbled in the distance after the storm, each distant boom reinforcing my jitters.

The developers had left a lot of the place untouched because the tourists liked to come and look during the day. See what a big quake could do.

Personally, I preferred not to remember.

Fortunately we didn't have far to walk through the crowds of street vendors trying to hawk everything from dubious fast foods to even dodgier datapads and entertainment loads. There was even an outdoor nanotatt parlor.

Talk about the height of stupidity.

If you were going to get drunk or stoned and pay for a cheap Dockside tattoo, far better to go for the traditional ink and, at worst, be up for a pricey skin regen to get rid of it later. Letting some street hack set you up with nanotech—which had the potential to do all sorts of permanently nasty things if it went wrong—was insanity.

It didn't matter how pretty and enticing the moving, sparkling, infinitely alterable nanotatts looked on the pictures hung around the booth. When it came to messing with tech, the old adage held true—you got what you paid for. At the prices flashing on the hover sign above the booth, you were getting third-rate chop-shop gear out of South America or Eastern Europe. And hygiene and training of the tattooists out of God knew where.

Just thinking about it made the healing scar on my wrist hurt.

Or maybe I was just getting old.

Nat had gone ahead of me while I was distracted by the tattoos. I jogged to catch up with her, slipped my arm through hers, then jumped when static sparked between us.

"Ow." I rubbed my arm. "Damn storm."

I always got static around thunderstorms. And for once my shoes didn't have rubber soles to counteract the effect.

Nat didn't seem to notice. Her gaze was fixed on a sign about fifty feet down the street. The simple white letters were halogen bright and stood out like a beacon among the flashing and whirling colors around them.

UNQUIET.

"That's where we're going?" I asked, pointing. Nat nodded, and my stomach twisted. Dumb. It was just another pretentious club name. Nothing more.

Still, my hand curled around the datapad in my jacket pocket as we approached. Help was just a call away if something did go wrong. I hoped.

The line was longer than you might expect from a Dockside club on a rainy Sunday night, and I relaxed slightly. It couldn't be too bad if lots of people were keen to play here. Could it?

Nat bypassed the line, ignoring the damp-looking scowls directed as us, and headed straight for the head of the rope line. The scantily clad bouncer held out some sort of scanner, and something glowed briefly on the back of her hand.

Damn. She'd purchased a pass or a membership to this place already?

"She's with me," Nat said to the bouncer.

"Guest fee is one hundred. Cash." His voice was bored, as was the expression on his overly painted face.

One hundred? For one night? Down here? One hundred was ridiculous for one of the Haight clubs. For a waterfront tourist trap, it was extortion. But Nat was already headed for the door, and I wasn't going to let her go in alone. I dug a hundred credit chit out of my purse and snapped it into the slot the bouncer indicated. He smirked, stamped my hand with a complicated squiggly symbol, and let me through.

As soon as I stepped through the weather shield around the club's entrance, I realized why the high price tag. And the attraction for the damp crowd waiting outside.

The air inside was scented with a throat-catching cocktail of smoky scents; I recognized tobacco and marijuana and Sandman, just for a start. There was also some sort of incense burning, adding sandalwood and something spicier to the mix. The tobacco license alone had to cost them a fortune.

"Filter?"

I nodded at the skinny girl dressed in the same sort of skimpy translucent outfit as the bouncer and took a filter pack from the basket she offered. "Anti-tox?" I asked as I snapped the tiny plugs into place in my nose and took a welcome unscented breath. She jerked her head at the other side of the door, and I saw another girl dispensing patches.

I slapped one on my arm and reminded myself to breathe through my nose as I moved deeper into the club, scanning for Nat.

Now that I was inside, I was even more confused about why we were here. Nat hated smoking and any hint of the drug scene. Most of her clubs were clean or only allowed gamer stims. I blinked repeatedly as the smoke stung my eyes. The haze in the air didn't make it easy to spot her.

I found her standing near the bar.

"Nice atmosphere," I quipped.

"Isn't it great?" She flipped her hand at the room behind us, grinning.

In what universe? I stared at her. Maybe she was high. If she'd spent last night playing here, then, even if she'd worn filters and a patch, some of the stuff could've gotten to her. And while I couldn't tell if she had filters in now, I definitely couldn't see a patch anywhere on the skin her game vest left on display.

She had to be high to like this place. The floor oozed stickily and it was crowded and noisy, with some kind of unpleasant metal pop blasting away. The smoke—and there were people smoking wherever I looked—hung in the air, giving everything a layer of hazy grime. I hoped my hundred had at least bought me top-class filters. I hadn't been to a club this low rent since college.

The bar guy—who fit right in with the crowd, with his

shaved head and red leather pants—came over to us and I asked for water. To my relief, Nat did the same.

"C'mon," she said after our sealed bottles were delivered. "The games are upstairs."

I hadn't realized there was another level, but the room did have kind of a low ceiling for a club. It added to the dive bar atmosphere.

Maybe there'd be less people on the game floor.

I followed Nat through the crowd to the far wall where another scan of the symbol on our hands gained us access to an elevator.

The noise level upstairs was mercifully quieter, more game club than the trash party vibe downstairs. There wasn't any music up here, just whoops and cheers and the muted bleed of game noises from the various bays.

I glanced at the screens in each bay as we walked past, recognizing one or two games. But most of them were unfamiliar, leaning heavily toward the violent bloody death genre.

My sense of unease returned. Like me, Nat was a quester at heart. She didn't usually do gore for the sake of gore. I was debating excusing myself to sneak off and call Damon when we reached the farthest bay. It was small, only four game chairs. Two were already occupied, though I didn't recognize either of the men, and the screen showed a desolate nighttime landscape, full of weird shadows and odd shapes. Two avatars —overly muscled scaly humanoids whose bodies were slung with various nasty-looking weapons—were standing motionless in the foreground of the screen.

"This is us," Nat said. She tapped something into the game port, and one of the monsters waved, then made a beckoning motion. "They've been waiting until we got here."

Hair rose on the back of my neck. "I'm not sure I feel like playing. Plus, no chip, remember?" The game chairs were state-of-the-art like the ones at Righteous. Apparently Unquiet didn't spend all its money on narcotics licenses.

Nat frowned. "You can use a headset."

Pushy. Which wasn't like her either. I shook my head. "I'm not ready after the last time. You go ahead."

Something almost hostile flowed through her eyes, and I fought the urge to take a step back.

"You said we'd hang out. That we'd have some fun," she said.

"We are hanging out." I cracked open my water and took a swig to ease my suddenly dry mouth. "What's with the pressure? You've never minded me just watching before."

"This game is really chill."

"I'm sure it is. But like I said, I'm not in the mood. I'm still feeling hinky since the surgery." I could see the figures on the screen making impatient gestures and couldn't shake the spooky feeling that they could actually see me.

Which was impossible.

But whether or not it was impossible, it gave me the creeps. I took another sip of water, feeling hot and vaguely nauseous even though the smoke haze was thinner up here.

Maybe the filters weren't doing such a great job after all. I had to remember to breathe through my nose or I was going to end up sandbagged, or worse. I didn't need—or want—any more weird experiences.

Nat was still watching me, anger lurking in the back of her eyes.

I wanted to tell her we should just go home but didn't think that was going to go well. "Look, how about you log in and I'll catch up. I need to go to the bathroom."

Nat's shoulders relaxed. "Promise?"

"I won't be long," I replied.

To my relief, she nodded and took a seat in one of the empty chairs, snapping her chip into place with an eager expression.

A third figure materialized on the screen. It wasn't quite the same as the other two, but it didn't look like any avatar of

Nat's that I'd ever seen. For one thing, it was male, and Nat usually stuck to girls. She sometimes used a guy if she was doing hand-to-hand combat games—she said they had better reach—but the landscape on the screen didn't look like the usual exotic arena format of a smash-and-bash.

So why the guy? I waited until Nat's breathing had slowed and all her telltales were green, telling myself to relax. Maybe the game didn't use custom avatars. Maybe it was an all-male scenario.

I watched as the three figures started moving into the distance and couldn't help hearing Cassandra's voice in my head, talking about intuition.

It was time to listen to mine and call for some backup. Someone who knew more about games than me. Someone with clout.

Only one name sprang to mind.

I found the bathrooms and called Damon.

"Maggie?" he said groggily. "I hope this is a booty call."

"Not exactly. But it is a chance to be a knight in shining armor." I slipped into an empty stall and shut the door, then tried not to touch anything. Unquiet didn't spend much money on bathroom maintenance, apparently.

"My armor's in storage." He sounded vaguely cranky. "What's up?"

"I'm down by the Piers. At a club called Unquiet."

"I've heard of it. What are you doing in a place like that? You don't . . . ." Maybe he realized that inquiring about my taste in drugs was an awkward question for him to ask an employee.

Better to clear that up. "No, I don't do drugs. Nat wanted to come. She's been here the last two nights. She said some of the Righteous guys brought her here."

"Possible. They have a license for a couple of our early games, but none of the later stuff, if I'm remembering correctly. They like the heavier stuff."

"Heavier?"

"More violent. Does Nat like slashers?"

Violent. Well, that explained some of the nastier-sounding graffiti gracing the walls in here. "Not really. That's kind of why I'm calling. She's acting strange. And she wants me to play this game I've never seen before. I don't recognize the other two players she's teamed up with. I don't know if they're from Righteous."

"Strange how?" All traces of tiredness had vanished from his voice.

"Just moody. And she's been out all night two nights in a row. Normally when one of us is sick, the other sticks around."

"You're still not feeling well?"

I lowered my voice as someone lurched into the stall next to mine with a muttered "fuck," followed by a string of less comprehensible curses. "No, I'm okay, but it's just weird that she didn't want to just hang at home after I'd had surgery."

"You don't think it's connected to the other testers, do you?"

"I don't know. But I'd appreciate it if you could come down here and help me get her home. We're in the last playing bay upstairs."

"Hang tight. I'll be there as soon as I can."

"Thanks." But he'd already disconnected. I took as long as I thought was plausible to wash my hands, racking my brains for ways to talk Nat into leaving. Maybe Damon could tell her she was needed at Righteous or something.

I made my way slowly back to the bay. All three of them were still hooked in, and the screen still showed the same dark landscape, only now they were running through it, weapons drawn and held ahead of them. Just visible in the gloom ahead of them was another figure, pale green and delicately built.

It was running too. No. *Fleeing.*

It kept looking back over its shoulder at the pursuers, its

face holding a desperate sort of hopelessness. The expression was way too realistic, like whoever had built the game was well versed in terrorizing their prey.

I shivered and turned away. No way was I plugging into that.

But hopefully I wouldn't have to. If none of them logged out, then they had no way of knowing I was back. And once Damon arrived, he'd know what to do. It was his area of expertise, after all.

Unfortunately, my luck didn't hold. I tried not to look at the screen too often over the next ten minutes, but each time I did, it showed nothing but blood and violence. The three of them dispatched the green thing and then flushed another similar victim from a stand of trees only to chase it off a cliff. Mercifully the screen froze at that point, and Nat and the other two started to move and stretch. Nat opened her eyes as she disconnected her chip.

"You're back," she said with a strangely pleased smile. "Are you ready to play?"

"Actually, I'm kind of thirsty," I stalled. "How about we get another drink? Or something to eat?"

Nat twisted in her seat, looking at the other two players. One was a shortish dark-skinned guy and the other one was tall with some sort of tribal tattoo covering half his face. I still didn't recognize either of them. "You guys want to take a break?"

They shrugged, stood, and moved off without saying anything.

Friendly. I was going to have a word with Damon about his hiring policies if these guys did work at Righteous. "Chatty, aren't they?"

"Just trying to stay in the zone," Nat said, combing her sweaty hair with her fingers. "Let's go. We shouldn't take too long."

"What's this game called?" I asked.

Nat either didn't hear me or was ignoring the question as we made our way to the bar. I ordered syncaf. Nat pulled a face at me and asked for vodka. I bit my tongue as she downed it in two gulps.

"What?"

"You don't usually drink much when you play."

"Sheesh. Relax, Mags. You should have one."

"The doc said no booze for a few days." A lie. But Nat didn't know that. I sipped my drink slowly, wondering where the hell Damon was.

I'd almost reached the bottom of the mug, stalling while Nat tapped her fingernails restlessly against the bar, when I spotted his dark head moving fast through the crowd. Relief made me smile.

"You're taking forever," Nat said, tugging at my arm as I swirled the dregs, waiting for Damon to reach us. "Let's go back."

"Almost done. You're the one making me stay up late, so you can't begrudge me some caffeine."

She tugged again. "C'mon."

"Why is this so important to you?"

Her grip tightened, and for a moment her eyes looked almost black in the dim lighting. Black and calculating. I stepped back but she didn't let go, just clutched me harder. "You'll see."

"Ow." I pulled my arm free just as Damon appeared by my side.

"Hello, ladies," he said. "What brings my two favorite employees to this neck of the woods?"

The look Nat turned on him was vicious. "What are you doing here?" she snapped.

"Just checking out the clubs. I like to keep up," Damon said mildly. He eased himself closer to me, and I resisted the urge to hug him. "What are we playing?"

"Nothing at the moment," Nat snapped. "Maggie's being a baby."

I clenched my jaw not to snap back. Her temper tantrum or whatever the hell it was she had going on was beginning to be seriously annoying. But I didn't want to make things worse if I could avoid it. I took a breath. "I'm not the one acting childish here. I'm just not in the mood to play."

"Not with me, anyway," Nat snarled. "Bad decision."

So much for not escalating. Well, if good cop wasn't going to work on her, maybe bad cop was the way to go. "What the hell are you talking about?" I said. "Are your filters not working or something?" If the drugs in the air were getting to her—and had been getting to her for the last couple of nights—that would be one explanation for her behavior.

"I'm just fine. I'm just trying to show you—" She broke off as Damon stepped between us. The look she directed at him was savage. "Get out of the way."

"Calm down," he said. "Maggie's tired. She just wants to go home."

"Home with you. Well, that doesn't work. I had her first." The words came out almost as a hiss, and I rocked backward as the hairs on the back of my neck stood on end.

"Is she high?" Damon asked, turning to me.

I shook my head, not knowing how to answer that.

"I'm taking you home," Damon said. He turned back to Nat, watching her carefully.

"Maggie's here to play." Nat's hands curled into fists, and I put mine on Damon's arm, trying to get him to move away.

"I'm going, Nat," I said, trying to sound calm. "I'll talk to you at home, when you're making sense."

"You heard her," Damon said, angling his body so he was between Nat and me. "Nat, you can get a lift with us if you want."

"As if I'd ride with you. This is all your fault."

I watched in horror as Nat swung her arm at him. Luckily, Damon saw it coming and blocked her, pushing her back.

"What the hell are you doing?" he asked, his voice dangerously flat.

Nat took a half step toward us and then stopped, anger twisting her face. "Take her, then," she spat. "Go home and see how much good that does you."

Chapter Twelve

"I'm sorry, I don't know what's gotten into her." Damon had hustled me away from Nat but fighting our way through the crowd was easier said than done. I shifted sidewise to avoid a couple staggering toward us, their unsteady gait suggesting they didn't believe in filters and anti-tox.

As soon as they'd passed, Damon moved closer, his hand firm on my back as he pressed us forward, heading for the door. "She was okay when you left home?"

"Other than being pretty insistent about going out tonight, but she can get hyper-focused about games sometimes."

"But you said the game didn't seem like her kind of thing?" He steered me through a small gap in the crowd.

I shuddered, remembering the hopeless expressions on the creatures Nat and her companions had slaughtered. Virtual or not, they haunted me. "No. Definitely not." I pressed closer to him, wanting warmth even though the heated smoky air and press of bodies in the club should've been enough to keep anybody warm.

"I'm going to call Ajax, see what she's been working with."

I stopped dead and he nearly cannoned into me, but side-stepped at the last minute and then pivoted to face me.

"You said she'd be working with a safe version. Are you saying this is what happened with the other testers?" I demanded.

He shook his head. "Not this specifically, but any strange behavior needs to be checked out."

Guilt made my stomach clench. I should have put two and two together. "We should go back. Get her out of here."

"Maggie, she just tried to punch me. I don't think she's going to agree to come quietly."

"We should still try." I turned but he caught my hand.

"No. She's not safe for you to be with right now." It was his master-of-the-universe tone.

"It's Nat."

"I know." This time he sounded gentler. "I know she's your friend, but I'm not letting you get hurt."

I tugged my arm free. "She wouldn't hurt me."

"Maggie, she just tried to punch me. I don't think you can assume anything right now. Look, I'll call Ajax and get him to come down with some of the other testers and talk to her, try to get her home. But you and I are leaving."

I hesitated, twisting back, trying to spot Nat. Nothing. "Let's wait for them to get here."

Damon caught my hand again and stepped toward the exit. "We will. Outside though. We'll take care of her, I promise. But I'm getting you out of here."

"But—"

He started walking, and it was either follow him or get pulled off my feet. I gave in and went, torn between my guilt and distinct relief to be getting out of there.

The air outside was weirdly stale until I remembered the filters and ditched them, breathing in the tang of rust and seawater gratefully.

Damon pulled out his datapad and spoke briefly with Ajax. I fought the urge to go back into the club and drag Nat out of there. I knew Damon was right, that she wouldn't come and that it could only end badly, but I didn't want to leave her in there. Damon stayed silent, waiting beside me.

Ajax and a couple of other Riley guys arrived faster than I expected. Damon pulled him aside. I couldn't hear what they said, but Ajax's expression turned grim.

When they came back to me, Ajax tipped his chin at me. "Don't worry, Maggie. We'll make sure she gets home okay. I'll let you know when she's there."

Nat liked Ajax, I reminded myself. She would be all right with him. And he'd keep her safe.

"Thanks," I said. "I appreciate it."

That earned me another chin tip. Then he and the others headed back toward the club.

I let out a breath.

"Okay?" Damon asked.

"Not really, but it'll have to do." I glanced back at the club's entrance, then made myself turn away. I couldn't do anything more here.

"We should get out of here too." Damon held out his hand and I took it, letting him lead me away. The crowds had thinned out, and most of the street stalls were closed down. He set a fast pace back toward the Embarcadero.

"Tell me what happened to the other testers," I said.

"Let's just get to the car. This isn't the place to stop for a chat."

I stopped walking, pulling my arm free to wave at the street around us. "There's no one around."

He stopped too, mouth flat. "What do you want me to say, Maggie?"

"I want you to tell me what you think might be wrong with my best friend."

His face twisted. "I don't know. I don't know what's wrong with any of them. The doctors can't find any medical reasons for their symptoms."

"You said Nat would be safe. You said the testers were

using a clean version of Archangel." Anger sharpened my words.

He scrubbed a hand over his head, ruffling his hair into spikes. "They are."

"Then maybe it's nothing to do with the game."

"I hope so. But it's not worth the risk. We'll get Ellen to check her out tomorrow."

"If we can get her to come to work. I'm not sure how cooperative she'll be." I stared out at the water, visible through the rubble-strewn gap where a building had been demolished. Lights flickered over the harbor. It was pretty in a warped sort of way, but I wasn't in the mood to enjoy the scenery. Instead I was battling frustration and anger and fear spiked with a healthy dose of worry.

The water was almost still, just the tiniest of waves rippling across the surface and making the lights smear into each other in sparkling blurs.

"She's your friend. You'll think of something. Besides, she really wants this testing job. Use that. Now let's go."

"Where's the car?" As I turned back to Damon, something about the movement of the water caught my eye.

"This way," Damon said. He took a step, then stopped again when I didn't follow. "What?"

I turned back slowly, staring hard at the play of light and shadow on the water. Yep, there was definitely a swell of darkness on the surface. A blot that seemed to soak up the sparkles of light as they touched it.

A blot that was moving in the direction of the water's edge.

Toward us.

That couldn't be good. I didn't know what it might be, but the hairs on the back of my neck stood on end as the darkness rolled toward shore.

"Damon?" My voice was tight, and I had to swallow hard to finish my sentence. "How far to the car?"

"A few minutes." He sounded puzzled.

"Okay." I stepped backward slowly, not taking my eyes off the blot. "I think we should run."

"Maggie?"

I pointed in the direction of the approaching darkness. "Don't argue." I walked faster, hoping my stupid heels wouldn't catch on the broken pavement. The blot oozed onto shore, slithered forward, and resolved into something with more legs than anything coming out of the ocean had any right to possess.

More legs than anything of this earth should have.

With each skitter of its legs came a sound like twisted iron scraping over concrete.

Simple instinctive terror flooded me. "Run." I turned and propelled myself forward, fleeing as desperately as one of those pathetic game creatures Nat had been hunting.

Damon's footsteps pounded behind mine, and in a few seconds he caught up to me, grabbing my arm and pulling me along. This time I didn't mind at all.

I didn't know where the car was, so I let him lead as we bolted through the broken buildings, taking as straight a line as the crazy architecture of Dockside would allow.

The screeching scrape still came from behind us, and I twisted my head as we ran, trying to see where it was.

"Don't stop," Damon ordered.

No chance of that. I'd spotted the thing following us easily enough, skittering too fast with a jittery gait, legs bending at angles that were all wrong. I accelerated and Damon kept pace as we bolted for a row of lights in the distance. I was all for lights. Until they suddenly went dark and every instinct I possessed screamed, *Not that way.*

I lurched to the right, into the mouth of an alley. "In here."

"Wrong way," Damon yelled.

I shook my head. "Trust me." The alley was darker and

full of God knew what, but anything was better than heading toward those dead lights and whatever had killed them. I sucked in air, ignoring the pained protest of overburdened lungs, and put on speed.

Over the harsh whistle of air as I gasped and the echoing pounding of our feet, the scraping sounds grew louder. I risked another glance back. At the far end of the alley, light glinted blackly off the creature. It was gaining on us.

Fuck. I didn't know how much longer I could keep up the pace. The alley narrowed ahead of us, angling so I couldn't see what came next.

"What is that thing?" Damon panted.

"No idea, but at a guess, nothing good." I wished I'd paid more attention to Sara—or anyone, really. What sort of creatures could a demon send after me? Because I was dead certain that was what was happening. And I was also certain that if it caught us, it was going to try and hurt us. Kill us even.

I had no idea what to do. Sara wasn't here. Cassandra wasn't here, and as far as I knew, Damon had about as much magical ability as me—aka zero.

But we had to do something.

Not that I had any idea what might work. But I did know that running would stop working at some point.

Probably sooner rather than later. We were slowing down, gasping for air. Neither of us could run forever.

Think, Maggie. Think fast. I scanned the alley, looking for something, anything to use as a weapon.

Nothing. Rotten cardboard was useless, and the rusted dumpsters weren't exactly the sort of thing you could pick up and throw at a nightmare.

Where was a witch when I finally needed one?

Maybe she was lying about your power.

The thought dropped into my head with the force of one

of Nat's death-strikes. I almost fell, but Damon caught my arm and kept me moving.

I ran on autopilot, trying to deny it might even be possible. I wasn't a witch.

"Emotion is energy. Energy is power. That's what we use." Sara's voice sounded clear in my head, and tears suddenly washed out my vision. I swiped them away with the back of my hand as another screech and clatter rose from behind me.

Emotion. Energy. *Power*.

Right now there was plenty of emotion. Our frantic sprint wasn't the only reason my heart was trying to leap out of my chest. Fear and shock ricocheted through me. What if it was true? What if I had power? I had no idea how to use it. Or even if you could use your own energy. I'd never paid attention. Hadn't *wanted* to pay attention to the things Sara did.

Everything she did involved trappings. Candles and herbs and oils.

Just for show, baby, the voice whispered again as my foot skidded on something noxious on the pavement. I scrabbled for balance, and Damon's hand clenched around my forearm, keeping me upright and hauling me forward as I flashed on a memory: Sara laughing to herself as she counted a stack of twenties. The client had been very impressed by her incense and candles and the reek of spice that rose from the potion in the fancy glass bottle.

But she'd started laughing almost before the trailer door had closed behind them. Laughed like a hyena as she tucked the money away. Then she'd grinned at me and said something about power coming from within.

What the hell did that mean?

We rounded another corner, gasping in unison. From behind us, the wind rose suddenly. It carried the stench of the creature, sweet and rotten and pure run-hide-flee that bypassed rational thought and spoke to the instincts deep within. I tried to speed up, my legs doing a remarkable impression of concrete blocks, fighting me every step. The stench filled my nose, alien yet somehow horribly familiar. Up ahead I saw nothing but brick.

Dead end.

Shit. Shit. Shit.

I stopped dead and twisted, hoping it hadn't caught up yet, that maybe we'd have time to backtrack and correct our mistake.

No such luck.

It rounded the corner as I turned, and I knew time had run out.

I had to try something. I'd always believed I had no power, but I'd also had no idea I'd been bound to a demon. What I believed wasn't worth a damn anymore. Trying something was better than nothing. I couldn't just stand here and wait to die.

"Get behind me," Damon said.

"No."

"Don't be—"

"Shut up." I needed to focus.

For one second his eyes met mine, and I drank in the shocked flare of blue in case it was the last time I saw it. Then I turned away, searching inside for any glimmer of anything.

I didn't know what power felt like.

Didn't know how to use it.

So I just hoped like hell, and reached for whatever might be there and, as I felt something blaze in response, screamed, "Burn," as I flung a hand toward the creature.

Then I just screamed as invisible knives slashed through my body, shredding me. I had just enough time to see the creature engulfed in a wave of flame before the knives cut the lights.

I came to with my head cradled on Damon's lap, the stink of acid and smoking rot stinging my nose, and sirens shrieking in my ears. My right arm burned, and as I cracked my eyes open, pinwheels of light bloomed across my vision.

"What happened?" I croaked. It seemed the obvious question. I rubbed my eyes with the arm that wasn't killing me, trying to clear them. Trying to see him.

The light in the alley wasn't good and it flickered like a fire. No, not *like* a fire—there was a fire. A small burning heap of something spat sparks about twenty feet away from us.

Maybe it was the weird light, but Damon looked terrible, eyes reddened and face smeared with ash and smoke. He brushed my hair back. "It's okay, the paramedics are on their way."

"I can hear that." I tried to sit up, but he pressed gently on my shoulder, holding me where I was. I gave in because the movement made everything hurt. "But what happened?"

"There was something chasing us and you—" He stopped, swallowed. "You did something and it burst into flames."

What?

I sucked in a breath as the memory hit me. The water. The creature. That noise. The overwhelming sense of terror and desperation. But I couldn't explain what I'd done.

"I don't understand."

"Me neither," he said, and the look on his face made me wish I hadn't asked. I closed my eyes again and listened to the sirens wail in time with the pain shooting down from my shoulder to my wrist and the rhythm of thudding footsteps running toward us.

The EMTs gave me something for the pain, and by the time we reached the ER I was floating. But not quite enough to completely block the fear lurking beneath the pharmaceutical calm.

My right forearm was burned and peeling like a bad

sunburn. The paramedics had muttered over it as they'd carefully wrapped a gelskin around it.

The doctors in the ER were umming and aahing over the injury when Meredith arrived.

She took one look at my arm and shooed everyone out of the cubicle. Well, almost everyone. Damon remained right where he was. Meredith shot him a look and then called Cassandra. I went from scared to completely terrified.

It felt like a very long time with me avoiding eye contact with Damon and Meredith, refusing to answer any questions, until Cassandra arrived.

Just like Meredith, she took one look at me and her expression turned grim. She turned to Damon. "I need to speak to Maggie alone."

His expression went mulish. "I'm staying right here."

"You can stay right here after we're done talking. Run along now." Her voice dripped ice.

I shivered, glad that particular tone hadn't been turned on me. Mrs. Claus as Ice Bitch Queen of the Universe was unnerving.

"It's okay," I mouthed at him.

"No, it's really not," Cassandra said as Damon departed through the curtains enclosing my bed. She moved closer and gently picked up my arm, running a fingertip very lightly down the gelskin before stepping back. "What the hell have you been doing?"

"I don't remember, exactly," I said.

"Try hard," she suggested in the ice queen voice as she lifted my chart from the end of the bed and studied it.

I decided it would be easier to start at the beginning. "I went to a Dockside club with my friend. Nat. It was kind of dicey and she was acting strange, so I called Damon to come help me get her out of there. Nat threw kind of a fit."

Cassandra looked up from the chart, eyes narrowed. "Define 'fit.'"

"She got all upset because I wanted to go, and then she tried to hit Damon."

"And she doesn't usually take potshots at people?"

"Not unless she's playing. She games." I reached for the water they'd left me and took a nervous sip.

"Go on."

"Anyway, we figured we weren't going to get her out of there, so we left after Damon called a couple of other people at work she knows to look after her. It was late, not many people around. We were walking back to Damon's car, and something came out of the water and started following us."

"A little more specific, dear."

"You'd have to ask Damon for a description. It's all a bit of a blur."

She put the chart back with a snap. "I'm not surprised. So something chased you and you did what, exactly?"

"We ran but eventually wound up in a dead end, and I knew I had to try something. So I—"

"You set it on fire?" Her tone was sharp as a blade.

"No power, remember?" I forced myself to meet her gaze, trying not to let the weight of her eyes make me burrow under the hospital blanket.

"Try again."

"I couldn't have. That would be impossible."

"No, just very stupid. What were you thinking? You have no training."

"I never needed any training." I twisted my hands in the blanket. "I don't have any power."

Cassandra nodded at my arm. "I think you just disproved that theory."

"But how? My mother told me I didn't." My voice sounded whiny, like a teenager protesting detention. "She tested me on my thirteenth birthday. She made me stay up until midnight on the night before my birthday so she could do it as soon as possible. It was a big deal because I'd only been home from the hospital a few days."

"I think we've established your mother wasn't exactly a beacon of truth," Cassandra said. She pursed her lips and stared at me for a moment. "Wait. Did you say hospital?"

I nodded. "Uh-huh, just before my birthday. I remember being worried that I might miss cake at school. I was sick for almost a week. They never worked out what exactly, just a really high fever and vomiting. I was mad when I got home and Sara made me stay up late."

Cassandra's eyes turned thunderous. "I see. I think your mother is lucky she is no longer with us, Maggie."

"What do you mean?"

"That I'm almost certain that she's the one who bound you to the demon. Just before your power showed itself."

The words hung in the air like tiny bombs. Then they zeroed in on me and exploded in my chest. I gasped and doubled over. I'd been trying to deny it but couldn't really, having recognized the truth somehow back in the alley when I'd wondered if she'd lied to me.

Still, the first words that came were "You're wrong."

"I don't think so. I'm sorry, Maggie."

"My mother wouldn't do that." My voice caught, the voice of an eight-year-old who'd just found out that Santa wasn't real. It hurt. The truth often did. And this felt true. Utterly and completely true. And if my mother could do that—could sell me to a demon—then she must never have loved me at all. Not even a little bit.

Which meant she wasn't going to get the satisfaction of making me cry about it now. I stared at the weave of the hospital blankets and let the anger burn away the hurt.

Cassandra sighed. "It makes sense. The illness just before you turned thirteen? It's too convenient."

"What does me being sick have to do with anything?"

"If I had to guess, I'd say it was most likely a reaction to whatever she gave you so you wouldn't remember the ceremony."

"But why?"

"Sara always was frustrated."

My head snapped up. "Nobody sells their child to a demon out of frustration."

"It would be nice if that were true. But for some people, the power is like a drug. They want more. Whatever the cost."

"Sara wasn't like that," I protested, wondering even as I spoke why I was still defending her when she'd completely failed to defend me.

"What I remember was that she was ambitious. She wanted things and didn't care too much about how she got them. There'd been rumblings about her over the years," Cassandra said. "Then she suddenly went off the radar. I guess that's when she got pregnant with you."

"Why bother even keeping me? She could've taken care of it." The bitterness must've shown on my face.

Cassandra pulled a chair over to the bed, taking my good hand as she sat. "This is hard for you."

The gentle warmth of her fingers felt too much like the things I'd never had. "You *think*? God."

"Once she was gone, she was gone. I never heard about her. We would've kept a much closer eye on her if we'd known she had a child but no one ever told us about you. Including her."

"Did she have to?"

"There's no official register of those with power," Cassandra said. "But most people let us know when they have children, so we know who to watch for if something ever happens."

"I guess if you're planning to make sure your child never show any power, then you wouldn't bother." I bit the inside of my cheek as tears threatened again.

"Even for Sara that sounds kind of far-fetched."

"Does it? You said it yourself. She went off the map when she had me. Left everything and hid out in small towns. Sounds like someone with a plan to me."

"Maybe. But I guess we won't ever know." She tilted her head as she studied me. "What we need to understand now is exactly what she did to you."

"Why? The binding is broken."

"That doesn't seem to be sitting too well with the demon concerned. Imps don't just randomly appear and attack people—"

"Is that what that thing was, an imp?"

"That would be my best guess. Imps have to be called or sent through. Unless you've pissed off any other witches lately, I'm betting on the latter. Which means a demon sent it. Your demon."

"I'm no good to him—it?—dead, surely?" My voice shook a little.

Cassandra patted my leg. "I don't think it would've killed you. It was probably carrying a spell of some sort."

I shuddered. "To do what?"

"My guess would be something to lower your will or get you to consent to the binding again."

Not going to happen. "Would that even work?"

"Consent under magical duress? Maybe. Maybe not. But lowering your will might."

"How?"

"A binding takes consent—at least when a witch casts one it does—but possession doesn't. The demon can overwhelm you psychically if you're not mentally strong. Maybe that's how they got around your consent in the first place. Maybe Sara gave you something to make you sick and that lowered your psychic barriers somehow." She looked a little rueful. "It's actually quite clever when you think about it."

"I don't want to think about it." I swallowed as nausea twisted my stomach. A demon was after me. Had sent that thing to attack me. And I was a witch. Right now I didn't know which was more horrifying.

"You're going to have to. And it seems it wants you back. Probably more now that you've used your power."

"Why?"

"Witches are an even more attractive energy source. For one thing, the demon can feed on the magic, not their life force. So a bound witch is a source that doesn't die." She perched on the end of the bed. "It explains why you've survived the binding. Especially if Sara limited it somehow."

"What do you mean?"

"Made sure the demon could only feed on your magic. I'm guessing that's why you've never been able to do anything before now."

"Why would she do that?" I doubted Sara had had any thought for my well-being. There had to be something in it for her if she'd limited my bond.

"Maybe she thought she could guarantee herself access to a demon's assistance for a lifetime."

"Until she died."

"Yes. And the demon was stuck with a binding that meant it could never use your full potential. A tame witch doing its bidding would be a prize. Witches can bind others to the demon. Give it enough energy to feed from and it might even break through. Trust me, we don't want that to happen again."

"Again?"

She shook her head. "A story for another time."

"A demon came through and it was defeated?"

"At a high cost." Sorrow swam in her eyes, and the pain seemed so real that I almost started to cry all over again.

Cassandra blinked and the emotion in her expression changed to resolve. "The important thing is to stop that from happening this time by keeping you safe."

Keeping me from becoming bound again, she meant. I

clamped my teeth together until I was sure I wasn't going to retch. "How exactly are you going to do that?"

She looked at me like the answer was obvious. "By teaching you to use your power."

"No." I shook my head violently, chest tightening. "I don't want anything to do with magic."

"You have to learn to control it or you're going to end up hurting someone. Or yourself." She looked at my arm. "That could've been a lot worse than a mere burn. You could've set yourself on fire."

The pain in my chest came back. Fear spread like icicles through my veins, and I pulled the blanket closer to me, desperate for warmth. "Isn't there another way? Can't you do something to take my powers away?" The demon wouldn't want me if I wasn't a witch, surely?

"Not without sending you insane or catatonic. You have power, and you're going to have to learn to live with it. You need to learn to control it before you can decide how exactly you're going to do that."

"But I don't want to." My inner teenager surfaced again.

She let go of my hand and straightened. "We all have to do things we don't want to."

"How long will it take?"

"Depends on how hard you work and how much talent you have."

"You can't even give me a ballpark figure? If the demon—" I stumbled over the word, fighting a terror-fueled adrenaline rush that had me tasting bile. "If it's going to try again to get me back, don't we have kind of a deadline?"

"We have some time," Cassandra said. "Sending an imp through will have cost it in energy, particularly so soon after losing you. Assuming it doesn't have enough others bound."

That wasn't exactly a cheerful thought. "How can we tell?"

"If it has others? I think we should just assume it does. Some, at least. The more powerful the demon, the more energy it needs. And Sara would've wanted to deal with a powerful demon."

"Why?"

"To deal with a demon at all, you need to be desperate. You have to want something very badly. And if Sara wanted more power, then she'd want enough to make the risk worth her while. Do you have any idea if she was in trouble at all back then?"

I shook my head. "No more than usual. Not that I could tell. We did move not long after my birthday." One of our harder moves. She'd dragged me from the heat and sunshine of Florida to the cold, wet mountains of Virginia, landing us in a small hill town that had been my idea of hell.

Those same mountains took her life when her car went off a bend a few months later. After that, Gran had taken me back to California and I'd spent as much time as possible soaking up the sun, feeling like I'd never get warm again.

Cassandra looked down at the gel on my arm. "In a way, it's too bad the binding is broken. We might've been able to tell something from the spell."

"You'll have to excuse me if I don't share that sentiment."

"Of course." She smiled. "Still, Sara did protect you in a way. If she hadn't limited the binding, you'd probably be crazy by now. Or dead."

"She probably thought she could get something out of me staying alive," I said. "Leverage maybe. Threaten to cut off the demon's food supply, so to speak."

Cassandra gave me a long look. "I'm not sure that's even possible."

I shrugged, not willing to cut Sara any slack. If there'd been an angle to work, she would've worked it. "Well, like you said, we'll never know, will we?"

"No, so let's focus on the present. You can come to me tomorrow and we'll begin."

"I have to work."

One gray brow arched. "Money is more important than your life?"

"This job is. After all, if the demon got to me through the game the first time, then it could get to others."

She looked concerned. "If it got to you through the game, you should be staying away from games."

"Trust me, I will be. But I need to keep working."

"After work, then. The sooner we start this, the better."

Chapter Thirteen

By the time Boyd—I'd finally found out his name—steered the car through Damon's gates, I was floating toward sleep, lulled into a haze by smooth suspension and painkillers. Cassandra and Meredith had done something to my arm to ease the burn, but I hadn't argued with the doctor's addition of a prescription for some pharmaceutical help.

"C'mon, Sleeping Beauty." Damon helped me out of the car and swung me into his arms despite my protests. I snuggled against his neck, fighting to stay awake.

"I guess we won't be having that talk right now," he muttered as he carried me into the house. I pretended not to hear, just made a sleepy noise. He'd tried to give Cassandra the third degree when she'd let him back into the room, but she'd shut him down. For which I was grateful. I wasn't keen to explain everything to him either. I wasn't sure I *could* explain it.

I knew I'd have to face the music in the morning, but for now, I was going to pretend that wasn't true.

By the time Damon slid me into cool cotton sheets, I'd slipped even further into the haze. The pillow was like a cloud under my cheek. A cloud that wanted to pull me under. But before I gave in to that pull, there was something I needed to know.

"Did you hear from Ajax?" I managed to ask without slurring more than a tiny bit.

"Not yet." He pulled the covers over me, and I knew I should be worried about Nat, but it was just too easy to let myself slide all the way into oblivion.

When I swam back to consciousness, Damon was a solid warm curl at my back, his arm carefully tucked around me so it supported my burned one. Not that he needed to. It didn't hurt.

Really didn't hurt. Which was . . . unexpected.

I wriggled my fingers and flexed my wrist experimentally, dislodging flakes of gelskin.

The flesh below what remained of the gel was pinker than normal, but nothing like the angry red of last night. Whatever Cassandra had done, it had worked. Which I would've been happier about if I wasn't all too aware of the fact that what she'd done had involved magic. Still, I was grateful it didn't hurt and flexed it again, wriggling my fingers carefully.

Damon shifted on the pillow beside me, and I froze. I didn't want to wake him. Not yet. As long as he slept, we didn't have to have the talk.

I really, *really* didn't want to have the talk.

Damon's arm tightened, pulling me back into him. As my butt hit his hips, it became clear that part of him was wide awake too.

I sighed happily, pressing against him. Drowsy morning sex might be just as good as more sleep. And required no talking.

"Is it morning?" Damon said in a sleep-slurred rumble that shot straight to my groin.

"Go back to sleep." I kept my voice low. As tempting as it was to jump him, sleep seemed the safer option.

He flexed his hips, his breath warm down my neck, waking every nerve it hit.

"How are you feeling?" he asked.

"Good." I tried to keep the rapidly blooming lust out of my voice. "Seriously, go back to sleep. It's early."

"You smell good." Breath stirred against my neck again, making the muscles quiver.

"Eau de hospital will do it every time."

His arm tensed, and I cursed my choice of words. Reminding him of the hospital wasn't exactly a good strategy if I was trying to avoid the talk.

"You're really feeling okay?"

I raised my arm, displaying the fading remnants of the burn. "Cassandra does good work."

More gelskin crumbled and drifted onto the covers as he ran his thumb up my forearm. "So I see."

He sounded more awake. I braced myself for the inevitable.

"Are you—"

"Can we not do this? Not just yet?" I wasn't ready. And if he wasn't going to sleep, then I needed a distraction. Sex seemed the obvious choice. I twisted in his arms, draped a leg over his hip.

"Maggie . . ." His pupils flared dark as I pressed closer.

"Not yet." I tugged his head down and pressed my mouth to his, hard. Then I pulled back. "Last night I kept thinking that I might never get to do that again."

He studied me for a moment, a mix of wariness and warmth in his eyes. "I thought you wanted time."

"I changed my mind."

"What if I still need some?"

I wrapped my hand around his cock. "This suggests otherwise."

He sucked in a breath as my hand stroked. "You can't put this off forever."

"I know." Up. Down. Soft over hard.

His eyes glazed. "Now who's beguiling who?"

I smiled. "Is it working?"

"Turn over," he said softly.

I rolled. Lips brushed my hair softly. Then he lifted it and I quivered again when his breath whispered over my nape. I wanted him to take me away. Wanted just to be. Not to think or worry.

"You don't smell like a hospital."

"No? Must be whatever fabric softener your housekeeper is using, then."

"No, it's just you." His voice was soft. So soft. It made me want to let my defenses down. To let him through. But I couldn't. Then he pressed his lips to my skin.

My breath hitched, heat seeping through me. Heat was good. Heat meant no thinking, a place to hide from everything that waited for me outside this room.

"You're sure you're feeling okay?" Another kiss. Right at the curve between neck and shoulder where I seemed to have a nerve that connected straight to every girl part I owned.

I sighed. "I'm good. But you could make me feel better."

"Really?"

This time his tongue traced the spot, and I couldn't stop my shiver of pleasure. "Yes. Please."

I tried to turn in his arms, but he tightened his grip and scraped his teeth against my neck.

"No, stay like that."

His free hand slipped upward from my waist, found a breast, and started tracing a pattern around my nipple that made me crazy.

"Just lie still."

I couldn't disobey. Couldn't think of a reason why I'd want to as he set to work with lips and fingers, playing my body like a master even though the options were somewhat limited by our positions.

I felt him behind me, hard and ready, his breath coming a little faster, a little deeper with each sigh or moan he coaxed from me.

By the time his fingers slipped between my legs, I was ready to melt. Or maybe explode. He stroked me softly and I started to soar.

"Not just yet. Slowly." His hand slowed down to an agonizingly pleasurable rhythm, and my world shrank to focus on his fingers and the sensations pulsing through me with each touch.

But it wasn't enough. I wanted him closer. As close as we could get.

"I want you," I said softly. "Please, Damon."

"Your wish is my command."

His hand moved to my thigh, coaxed it upward. He pressed against me, teasing, drawing out the moment before he finally slid home and filled the ache.

I tightened around him, trying to draw him closer, but he kept control, moving softly and slowly. Steady like a train. Sliding and stroking. And all the time his lips skimmed my throat and ear, as he murmured to me, driving me upwards.

Time went away. The world went away. Nothing was real but him. It had been a long time—maybe never—since I'd felt like this about a man. Like he was the whole world.

Dumb, perhaps. Crazy when it might all be about to slip away.

But crazy felt better than anything I could remember.

"Come for me, Maggie," he said softly as he quickened the pace, driving deeper and harder. "I want to hear you."

It was irresistible, that voice, and I let it take me where I needed to go.

We stayed curled around each other until Damon's datapad buzzed into life twenty or so minutes later.

"Ajax," he said as he looked at the screen.

Ajax. Nat. Reality came speeding back, dragging a load of worry in its wake that hit me like a truck.

I listened to the conversation and, when I worked out what was going on, scrambled out of bed, headed for the shower.

"Where are you running off to?" Damon asked when I reemerged, clean but still kind of damp.

I twisted my hair up into a soggy knot, wanting to get moving. "It sounded like he got her to agree to come in to work. I need to be there when she arrives. I'm her best friend. I should be the one to talk to her, get her to agree to see Doctor Chen."

Shoes. Purse. Was there anything else?

Damon looked like he wanted to argue, but then he nodded. "Boyd will take you in."

The drive from St. Frances Woods seemed to take even longer than normal, the traffic grindingly slow. I envied those zipping along in the hover lanes.

Boyd had barely stopped the car outside the tester's building before I opened the door and scrambled out. I hit the testing rooms at a near run, only to find Ajax and the rest of his team but no Nat.

"No sign of her yet," he said. Stubble coated his jawline, and his hair stuck up at odd angles. His clothes reeked with the bite of Sandman.

"You didn't bring her with you?"

He grimaced. "We got her out of the club. Took her to a pizza joint to get some food into her. She was acting fairly normal. Said she wanted to go home and change."

"And you let her?" I said, voice squeaking with disbelief.

He scrubbed a hand over his jaw, expression unhappy. "I argued, but she wanted to go home. I didn't want to upset her and have her disappear again. I took her to your apartment in a cab, but she wouldn't let me come into the building. Told me she'd meet me here."

At least she'd gone home. But damn, I could've been there. I shouldn't have let Damon take me back to his house. I looked back at the door. "Maybe I should—"

Ajax shook his head. "I don't think that's a good idea. She was kind of slipping. Nervous. Let her come to you."

I didn't want to take his advice. I wanted to run home, scoop Nat up, and get her somewhere safe. But he was right. Nat's stubborn streak could be Grand Canyon–wide, and nothing made her dig in her heels like being pushed when she wasn't ready. "I want to know as soon as she gets here."

All I could do was wait, so I hunted down coffee and made my way across to the main building. The thought of facing my team with no chip didn't improve my mood as I descended in the elevator.

Eli and Benji and Trista were already at their desks, hard at work. Their varying looks of concern, surprise, and faint annoyance told me I wasn't exactly expected.

"Hey, you're back. Are you okay?" Eli stepped back and gave me the once-over. The shower had dispersed the rest of the gelskin, but there was no way to hide the surgical shield on my left wrist. His eyes widened and a grimace twisted his face.

"They took your chip?" he breathed.

"They jacked your chip?" Benji said, swiveling on his chair. "Shit, that rips."

"Pretty much," I agreed. "So we're going to have to do this the old-fashioned way. Or I am, at least."

"That's chill. We can do that." Benji frowned, but then his expression lightened. "Or one of us can run the data and you can watch on the screen." He turned back to his desk as his screen chirped at him. "In fact, let's do that," he added with a decisive nod that sent his newly green dreadlocks bouncing. "Boss man says you're to take it easy."

"What?" I headed for Benji's desk. Sure enough, there was a message from Damon telling the three of them to basically babysit me.

"Hang on." I picked up the phone and dialed Damon's extension. Cat answered. "Put me through, please."

"Ms. Lachlan? Is that you?"

"Yes. I need to speak to Damon. Now."

Benji grinned as I snapped the words. God knew what Eli and Trista thought.

"What's up?" Damon asked. He sounded distracted.

"I don't need babysitters," I ground out.

That got his attention. "I don't remember hiring any."

I fought the urge to bang my head on the desk. "You sent my team a message saying I have to take it easy."

"Well, you do. Doc's orders."

"I'm well aware of that. I can look after myself." This was exactly why leaning on Damon was dangerous. Give the man an inch and he'd take a mile—and probably stage a takeover bid for the next ten.

"But it's more fun if you let me do that."

I counted to three before I answered. Slowly. "You need a new definition of fun."

Benji's expression changed from grin to something more thoughtful. Assessing even.

Shit. I was talking to Damon like he was my boyfriend, not my boss.

Apparently morning sex and worry addled my brain.

"I would appreciate it if you'd trust me to know my own limitations," I said in a more professional tone. "After all, that's what you pay me for."

"When you talk like that, I start imagining you in a sexy little suit and glasses. And then I imagine taking them off you . . . ."

My palms started to sweat and I swallowed hard. Damon and I were definitely going to have another discussion on keeping things office appropriate. In the meantime, I wasn't going to play along.

"I'm glad you see my point of view," I said briskly.

"Did Nat turn up yet?"

"No. Goodbye." I hung up the receiver before he could say anything else to stir my hormones into rebellion.

"You and the boss man sound kind of slick there, Maggie D," Benji stage-whispered, winking at me.

"You're imagining things," I said. Beating my head against the desk still seemed like a good option. Though really, it was too late for that. I knew better than to mix business and pleasure, and this was why. These guys weren't going to go all out for me if they thought the only reason I got the gig was boning the boss.

Of course, that problem might just go away after Damon and I finally talked about what happened in that alley.

Something to worry about later. I had a job to do. Focusing on that might just keep me sane.

"Do you need to do anything to reset my system for me to work without a chip?"

Benji shrugged. "Couple of tweaks. No biggie. Thirty minutes tops."

"Great." My fingers itched to call Ajax for an update, but I didn't want Benji and the others listening in. "I need to check something with the testers. Buzz me when you're done."

I sped back to the tester's building. Still no Nat. I nibbled a fingernail as Ajax called her datapad.

No answer.

I double-checked that he had the right details. He did. He had our house comp's message service link too.

Still nothing.

"Let me try." Maybe she was avoiding work. I had no idea

whether she would also be avoiding me or not, but I had to try.

My call was no more successful than Ajax's. And when I used the tracking app Nat and I shared, it told me her datapad was offline. I chewed my lip, trying to ignore the sick roll of my stomach. Nat was never offline.

I commandeered a screen and logged into our house comp. No entries or exits recorded since Nat and I had left the night before. So if Nat had gone into the building like Ajax said, she'd obviously just waited until he'd left and then headed out again.

Or had she? What if something else had been waiting for her? The sort of something that had come after Damon and me? There was no reason to think Nat might be a target, but what if it had been waiting for me?

I swallowed hard, suddenly terrified. "I don't like this. I'm going home to see if she's there."

Ajax didn't try to stop me.

There wasn't a cab outside the Righteous campus. Typical. I grabbed my datapad to call a ride-share.

I had a mini heart attack when it buzzed to life in my hands just as I was punching keys to book the ride.

"Maggie Lachlan," I answered, trying not to sound too annoyed at the interruption.

"Where are you going?" Damon asked. "Cat said she saw you heading out."

"Home. Nat still a no-show."

"Wait there. I'll be two minutes."

"But—" I was talking to dead air. I toyed with the idea of leaving without him, but he'd probably just follow me. Plus, according to my datapad, he'd be here faster than the closest driver. So I stayed put.

Luckily, he was true to his word. Two minutes later, his car drove through the gates and stopped next to me.

The passenger door opened. "Get in," Damon said from the driver's seat.

"Where's Boyd?"

"I can drive."

Of course he could.

I climbed in. He nosed the car onto the road and disobeyed the posted speed limit as he headed for the gate. Once we were off-campus and back in the city traffic, he proceeded to give me another near heart attack as he wove between the cars around us, heading down the street at a speed I wouldn't have thought was possible downtown.

"Have you tried calling Nat?" he asked.

"Ten minutes ago. I was going to try again from the car." I fiddled with my datapad, willing it to give me the right answer this time. It still said Nat was offline. I sent her a message anyway.

"Call her now."

I did just that and listened to the house comp route me to Nat's voicemail after the obligatory five rings.

"No answer?"

"Voicemail." I pushed the datapad back into my purse and tried not to shriek as Damon shot through a gap barely wide enough for the car.

"Do you want to go home or to the club?"

"Dockside? No, thanks." Even in the light of day, I wasn't in a hurry to return to the scene of last night's terror. "Just home. Preferably in one piece."

He just gunned the engine and shot through a yellow light. "And if she's not there?"

"We'll cross that bridge when we come to it." I shut my eyes so Damon's kamikaze driving couldn't push my anxiety levels into the red zone.

Maybe Nat was just passed out somewhere at a friend's

house, oblivious to all our attempts to reach her. She slept like the dead at the best of times. Add a couple of late nights gaming and the cocktail of narcotics swirling around the air of Unquiet last night and she'd be practically comatose even if Ajax had stuffed her full of pizza.

It was a nice theory, but it didn't ring true. If she was safe, I wouldn't have knots in my stomach and a growing sense that something was very, very wrong. We finally turned into my street. The lights on all the parking stacks glowed red. Full. Damon circled the block a few times.

"Let me out," I said on the third go-round.

He hovered a finger over the lock release. "Only if you wait for me."

"I want to see if she's there. Unlock the damn door." I glared at him.

"I don't want you going up there alone."

My frustration eased. He was trying to protect me. Any other time, I might've found it hard to resist, but I was trying to find Nat. My instincts told me she was the one who needed protection. "It's just Nat."

"Nat who took a swing at me," he reminded me. "And there could be other things. Like last night."

So I wasn't the only one to have that thought. And, if Damon was bringing up last night, I got the feeling that my avoiding-the-subject time was about to run out. I looked away. "I'll wait for you."

"Don't have to." He pointed at a car pulling out ahead of us, then slid into the empty space.

"Nat, are you here?" The house comp had said she hadn't entered the apartment, but I couldn't help hoping that she'd somehow hacked it.

No such luck. The apartment was stubbornly silent. Nat's

bedroom door was wide open, and my heart slid to my shoes as I reached the doorway.

Neatly made bed. No sign of it having been slept in. No sign of Nat either.

"She's not here," Damon said from behind me.

I didn't tell him I already knew that. If I said it out loud, I'd be admitting that Nat was just . . . gone. "Maybe she's on her way to Righteous after all."

"I'll call the office." He moved out to the hallway. Nat's room screen sprang to life as I waved at it. Her inbox showed a stack of messages, all from me, Ajax, and other Righteous employees.

"Time of last access?" I asked the computer. I couldn't get into Nat's personal system, but the access logs were on the house comp.

"10:05 p.m."

No change. Nothing since last night. Before we'd left. She hadn't even accessed her system since then. Bad sign.

Damon stuck his head into the room. "Still a no show at work. Cat's going to call the club, see if she went back there."

"Ajax said he brought her back here, but obviously she didn't stay." I doubted she was at a club. Even for Nat, twelve hours straight of game time would be extreme. I tried to think where else she might hole up. In the weird mood she'd been in last night, it didn't seem likely that she'd go to her parents' house. And I didn't know quite how to check with her mom without freaking Mrs. Marcos out.

"Where else does she play?" Damon asked. "Cat can start checking those clubs as well."

"Thanks." I reeled off Nat's favorite clubs but didn't hold out much hope that she was at any of them. My gut was telling me this was something more.

"Maybe Cassandra can help. She might know somebody who can . . . ." He made a vague gesture in the air.

"What's . . . ?" I copied his movement.

"You know, can't some witches locate objects or something?"

How was I supposed to know? "I guess. Okay, good idea. I'll call her and you call Cat."

The conversation with Cassandra didn't take long. Yes, she could try locating Nat, but I needed to bring something that belonged to her to the store.

"Like what? Clothing? Jewelry?"

"That would be best. Something she wears a lot like a ring or a necklace. If you can't find one of those, then dirty clothes or a hairbrush."

Hairbrush? I went cold. Weren't witches meant to be able to do bad things if they had a piece of your hair or nails? I didn't like the thought of handing Cassandra that level of power. She seemed trustworthy, but I barely knew her. Nat wore plenty of jewelry, so I'd try and find a ring or something. "People can really do this? Tell where someone is from an object?"

"Sara didn't do finds? I guess not. Yes, some of us can do that. It's an effort though, and doesn't always work."

"But you'll try? I'm worried."

"Of course. Just find something and bring it with you. Don't handle it more than you have to. If you can wrap it in silk or cotton, that's best."

"Okay. We'll be there soon."

"We?" Cassandra sounded surprised.

"Damon and I." I flipped open the Chinese lacquer jewelry box on Nat's dresser and spotted one of her favorite rings. Now all I needed was something to wrap it in.

"I see. Maggie, does that boy know what he's getting into?"

"What do you mean?"

"Did you talk to him yet? About what happened last night? Does he know about you?"

I snapped the box shut, guilt washing over me. Damon was still in the living room. He couldn't hear me, but I lowered my voice anyway. "About me being a witch? We haven't really had a chance to talk about it." My thoughts tangled like the strings of beads Nat had piled on her dresser. How could I tell him? Then again, how could I not? What the hell would I say?

"I would've thought the demon was the bigger problem," Cassandra said dryly. "Unless he's an anti?"

She meant the religious crazies who sometimes rose up claiming magic was a scourge on the world. I wasn't a fan of magic either, but that just meant I avoided it personally, not that I wanted all witches thrown in jail or something. "No. I'm not sure he's much into the magic, but I don't think he's prejudiced."

And if I really believed that, why did I keep putting off telling him? Or was I worried about my own prejudice?

I picked up the beads and tried to untangle them.

"You need to tell him. You can't drag him into the middle of this without warning. Demons are dangerous."

One of the strings parted with a snap and beads sprayed everywhere. "You think Nat going AWOL has something to do with the demon?"

"I hope not, but it's a strange coincidence. I've never liked coincidences. Talk to him."

I looked down at the beads sprinkled over the floor and sighed. Time to clean up the mess. "I will. We might be a bit longer."

"I'll be waiting."

I hung up and stood frozen for a moment, trying to figure out how exactly you told your fairly new lover that you were a) a witch and b) potentially being hunted by a demon.

I still hadn't come up with an answer by the time I'd gathered as many beads as I could and found a silk scarf to wrap Nat's ring in.

Damon was just pocketing his datapad when I reached the kitchen.

"All set?" he asked. "Cat's got the list of clubs so she'll get the calls out. If Nat's not at a club, I'll send some of our security team to look around in the neighborhoods near them."

"That's great." I rocked on my toes, trying to find a way to say, "Hey, guess what? I might be a witch." Then I wimped out. "I appreciate all this. You don't have to."

His headshake was dismissive. "What did Cassandra say? Can she help?"

"Yes. Maybe. We can head over there in a minute." I patted the pocket with the silk-wrapped ring a little nervously.

"Don't you want to go now?"

"There's something I need to talk to you about first." I pulled out a chair from the kitchen table. "Maybe you should sit down."

He sat slowly. "Is this the conversation you've been ducking since last night?" His eyes seemed to be a cooler shade of blue.

I took a seat across from him, picked up a napkin ring to distract myself with. "I guess."

"Am I going to like it?"

I made myself meet his eyes. Cool. Very cool. "I don't know."

"Then you'd better tell me."

"Will you promise to hear me out before you say anything?"

He frowned. "All right. This isn't a 'Dear Damon' speech, is it?"

I managed half a smile. Because half of me was afraid that after he heard what I had to say, I might be the one getting dumped. "No."

"Then what?" He leaned back in his chair, the fingers of his right hand drumming a tattoo on his thigh.

"I don't know if your background check on me showed this, but I'll assume it didn't. My mother was a witch."

He went very still. I couldn't read a thing from him.

"Go on."

I sent the napkin ring spinning. "The thing is . . . the thing is, it turns out that maybe so am I."

Chapter Fourteen

THE NAPKIN RING spun and spun, the whirring clatter the only noise in the room as Damon stared at me, disbelief clear on his face.

Eventually I couldn't take it anymore. I slapped my hand over the ring. "Say something." The edge of the plastic dug into my palm as I willed him to say, "It's okay."

Silence.

Until he pushed back his chair with enough force that it almost fell to the ground before he caught it and jerked it back into place. My heart went into free fall. Somehow I didn't think he'd be reaching to catch that.

"Say something. Please." My voice came from far away.

"Like what? Congratulations?" His voice was strained. Tension rode his neck and shoulders. Maybe I'd been wrong when I'd told Cassandra he wasn't anti-magic.

I closed my hand around the napkin ring and the pain increased. Somehow physical discomfort was a welcome distraction. "I didn't say I was happy about it."

I thought I saw his shoulders relax, just a fraction of an inch. "You're not?"

"No. This is the last thing I want."

His knuckles were white where he gripped the chair. "Is that why you didn't tell me?"

I hesitated, not knowing what to say when there was so much riding on how he might react to the answer. "I didn't tell you because I needed some time to deal with it by myself first. That's all." My fingers were turning numb. I forced myself to open my hand. The vivid red imprint of the napkin ring stood out like a burn. The sensation as the blood rushed back in to my hand burned too.

"You do that a lot." Damon was staring at my hand, not meeting my eyes.

"What?" I rubbed my palm, trying to ease the ache.

"Deal with things yourself." He lowered himself back onto the chair.

"I'm not sure I—"

"You sleep with me, you need some time. You find out you're a witch, you need some time. Do you ever let people in? Ever turn to them first?"

My spine stiffened. "And if I'd turned to you last night? Told you I was a witch? Would your reaction have been better than it is now?"

His face went very still. Then he cleared his throat. "I don't know."

"That's why I needed the time. I didn't know how you were going to take it. I didn't want to—" I stopped myself. Maybe he was right. Maybe I was slow to let people in. But Sara had taught me to be cautious, shown me that life could be messy and nasty and that lots of people would go to extremes to get what they wanted, no matter who they might hurt. Losing my grandparents to the quake had reinforced those lessons. I'd learned well enough that the fact that I wanted to let Damon in so fast, that I didn't want to lose him, scared me silly.

"Didn't want to what?"

I shook my head. "Look, I was scared. And freaked out

and, honestly, kind of spaced out from the drugs. I made a choice. Maybe it wasn't the greatest choice in the world, but it wasn't exactly a normal situation. So maybe you could cut me some slack?" I looked across at him, into those blue eyes that suddenly seemed so distant, willing him to understand.

"Is there anything else you haven't told me about last night?"

I swallowed, feeling like I was standing on the edge of a cliff that was beginning to crumble beneath my feet. I had no idea how to get back to solid ground. "Yes."

"What?"

"The truth, the whole truth, so help me whoever?"

He nodded curtly. "If it's not too much trouble."

I knew I had to tell him. A lie now would ruin any slim chance we might still have of making something out of whatever this was between us. But I couldn't help feeling like the truth might just have the same effect.

Time to choose again.

I took a deep breath and told him about the demon.

The car echoed with silence as Damon drove us to Cassandra's. Too much silence. It made me want to babble stupidly to fill the yawning empty space between us.

"I could go by myself. Drop me off anywhere. I'll catch a cab," I said for about the third time since I'd finished my confession slash explanation slash half-garbled lesson on what little I knew about demons.

"Don't be ridiculous."

Exact same answer. Third time in a row. The only thing that had changed was his tone growing colder with each reply. Not a good sign.

I twisted in my seat so I was facing him. "You're quiet."

"You gave me quite a lot to think about." He gunned the engine, waiting for the light to turn green.

"I'm sorry I didn't tell you sooner." I'd said that about five times already. Apparently we were trapped in the conversation from hell.

"Don't worry about it." We roared through the intersection, the speed making me wonder if he was trying to get airborne down the hill. Or maybe just scare the crap out of me. He was certainly succeeding at the latter; my knuckles were white where they wrapped around the armrest.

"Cassandra isn't going to close the store before we get there," I managed through gritted teeth as we just made it through another set of lights.

"I'm sure she won't."

"Then can you slow down a bit? I get that you're mad, but I'd rather not die just now."

"I'm not mad."

That was a big fat lie. But he did ease off the accelerator. Which left me free to concentrate fully on just how mad he might be. And how the hell I was going to get him to talk about it?

Cassandra took one look at us and insisted on making us tea upstairs.

"You'll like this," she said, handing us mugs. "It's very calming." Her tone suggested it had better be.

I took the mug and sniffed gingerly. Nothing suspicious, just the usual wet grass and green things smell of herbal tea.

Damon didn't look any happier with his than I was, but he took a sip. Then another. I tried not to watch him too closely, but I still noticed when he eased back ever so slightly on the sofa.

I didn't want to push him. He needed to process. So I turned to Cassandra.

"Did you bring something that belongs to your friend?" she asked.

I handed over the small silk-wrapped ring. "Yes. Nat wears this most days."

Cassandra put the bundle down gently, then placed her hands on either side. "But not today?"

"She didn't have it on at the club last night. She doesn't wear rings when she games."

"All right." She peeled back the silk. The ring—a twining band of silver leaves—looked tiny against the expanse of fabric. Thin and fragile.

Please let her be okay.

"What's her full name?"

"Natalia Imogen Marcos."

Cassandra nodded, then closed her fingers around the ring. Her eyes took on a faraway expression.

I stayed still, not wanting to do anything to disturb her. It wasn't easy. As the seconds ticked by, a weird pins-and-needles sensation flowed across my skin. I wanted to scratch something—though I didn't know exactly what—but I didn't want to risk distracting Cassandra.

Damon watched Cassandra too, his face arranged in the same distant mask it had worn in the car. I wondered if he ever played poker. Apart from "not happy," I didn't have a clue what he was thinking or feeling.

After about five minutes, Cassandra took a deep breath and opened her hand. The ring looked exactly as it had. "I'm sorry, Maggie. I'm not getting anything."

I looked at the silver leaves in dismay. "What does that mean?"

"She might be out of my range. She might be—"

"Dead?" I whispered. Damon started to move toward me

but stopped, which did nothing to ease the dread crawling my skin and gripping my lungs.

"No." Cassandra shook her head decisively. "No, I don't think so. She might be shielded."

"Shielded by what?" Was there something that could block attempts to do a location spell or whatever it was Cassandra did?

"That's the million-dollar question," Cassandra said. "I need to think about this. I have some friends who may help. One of them is better than me at locating."

She put the ring down on the scarf and wrapped it back up without touching the metal. "I'll keep this for now."

"No problem." It made more sense for Cassandra to keep it. Then I wouldn't have to bring it back here again if she needed it. Presumably the less contact it had with other people, the better, so me carting it around in my purse seemed unlikely to be helpful. The worst thing that could happen would be Nat turning up and me having to explain where her favorite ring was. I'd happily take any shit she might give me for handing it over to a stranger if that happened.

"Good. Now, seeing as we can't go any further in this direction for the time being, perhaps we should talk about you."

"Me?" I swallowed tea too fast and began to cough.

"You need training."

That pronouncement didn't help me get my breath back. It was true, maybe, but truth wasn't always what a girl wanted to hear.

I slanted a glance at Damon. No change in the poker face. Apparently the announcement that I needed to learn some magic hadn't improved his mood. It hadn't really improved mine either, but I wasn't stupid. I killed the imp through sheer dumb luck. If more things like that—or worse—could be coming after me, I needed to know what I was doing, even if I didn't like it.

"Right now?"

Cassandra nodded firmly. "The sooner, the better."

Damon stood. "I'll head back to the office, see how the search is going."

"Not just yet," Cassandra said, holding up a finger. Damon stayed still as she rose.

Ice Bitch Queen versus Master of the Universe round two. If I hadn't been so tense, I might've enjoyed it. As long as I didn't have to put money on who might win.

Blue eyes clashed with brown. Cassandra stood her ground, arms folded against her floral-cotton-covered chest.

Damon didn't budge either. "I can't do anything here."

"No, but there are some things you need to know. Maggie told you what's happening?"

His gaze flicked toward me for a second, then focused back on Cassandra. "She told me she was a witch. That she was bound to a demon."

I tried not to wince at the disapproval in his voice.

She smoothed a hand over her bun. "Yes. And because of that, you need to know how to protect yourself."

This time the folded arms were his. "From what?"

"If the demon is trying to recapture Maggie, it will use any method it can think of. It may try for those close to her."

"How would it know who I was?"

Good question. And the better one was, why hadn't Cassandra told me this yesterday? Or earlier? I hit her with the same sort of flat stare as Damon. It had about as much impact on her as his did.

"While the binding was active, it would've had an awareness of the people in Maggie's life. Demons are very intelligent."

"Then wouldn't anything I do to protect myself be a waste of time?"

Cassandra clucked her tongue denial. "Intelligence doesn't mean they don't have limits. Let's go downstairs and I'll give you a few things that may help." She turned to me and made a "hurry up, get your butt off the sofa" gesture.

I stood and managed to not actually wobble despite my legs feeling like not-quite-set Jell-O. I didn't think Damon would leap to help me if I stumbled, and I didn't want to make a fool of myself.

We all trooped back downstairs with me in the lead.

I took two steps onto the shop floor, then froze. Cassandra almost cannoned into me.

"What?" she said with a snap in her tone.

I pointed at the door. The open door.

And the creature that hovered, drooling black slime, at the threshold.

Another nightmare—an imp? I didn't know if that was right, but I knew it was nothing good. The sight of it brought an immediate rush of fear, souring my mouth and cramping my stomach.

I flung out a hand instinctively.

Cassandra smacked my arm down. "Don't be an idiot. You don't know what you're doing."

"What is that?" Damon demanded as he moved to stand beside us.

"An imp. Don't go any closer," Cassandra warned as he stepped forward.

He obeyed but didn't look happy. "Why is it just standing there?"

"This shop is well warded. It can't cross." She raised a hand and the door swung shut with a thump, knocking the imp back a pace. Its mouth opened and a gibbering moan came from behind the glass.

My brain kicked back in as the fear receded. Apparently I equated glass with safety, which seemed overly optimistic, really.

I stared at the critter as it pressed closer, leaving a greasy smear as it dragged a misshapen limb down the glass, still moaning. An imp. Like last night. Which meant it could be killed.

I looked at Cassandra, waiting for instructions.

She was watching the imp's movements with a smug smile. "Just opening the door would've hurt it."

The creature hissed and chattered outside the door.

"It doesn't look hurt." I stared at it warily. It didn't look exactly like the creature from the night before. Fewer legs, for a start. And it wasn't really black in the sunlight, more a deep, oily shade of green. Colors coalesced across its skin, hints of purple and red and blue and yellow, all in not-quite-right shades that made my eyes hurt and my skin crawl.

I stepped sideways and bumped into Damon. His arm clamped around me.

"How did it know we were here?" I asked.

Cassandra's eyebrows drew together. "The demon may have others who are bound. They could be watching. Or it could be following your energy pattern. There are several ways it could track you."

"Great," I muttered, fighting not to huddle closer against Damon.

"Now do you see why I said you needed protection?" Cassandra said to Damon.

He didn't answer. I figured he didn't need to. To say no at this point would be pointless.

I had a sudden nasty thought. "What if someone else comes past?" I didn't want some innocent bystander becoming an imp snack because of me.

"Don't worry, when something sets off my wards, it automatically sets off some other protections. No one will come down the street right now."

One small piece of good news, at least.

We all studied the imp while it stared at us, baring a mouth full of rows of jagged teeth that made a great white look like a gummy bear. Damon's arm tightened around my shoulders. "Can you get rid of it?" I asked.

Before Cassandra could answer, the imp sprang forward again, hitting the glass with enough force to rattle the door. But it held, and the imp fell back with a pained yowl.

Cassandra grinned. "Slow learner, it seems."

"Let's hope it's got a low pain threshold," I said. "Or gets smarter fast."

"We don't have to worry about that. I'm hardly going to leave it there. If we chase it off, it's still loose in the city. They'd have my hide."

"Who is 'they'?" I asked as the creature prowled a path along the storefront and back to the door, making a noise that made my teeth ache. A memory tickled at me. Cassandra had said something like this when we'd first met. I wanted to know who she was talking about.

"Never mind about that. Come back here behind me."

Damon and I moved. Fast. Cassandra nodded approval, then turned to face the door, raising one hand. Light flashed and the imp shrieked as it burst into bright white flame.

I winced away, shielding my eyes. Damon let me go. When I looked back at the doorway, there was nothing but smoking ash. Awe swept over me, like I'd just seen something I'd never known I'd been looking for. Quickly followed by a healthy dose of shock as the smoke wafted upward.

What the hell am I getting myself into?

I turned toward Damon. His face was still set but paler than it had been.

"You might notice that I managed not to set fire to myself in the process," Cassandra said, turning back to us. "Which is why you need training."

"I don't have to do—" I waved a shaky hand in the direction of the ash. I felt vaguely nauseous at the idea of ever having to burn something alive again. Even if the something was an imp.

"You don't have to use your powers to harm—or defend, rather. Of course you don't. But knowing how is important, if only to prevent accidental singeing."

I threaded my fingers around the pendant she'd given me. "What else?"

"Depends what you have a talent for." She studied me for a moment. "Obviously fire is not going to be a problem. But first, let's take care of Mr. Riley. Then you can watch while I cleanse that mess." She bustled around the store, picking up various candles, oils, and stones and piling them on the counter.

"Maggie will explain what to do with these." She opened the counter tray, pulled out a leather cord with a chunk of the same black tourmaline she'd given me hanging from it, and held it up toward Damon. "Bend down. I'm not an Amazon like her."

Damon dipped his head and she fastened the leather around his neck. It suited him somehow. But judging by the speed with which he unbuttoned his collar and hid the thing out of sight beneath his shirt, he didn't agree.

"Next to the skin, very good. Keep it there and you should be fine." Cassandra held out a datapad. "Here, transfer my contact details to your system. If you notice anything strange or out of place—anything at all—call me. Any time."

"Thank you," Damon said politely. He didn't meet my eyes as she handed him a bag with all the supplies she'd gathered. "How do I know there won't be another of those things waiting for me at the office?"

"I can shield you a bit," Cassandra said. "And the demon's lost two imps in two days. I'm hoping it's not going to have much energy to spare for anyone but Maggie."

Lucky me. But it seemed to satisfy Damon.

"I'll see you later?" I asked.

His response was a noncommittal grunt.

"You'd better use the rear exit," Cassandra said diplomatically. "You don't want to track through imp ash. It stains." She ushered Damon out back.

Stained? Did she fry imps regularly? I didn't think the opportunity would come up that often. According to what she'd told me, not many witches would risk summoning one.

I rubbed my arm where I'd scorched myself as I stared at the pile of ash. Cassandra was right—I needed to learn what I could do, if only so I could avoid ever having to do any of it.

Cassandra returned before I had too much time to brood.

"He's quiet," she said with an inquisitive tilt to her head.

It was tempting to unload on her, but unloading might just make my fears about him come true. I gestured at the ash. "This is a lot to deal with."

She let it go. "How are you dealing with it?"

Right now I wanted a drink. Or a vat of chocolate. And possibly to be knocked unconscious so I didn't have to deal with even one more thing. But short of letting the next imp catch me, none of those seemed likely options. "I've had better days."

"Haven't we all." She frowned in the direction of the door. "Right, let's get this mess cleaned up."

"What about my lesson?"

"We can do both at once. There are a couple of buckets and rubber gloves upstairs under the sink in the kitchen."

I went to fetch them. By the time I came back downstairs, Cassandra had a vial of oil, a pile of herbs, and a sack of salt on the counter.

"Wouldn't Lysol be easier?" I asked as we both pulled on purple gloves.

She smiled. "Probably. But that would only take care of the physical side. And that's the easy part."

"What's the hard part?" It seemed the obvious question.

"Clearing up the energy signature so nothing else can home in on it."

I wished I hadn't asked.

Cassandra ground the oil, herbs, and salt together in a big stone dish until the whole room smelled like clary sage and rosemary and lavender and other things I didn't recognize, then dumped half into each bucket before filling them with hot water.

"How does this work exactly?"

"Remember what I told you about energy?"

"Every person or thing has an energy field," I said slowly. "Witches have the ability to manipulate those fields."

"Close enough for now," Cassandra replied, lifting a bucket.

"If witches can manipulate energy fields, why do you need all the herbs and things?"

"We don't is the short answer. You used your own energy to burn that imp last night, didn't you?"

"Then why?" I picked up the other bucket and followed her to the door.

"Firstly, all the things we use have energy of their own, which can help with the working. Secondly, going through a ritual of preparation helps you focus your intent. Thirdly, depending on what you're doing, the herbs and crystals have other properties besides energy that can help." She flexed her fingers in the gloves. "And lastly, any doctor will tell you that the placebo effect is real. Making someone take a tonic or wear a talisman helps belief, which in turn helps the working influence the energy field."

I fingered my pendant. "So this is really just a magic sugar pill?"

"Not entirely. The energy of the crystals helps shield your own. How well it does, well, that depends on your belief." She paused, one hand on the door handle. "Do you believe, Maggie?"

"In magic?" I nodded at the pile of ash. "It's kind of hard to argue with that."

"Good. Then maybe we'll get somewhere. Now help me

clean this up. We'll put it in this." She indicated the bucket nearest her foot.

I knelt, the sun beating down on my back as I eyed the ash warily. Imp ash. Still faintly warm. Ash caused by a fire lit by magic. I couldn't help feeling like maybe I was asleep and having a particularly weird nightmare. But around me, hover whine and sirens and the background hum of lots and lots of people—all the familiar sounds of the city—told me I was awake. The breeze blew hair into my face and the stink of the ash grew stronger.

Not a dream. Reality. I had to deal. So I leaned forward and scooped ash. "Tell me about imps," I said as I lifted the first handful. I'd expected it to be hot, but it was already cool enough to touch. "Do you think this one was trying to do the same thing as the other?"

Cassandra scooped ash herself. It smelled disgusting, cutting through the oils, and had a weird, slightly greasy texture rather than being light and crumbly like wood ash. The water in the bucket bubbled briefly with each scoop. "I think it's fairly clear they're after you. And yes, I say they're still trying to do something that would let the demon possess you or bind you again."

"A spell to lower my will, right? Is that the only way it can possess someone?"

"No. Certain people are susceptible, those whose natural psychic barriers are low. And resistance is sometimes weakened if you're depressed or sick. Mentally ill. Demons prey on the weak."

"But they can't get to you if you're strong?"

"The stronger the demon, the more powerful its influence. A weaker demon would need the imp to touch you to establish a link if you were susceptible. A stronger one can do it without a physical connection if there's weakness to exploit."

Like being bound to one? I took a deep breath, suddenly dizzy. Bad idea. The imp stink made my stomach churn.

Cassandra put a gloved hand on mine. "You're a witch. Your barriers are strong. It's not going to sneak up on you that way. It wouldn't be wasting energy on sending imps if it could."

I nodded slowly, wanting to believe her. But my spine prickled as I wondered if the demon was already watching me, planning another attempt.

One step at a time, Maggie. Scoop, dump, fizz, repeat. If I concentrated on just that, I could get through the next few minutes.

When Cassandra was happy that we'd gathered as much ash as we could, she put her hand over the bucket and I got the weird tingly feeling again as she closed her eyes.

"Good," she said after a few moments. She pointed at the other bucket. "Pour that one over the mark."

The hypercrete was scorched and blackened where we'd cleared the ash. I poured the water and oil over the marks gingerly. Again there was a hissing, bubbling mess but, to my disappointment, once the foaming subsided, the black smears were still there.

"Can't do much about the appearance. I told you it stains." Cassandra crouched and held her hands out again. "But at least it's done the trick."

"Is it even worth me asking what you just did?"

She stripped off her gloves and put them in the empty bucket. "Bring that along with you and I'll try to explain. Though it might be just easier to start with the basics."

The basics, it seemed, after we had emptied and cleaned both buckets with more herbs and hot water and then thrown them and the gloves into the recycler, involved still more herbal tea.

"You know, I'd really prefer syncaf," I said hopefully.

"You're already running on adrenaline. You don't need to strain your energy field any more with caffeine. You may, however, have a cookie. Low blood sugar is bad." She held out a plate of oatmeal raisin.

I really wanted the caffeine, but I took the cookie anyway. Once I took a bite, I realized I was actually starving. Three more cookies disappeared in quick succession. The sugar wiped out the taste of the tea as well.

Bonus.

I eyed the cookie plate, wondering if I could manage a fifth. Without Nat to yell at me about eating white flour and fat, I could eat guilt free. Except that thought brought back the fact that Nat was missing with a vengeance. Along with all the stress and worry I'd managed to forget for a little while.

I straightened in the overstuffed armchair. "Okay, let's do this. How do we start?"

Cassandra finished her cookie. "Every witch has to learn how to perceive the energy fields."

That seemed about as useful as being told I had to learn how to fly when I had no wings. "How, exactly?"

"Everyone is different. Some people feel the energy, some can see it. I know one witch who seems to hear it. She says everyone has their own song."

Great, more variables. Magic had far too many buts and maybes. I wanted some nice clean logic. Rules. I could deal with those. In fact, I kicked butt at rules and logic. There was a reason I dealt with code, after all. So far where magic was concerned, I was the one getting my butt kicked.

"How do I know which will work for me?"

"Ever seen an aura?"

"No." Not unless seeing stars after banging my head against a cabinet door once counted.

"Then sight probably isn't the strongest way for you. Which is a pity, because it's the most useful. Most healers see the fields."

I had less than zero desire to be a healer. Spend all my time in hospitals? No thanks. Unless I could voodoo sick computers into behaving. Which I doubted.

"Can you sense it more than one way?"

Cassandra smiled. "Yes. I can see the energy fields and feel them."

"What do they feel like?"

"That's something else that varies. A breeze, a sensation of warmth, pins and needles."

Pins and needles. Bingo. "I felt something like that when you were trying to find Nat."

"Really? That's good. We'll start there, then. Hold out your hand, palm up."

When I did, she held hers, palm down, above mine, about an inch apart. "Now close your eyes and tell me if you can feel anything."

I concentrated hard. Nothing.

"Relax," Cassandra said softly. "Breathe deeply. Picture energy flowing through and around your body. And through and around mine."

I was glad my eyes were closed so she couldn't see the eye roll. It all sounded like the sort of airy-fairy bullshit the instructors at the ultra-zen yoga classes Nat dragged me to droned on about.

But this was real. I'd set fire to an imp using something other than matches and lighter fluid, and I'd seen Cassandra do it too. Plus she'd helped my arm heal overnight. So there had to be something there to feel.

I focused on slowing my heartbeat, trying to do as Cassandra had asked and think about energy. My mind came up with an image of little sequences of ones and zeros zipping between chips. Not quite the metaphor I was hoping for. I wasn't a computer, after all . . . but maybe it wasn't so silly. Energy had to be a type of information flow. Nerves used electricity to communicate, didn't they? So this energy field had to be data of some sort.

Maybe it would be like using the chip to plug into a code. The same sense of standing in the middle of a swirl of information flowing around and through me.

To my surprise, as soon as the thought crossed my mind, I could see it in my head, a cool blue light flowing around me, little dots and swirls of darker blue floating in the light. A warm sensation moved across my palm, tingling. Better still, another sort of sensation—one that felt greener somehow—floated about an inch above the warmth.

"I think I feel it," I said, voice full of wonder.

The sense of green warmed a little, like it was . . . happy, maybe.

"Let's see," Cassandra said. "I'm going to move my hand. Keep your eyes closed and move yours to stay the same distance apart from mine."

"Okay." I focused on my hand and the sensations, trying to see in my head where blue faded out and green began.

"Think about the connection," Cassandra continued. "Feel where the fields intersect. Try and keep that feeling—keep the same distance."

As she spoke, the sensation changed, the feel of her hand becoming more distant. Feeling like an idiot, I lifted my hand, only to smack hard into hers.

Cassandra laughed. "Slowly. The idea is to maintain the gap. Let's try again."

We played the game for a few minutes, me trying to follow her hand by feel alone and half the time only managing another collision. After about the tenth attempt, I was starting—maybe—to get the hang of it. I had a vague sensation of something more than just Cassandra's hand above mine, a sort of shape of where she was in my head. I was also out of breath from the effort.

"That's enough," Cassandra said abruptly. "Open your eyes."

For a moment, everything was dazzling. I squinted as the room returned to normal. Except for Cassandra. She seemed to glow faintly, the light the warm green of ancient computer text.

"You're glowing," I said stupidly.

"So are you."

I looked at my arm and almost gasped. There was a faint glow of blue flowing across my skin.

"Seems like you can see and feel too," Cassandra said with a smile.

"How do I turn it off?" I didn't want to walk around gaping at glowing people.

"It will probably fade once you start doing something else. You have to focus at first. Once you get better control, you can sort of choose to filter it out."

"How long is getting control going to take?"

"We'll see. But that's enough for now. You're tired." She watched me for a moment. "Though your field looks better now. Keep practicing your breathing and visualizing the energy flowing around you, see if you can make it wider and brighter. And try not to set anything on fire between now and tomorrow morning. I'll send you some texts to read."

I watched the blue glow surrounding my hand and got the not-quite-real feeling again. "What's happening tomorrow morning?"

"Your next lesson."

Chapter Fifteen

I LEFT Cassandra's exhausted and starving again despite the cookie binge. A quick glance at my data pad established it was close to three. Apparently cookies didn't count as a proper lunch when you were doing magic. Not that I knew whether what we'd just done counted as magic.

The energy field thing was kind of cool, but I wasn't sure I wanted to do actual magic.

Learning enough to protect myself made sense. But that was it. Magic had never brought anything but trouble and darkness to my life.

What I actually wanted was to find Nat. There were no messages on my datapad, so I didn't hold out much hope that Damon's people had found her. But I had to check in anyway.

I dialed Damon and headed down the street, looking for a cab. The few people I passed didn't glow, which was a relief—hard to ignore glowing people when you're trying to pretend everything is normal.

"It's me," I said when Damon answered. "Any luck with Nat?"

"No. There was no sign of her at any of the clubs."

My heart sank. "Are you still at work? I'll come in."

"Actually I'm home."

I waited for an invitation to come over. Silence. Which made my stomach twist in a not so good way. "Can I come over?"

"Yes, you probably should."

Hardly an enthusiastic invitation. "Okay. I'll swing by the apartment first, in case Nat's gone home."

"See you when you get here."

He cut the call before I could say anything else. Damn. I didn't want to admit it, not after such a short time of knowing him, but wondering if I was about to get the "it's just not going to work" speech hurt.

A lot.

My stomach was telling me that maybe dinner might be in order despite my late lunch by the time I'd made it to the apartment—still no sign of Nat—and back across town to Damon's house. I'd half expected his house comp not to let me in, but the door swung open after the scan flashed over me and the system announced that Damon was in his office. It took some time to find my way through the house, and by the time I reached the office, there was no sign of him. The bedroom was the only other room I was familiar with, so I headed there.

Bingo.

Damon stood by the window, staring down at the garden in the twilight. He was barefoot and wearing old faded jeans and a plain gray T-shirt. The shirt he'd worn to Cassandra's was balled up on the chaise beside him.

"Hi," I said softly from the door.

He turned, backlit by a golden halo of light from the setting sun. I couldn't see his expression.

"Hi, yourself," he said neutrally.

I came into the room, took a seat on the bed. Mistake. The urge to just lie back and fall asleep hit hard as my butt sank into the softness. But I forced myself to remain upright, not sure of my welcome.

"Nat wasn't there." No sign of her. No messages from her or any of our friends. I'd have to call her parents soon. I'd almost rather face another imp.

Damon didn't respond. I didn't think I could do any more awkward silence.

"How was your afternoon?" It sounded weirdly formal to my ears.

"Unproductive." His voice was overly polite.

I patted the bed. "Why don't you come over here?"

He stayed right where he was.

I bit my lip. "O-kay then. Do you want to tell me what's wrong?" I held up a hand to block the glare, squinting to try to see his face.

"No."

Okay. So the anger hadn't really gone away. I understood that, kind of. I'd lied to him, after all. But I was trying to make up for it. "Want to come over here and shag me senseless?"

"No."

I stood. "I guess I'm out of luck, then. I should go."

"Don't," he said reluctantly.

I held up my hands, palms out. "Then talk or tango, because I don't want to play guessing games. I already have enough puzzles to deal with."

"You're a witch. Can't you tell what's on my mind?"

"I'm hardly even a witch. I know basically nothing about magic." I moved around the bed so the sun wasn't blinding me. "But I do know telepathy isn't part of the package." As far as I knew. Maybe a lifetime of avoidance of magic hadn't been such a good strategy. There was a vast gaping abyss where anything beyond a very basic knowledge of witches and what they could do should be in my brain.

Damon rubbed his fingers over the back of his left hand. "You're not going to like this."

"I'm not exactly enjoying life right now anyway. You've been acting freaked since I told you what was going on. Just spit it out, Damon."

"You're a witch," he said.

"And?" I waited for the rest of the statement. Then, as the silence stretched between us, I realized there was no rest of that statement. It wasn't the lying he was mad about, it was the magic itself.

My stomach clutched. I might not intend to use my power, but I couldn't change the fact that I had it. It wasn't something I could turn off like a faucet.

Damon stayed silent, staring down at his feet.

"You don't like magic?" I needed to understand, to see if there was anything I could work with, or whether I might lose him just when I'd accepted that I really didn't want to. Because of something I couldn't control.

"No."

"But there's magic in most of your games."

He lifted his head. "That's not real. It's clean. There's no cost."

Frankly, when you get blown apart by a lightning bolt cast by a mage in a game, it feels pretty costly. "I don't understand."

"Magic in games is just that—a game. No one gets hurt."

His voice was bitter, and I sank onto the chaise. I knew that tone. I'd heard it in the voices of Sara's most disgruntled customers.

My mother was a witch. That much was true. She had power. But she didn't always bother expending it on clients when she thought she could blow them off with sugar water and a few vague made-up phrases. She was very clear up front with them that magic didn't always work. Which was absolutely true. And one hundred percent guaranteed not to work when she didn't intend to actually waste any of her power on them. Of course, none of them believed it wouldn't work for them, so we'd had our share of angry people knocking on the door of whatever hole-in-the-wall apartment or trailer we were living in, demanding their money back. Which usually resulted in Sara promising they'd have it soon and us promptly doing a midnight flit out of town.

Damon sounded like someone who'd been burned.

"Did someone you know get mixed up with something magical?"

His eyes bored into mine. "Not someone. Me."

I wrapped my arms around myself as my gut turned cold. We had to play this out. Real life didn't come with a quick release. "What happened?"

"I don't know why we're talking about this."

"Because I'm a witch, like you said. If you don't like witches, then that doesn't leave us many places to go. Is that what you want? For this to be done? Do you want me to just leave?" I wasn't sure if I meant leave the house or quit or both.

He made a noise halfway between frustration and confusion. "No."

Okay. So he maybe wasn't going to fire me. But we still had to deal with the fact that we were sleeping together.

I gripped my pendant, wondering if it could ward off emotional train wrecks. "Then we need to talk." I jerked my chin at the bed. "Sit. Unless you do want me out of here."

He sat, rubbed his hands over his face. "That's just it. That's part of the problem."

I was lost again. "Talking?"

"No, me not wanting you to go. Hell, I've only known you what, a week? It's too fast. Too hard. I shouldn't feel like this."

I could relate to that argument. I'd made it myself. "Sometimes people click," I said quietly. "Nothing we can do about that."

"And sometimes they're helped," he snarled.

My jaw dropped and a spike of anger followed my initial rush of disbelief. "You think I've done something to you? A working? Screw you, Damon. I didn't even know I had any power when we met." If he thought the only reason he could fall for me was magical influence, then we definitely had a problem.

"You don't need power to buy a love potion."

There was the bitterness again, and everything suddenly made horrible sense. "Someone used a potion on you." It wasn't a question. I knew I was right.

His hands balled into fists, knuckles stark white. "And it worked. I was so messed up by her, I could hardly see straight. Could hardly think straight."

Was that how he felt about me? It would explain his freaking out. Hard to feel like master of the universe when your hormones are spinning out of control and you only want one thing. "Potions don't last long." That much I did know from Sara. Even a real love potion couldn't work forever. And real magic cost a fortune. "Maybe it was real."

"They last long enough."

"How long exactly?" I held my breath, praying it had just been some bad teen crush gone wrong.

"Until shortly after our first wedding anniversary. Long enough for her to take half my assets when she left."

Wedding? Wife? My heart ached. "You were married?"

"Not really." He stood and stalked back to the window, staring out.

"You were married," I repeated. "When?" My research hadn't brought up anything about a wife. The records must've been buried deep.

"I was twenty when we met, almost twenty-one when we married."

"Just a baby." But old enough to learn never to trust magic again. The ache in my chest doubled. I had no idea how to fight that sort of lesson. I'd learned it too well myself.

"Old enough to know better."

Oh, I knew this dance. Knew the taste of the bitterness in his voice.

I got up and crossed the room, stopping just beyond his reach. I wanted to touch him, to help, but if he thought I'd spelled him, I doubted my touch would be very comforting. "How could you possibly know?" I said gently. "Who does that?"

He turned. "A witch, obviously." Bitterness edged with rage this time.

I swallowed, fought to hold my ground. "You really think I would do that to you? Force you?"

"I don't know. That's the problem. But you're a witch."

"Your wife wasn't," I pointed out.

"A witch sold her the potion. A witch didn't care that she was taking away my free will. She just made a potion, no questions asked. She got paid and didn't care that my life was destroyed."

I swallowed hard. I knew all about witches who didn't care about morality. After all, one had given birth to me. And once again my lack of magical knowledge was screwing me. I didn't know anything about love potions, but for one to last a year, surely there had to be some real emotion involved. Otherwise it wouldn't have hurt him so much.

I didn't want to point that out. It might just make things worse. "Your life isn't exactly a disaster. You're one of the richest men on the planet."

His mouth thinned. "I worked damned hard to get here."

"I know. You moved on. And to get where you are, you've had to trust your instincts. Those instincts told you to hire me. What makes you think I would do anything to hurt you?"

"I—I just don't trust magic."

"I'm not that fond of it myself," I snapped. "Think about

it. Apparently I spent sixteen years bound against my will to a demon. A demon that wants me back. I'm scared to death. I want to run away. I want to punch something." Or someone. But Sara was dead. Safe beyond any retribution I might want her to suffer for doing this to me. "You think I'd do anything to anyone else to make them feel the same way I feel?"

Damon looked away. I might as well have been talking to a brick wall.

"Because if that's what you believe, then I was right in the first place. I should just go."

He took a deep breath and looked back at me. The last of the sun glowed around him, a golden aura spotlighting everything I stood to lose.

"I need time to think," he said.

I choked back a pained laugh. Shoe was on the other foot now. "What happened to having to turn to people? Having to let them in? Isn't that what you said to me?"

His gaze didn't falter.

Fair was fair. I had to give him what I'd asked for. No other choice if I wanted to give us a chance. But it hurt. Grief flared in my chest as I tried to convince myself that it would be okay if he just had time to think. That he'd change his mind.

Apparently my intuition didn't believe me.

"You're right. This has been fast, but trust me, there's nothing magical involved."

My voice cracked and I swallowed. Hard. I wasn't going to cry. Wouldn't make a scene.

I stepped closer, put my hand on his cheek. The beginnings of stubble scraped my palm as my skin warmed, and I had to blink as tears prickled my eyes. Even though he'd just told me to go, I couldn't pull my hand away.

"Feel that? Nothing magic at all. Just good old-fashioned chemistry. Whether that chemistry is something you want to fight for is up to you."

He leaned into the caress, just for a second. "You don't understand."

I wanted to stay. To wrap myself around him so tightly that he'd see what we could have. But he had to be able to see it. If he couldn't, walking away now was the only way to survive.

I lifted my hand. "I do. You trusted someone. They betrayed that trust. Believe me, I know more about that than almost anyone you're likely to meet. But I'd like to trust you. Trust you to see beyond the past. Trust you to trust me."

"Maggie." His voice was raw with the same pain tearing through me.

"Don't talk. We're done talking." I bent and pressed my lips to his, breathed in the taste of him for a long moment and tried not to think about what I'd do if he never wanted me back.

Because I knew I was ensnared as thoroughly as if he'd brewed a potion himself.

"I have to go. You know how to find me."

I turned and headed for the door before he could see the tears threatening to spill over. If he didn't trust me—*couldn't* trust me—then he didn't get to see me cry.

My resolve lasted until I'd climbed into a cab and given the driver my address. Then I buried my face in my hands and choked back sobs, waving away the cabbie's concerned questions.

We were halfway home when my datapad beeped into life. For a wild moment I thought it might be Damon asking me to come back, but it wasn't his number on the screen.

I swallowed hard, trying to get control over my voice. "Hello?"

"Maggie, it's Cassandra. I've spoken to a friend of mine,

someone better than me at scrying. She's agreed to look for Nat."

It was good news, and it should've made me happy, but instead I just felt numb. I didn't want to keep looking for Nat. I wanted her to be here now. I needed my best friend. Needed her to tell me it was all going to be okay and then feed me wine and chocolate and help me forget Damon Riley once and for all.

But she couldn't. My best friend was missing.

"That's great," I managed, digging my fingers into the cracking vinyl seat as I fought for control. No time for a meltdown. There was no one around to pick up the pieces. I had to stay strong.

"They want to do it tonight, and you need to be there. Can you meet me at the store?"

"Of course." I hung up, allowed myself one shuddering breath, and then leaned forward in my seat to give the driver my new destination.

Cassandra opened the door and jumped in as soon as the cab pulled up at the curb, giving the driver a Pacific Heights address as she buckled in.

As the taxi moved back onto the road, Cassandra turned to me and pursed her lips. "You've been crying. What's wrong?" She fished in her battered leather purse for a Kleenex.

I wiped my eyes. "Nothing important. It's just all getting to me."

She shook her head. "You're not a great liar, are you? Does this have something to do with your young man?" She leaned forward and hit the button to activate the privacy shield. The static hum buzzed in my ears as the view into the front of the cab blurred.

I sighed. "He's not my young man. He doesn't like witches."

"As in 'death to all witches'? I didn't get that vibe from him."

"No, as in 'someone used a potion on me to get me to marry them and witches can't be trusted.'"

Cassandra frowned. "A love potion? I guess that's not surprising. A guy as rich as that, he'd be a tempting target."

She was right. And I had to wonder if he hadn't told me everything. Damon had told me about one spell, but had there been others? "This was when he was younger."

She looked surprised. "Someone must've wanted him badly if the potion really worked. Such things don't come cheap."

I knew that well enough. Sara had gouged people even for her fake spells. "I don't think he'd take the cost as a compliment." Quite the opposite in fact.

"One day maybe we'll be able to stop people being hurt. Not much you can do about it now though. Give him some time. He'll come to his senses. And if he doesn't, then he isn't the right one for you."

Easy for her to say. She had her Mr. Claus. Or so I assumed.

"Worry about it later, dear," she advised with a pat on my knee. "Right now there's something else I have to tell you." She frowned toward the driver, as though testing the audio shield was working. The man's head didn't move an inch as far as I could tell, his gaze fixed on the traffic ahead.

"Something else?" My pulse was bumping up into what was rapidly becoming unpleasantly familiar territory.

"Where we're going, it's not just a friend. More like a group."

Ah, the mysterious "they." My attention sharpened. "What sort of a group?"

"People call us the Cestis."

That didn't ring any bells with me. "And?"

"You haven't heard of us?"

"Nope."

She sighed. "I thought Sara might've mentioned us."

"Why would she do that?" Cassandra should've figured out by now that my mother told me as little as possible when it came to witchcraft and magic.

"The Cestis polices magic in this country."

Definitely a reason for Sara never to mention them. To anyone. "So you're magical cops?"

"Not exactly."

Oh good, we were back to the vague and mysterious part of the magical world. Just what I needed. "What does Cestis mean, anyway?" It sounded Greek, or maybe Latin.

"It means a girdle, because our power encircles the country. In theory."

"And in practice?"

She grinned. "In practice I always say it's because we hold things together underneath and keep things looking smooth on top."

I laughed. I had to. "That sounds like magical cops to me. Just in the US?"

"Yes. Though there's a Cestis in each country."

"But no group oversees all of the others? No one magical Spanx to rule them all?"

Cassandra narrowed her eyes. "One country is quite enough trouble, thank you very much."

I wasn't sure I believed her, but before I could ask any more questions, Cassandra passed me more Kleenex.

"Fix your face. You look like a hung over panda."

By the time I'd succeeded in removing my smudged mascara with spit and Kleenex, we'd reached our destination: a very expensive condo complex, complete with security shield, doorman, robo-concierge, and palm scan–activated elevators.

"How many of you are there?" I asked nervously as our elevator slid smoothly skyward.

"Five," Cassandra said.

"Always?"

She shook her head. "The number is flexible. Always an odd number though."

"Why?"

"No tied votes that way."

My pulse bumped again. "What exactly are you voting on?"

"How to act in a particular case, that sort of thing."

Were they going to vote on me? What to do with me? Whether to help me? Not that I had any idea how they might help, or what else they might decide to do. Were they magical cops, or maybe more than that? As in maybe judge, jury, and, executioner in one?

I rubbed my hands on my jeans as the elevator slowed to a halt. A low male voice with a British accent informed us we had reached our destination and wished us a pleasant day as the doors slid open.

We stepped out into a hallway as lushly appointed as the rest of the building. "Nice," I said, more to break the silence than anything else.

"Don't get the wrong idea. Ian just happens to be able to afford a place like this. The Cestis itself couldn't." She tilted her head to the right. "This way."

I followed her down the hallway. *Ian.* I committed the name to memory. Which meant I knew two of the mysterious five. "Who are the others?"

"You'll find out soon enough." Cassandra paused in front of an ornate wooden door and put her palm against the scanner pad. The door swung soundlessly inward.

Inside, a young man in a slick navy suit took our coats and asked if we wanted drinks. Cassandra waved him away while I tried not to gape as I looked around. Damon's place was huge, yes, and full of sleekly expensive things, but this place had nothing sleek about it. It looked like someone had raided an ancient French palace, taken a side trip to knock off Aladdin's cave, and then topped off their plunder with enough art to fill a museum.

Every corner and surface sparkled with gilt and mirrors, making it hard to tell exactly how big the room was. The floorboards were overlaid with oriental rugs and spindly furniture upholstered in ornate fabrics. Huge flower arrangements overwhelmed delicate tables, and candles flickered in hanging lanterns and chandeliers, supplementing the light from stained glass-shaded lamps and discreet LEDs in the ceiling. The place smelled like a flower shop crossed with a spice den.

"Ian is a little ostentatious," Cassandra said with an indulgent smile as I raised my eyebrows.

"I heard that." A deep male voice with a hint of something other than good old USA in his accent came from our right, where a carved wooden screen inlaid with an intricate pattern of pearly flowers hid who knew what.

The man who stepped out from behind the screen was younger than I'd expected from the voice. Mid-forties, maybe. He wore dark trousers, a black shirt, and a blazing red and gold velvet . . . well, a robe was what I wanted to call it. It swept to his knees and flared around his wrists.

"Cassandra, always good to see you." He leaned in and kissed both her cheeks. Then he stepped back to study me. "And this is Ms. Lachlan?"

I got the same treatment as Cassandra before I could reply.

"Welcome to my home. I'm Ian Carmichael."

"Nice to meet you," I said, studying him. A faintly golden stain hung in the air around him. I could see Cassandra's green as well. Why had my sight just kicked back in? My mouth dried. "Your home is gorgeous. And please call me

Maggie." At this point, I figured being friendly with the Cestis was the safest approach.

Ian waved a hand deprecatingly. "I'm a bit of a magpie. Now come along, the others are waiting."

We followed him out of the room and down a corridor lined with paintings and sculpture of all shapes and sizes. I saw a Monet, a Pollock, a Mondrian, Chinese vases that no doubt belonged to some ancient dynasty, an Egyptian cat statue, and what I thought were a couple of Donovan Harley's moonscapes. Somehow the kaleidoscope of old world and modern worked.

The room Ian ushered us into was practically bigger than my apartment and dominated by a huge circular table. Two women and another man stood together near an honest-to-God working open fireplace—something I'd never actually seen in a home before. Flames crackled and danced, adding warmth to the light in the room.

The second man was older than Ian, silver-haired like Cassandra but olive-skinned and hawk-nosed. He didn't look like Santa to her Mrs. Claus, more like an ageing movie star. A Greek god gone slightly to the seed as he'd sauntered over the hill. The glow around him was a warm red.

The women next to him were a study in opposites. The older of the two had deep brown skin, brilliant blue eyes, and was taller than either of the men. Cropped dark hair skimmed the curve of her head, and she wore gold and multicolored crystals in strands and loops and hoops at her throat and ears and wrists and waist. The crystals sparkled, as did the deep earthy colors glowing around her.

The second woman—well, she hardly looked old enough to be called that. If I had to guess, I'd say her freckled face and big brown eyes had at least eight years fewer on them than mine. Twenty or twenty-one, tops. Her hair shimmered with a mix of electric red and pink caught back into twisted knots that stuck out at random angles all over her head. Her aura was the same bright pink. She wore a pair of red Vivianne boots Nat would've loved, and a black sleeveless tee that read WITCH HARD OR GO HOME.

I really wished I could take the latter option.

"Maggie, may I introduce our fellow members?" Ian said.

"Antony Donato, Radha Morgan"—the tall woman nodded at me—"and Elizabeth—"

The redhead grimaced. "Call me Lizzie."

"Elizabeth Reagan," Ian finished.

"Lizzie's the one who's going to scry for you," Cassandra added. "She's very good."

I could almost hear the "for someone so young" hanging in the air.

"I am," Lizzie said with a grin. She held out a hand. "Welcome to the madhouse."

"Thanks. Do you think you can find my friend?"

She bounced on her toes for a moment. "I'll try. Cassandra's good though. If she couldn't find her . . ."

"No guarantees. I understand."

"We have some other business first," Ian interrupted. "Why don't we all sit down?"

Business? What business? I turned to Cassandra, but she just nodded at me. Her expression brooked no argument.

The five moved toward the table, pulling out chairs in what I assumed was a familiar order. Ian at twelve o'clock with Cassandra and Radha flanking him. Lizzie and Antony took the outer edges. They made a formidable-looking semicircle.

I rubbed my hands down my legs.

Directly in front of Ian sat an odd-shaped white ceramic container, some kind of bowl with a domed lid.

I took the chair opposite Ian's, feeling like a child about to face the principal. Or five principals. Five glowing principals. The energy flowing around them seemed brighter—maybe because they were closer? The colors swirled and bled around each other, making me a little dizzy.

"Am I in some sort of trouble?" I said, trying not to stare at the fields too hard.

Ian shook his head. "Not at the moment." He looked at me for a beat, then shook his head again. "Lord, you look like your mother."

I straightened. "You knew Sara?"

"A little. When she was younger. Before she . . . ."

"Went rogue?"

He nodded. "To put it bluntly."

I got the feeling I knew where this was going. "I might look like her, but I'm not her." In fact, I didn't even think I looked like her, apart from the eyes. Sara had been shorter than me, and beautiful. I was just kind of pretty. I'd never made a man walk into a light pole or a mailbox—something I'd seen happen around Sara more than once.

"We appreciate that. But the fact remains that you were bound to a demon for many years."

For a moment their collective glow flared, and I winced. "So? Cassandra says the bond is broken now."

"We need to know that you're truly clear of its influence," Ian said.

That couldn't be good. My mouth dried. I looked at Cassandra. "You didn't say anything about this."

"I'm sorry, Maggie. This is a Cestis matter," she replied.

Ian held up a hand. "Cassandra has already told us she believes you're trustworthy. We're here to determine if her judgment is sound."

I stared at him. "How the hell am I meant to prove that I'm just me?"

"There's the easy way and the hard way," Ian said, putting his hands around the white bowl in front of him.

"What's the easy way?"

"This." Ian lifted the lid off the bowl, revealing a pool of silvery liquid that shone eerily, as though it was both reflecting and absorbing light.

I pressed back in my chair, fighting a distinct urge to run. "What's that?"

"Demon stone."

"It's liquid," I pointed out. Liquid and semi-alive, judging by the way the surface rippled even though the bowl was perfectly still. I wrapped my hands around the sides of the chair as I fought to stand my ground. Something about the demon stone had my instincts on high alert.

"Liquid at room temperature," Lizzie piped up. "Like mercury."

I gulped. "Mercury's poisonous."

She nodded. "So is this. If you're a demon or under the influence of one, that is."

"The easy way is being poisoned?" The words sounded high and thin.

"Chill. It's treatable, usually. If you're just possessed. Not if you're a demon."

Okay, so the weird and creepy silvery stuff was poison for demons. Got it. "So why doesn't everyone just carry around some demon stone?"

"It's very rare. And very expensive," Cassandra said. "It needs magical containment. It's not toxic to humans and won't harm them, but it has an unfortunate reaction with most inert substances."

"Define unfortunate." I was liking it less and less.

Lizzie grinned at me. "It eats them. Like hydrochloric acid on lots and lots of steroids. It'll eat through a foot of steel in seconds. It eats hypercrete too."

Not good news for buildings and cars and, you know, life in general, then. "Okay. Not safe for public use, I get it. So why doesn't it eat through flesh again?"

"Magic," Cassandra said.

"How exactly?" If I was going to do this, I wanted to know how it worked.

"I could give you the long, complicated explanation, but it wouldn't make much sense to you at this point. Just trust me."

I swallowed again, looking at the bowl. "How would this work?"

"You put your hand in the dish." Lizzie snapped her fingers with another grin. "Easy."

Unless I was a demon, of course. Or irreversibly tainted by the binding. I was pretty sure I wasn't a demon but I had no idea about the second part. Plus, I wasn't too keen on dipping my hand into something that could eat through steel, no matter what they said about it not harming flesh.

"And what exactly is the hard way?"

Chapter Sixteen

"You let each of us read you." Radha's voice was low and sweet.

The surface of the demon stone shivered almost hungrily. My stomach answered with another wave of queasiness. "That doesn't sound so hard."

Light caught Radha's earrings as she shook her head. "It can be unpleasant for some. And draining."

"How exactly do you 'read me'?" I asked, keeping my eyes on her rather than the demon stone.

"Each of us will make a connection with you—with your energy field, if you want to be technical about it—and through the field, we can sense what's in your mind—"

"You'll read my mind?" I interrupted.

"Not exactly. It's more a matter of feeling for any demon trace within you."

I shuddered, not liking the thought of demon trace or having someone else in my head. "Isn't letting someone connect with your field kind of like what the demons do?"

"We don't try and take you over," Ian said with a piercing look. "Or feed off your energy."

"Then why is it draining?"

"It takes energy just to maintain the connection. The fields effectively flow around both people while they're joined. A bigger field takes more energy to sustain, just like using energy for a working does."

Demon stone or sharing my head with five strangers. Hello rock, meet hard, hard place. I'd had a demon piggybacking on me for years; I wasn't keen to let anyone else attempt anything similar, magical cops or not.

So it mostly boiled down to whether or not I trusted Cassandra's assessment that I was truly free of the demon and therefore the demon stone couldn't hurt me.

Cassandra's eyes held a quiet sort of strength. I latched on to that. She'd helped me. Healed me. If I trusted any of them, it was her.

"Thanks, but I'll take my chances with that." I nodded at the bowl.

Cassandra's eyes crinkled at the corners, deepening her wrinkles as she smiled approvingly. The others all looked surprised. My stomach flipped and churned again. Did they really think I might still be under the demon's sway?

If they were right, I could be about to die. Then again, if they were right and they found the demon trace by reading my mind, I doubted they'd go easy on me either. This was quicker. A binary situation.

I eased my fingers free from the chair and straightened, smoothing my shirt as I looked at the demon stone. "What do I do?"

"Stay right where you are." Antony picked up the bowl with two hands and carried it around to me, each step slow and cautious. Ian watched with great concentration. I didn't blame him. If they were right about what demon stone could do, then the amount of damage it would wreak on the art and furniture in this apartment if it spilled was not pleasant to contemplate.

"Cassandra, go help," Lizzie suggested.

I waited for further instructions. Cassandra came over to us and took up position behind me, her hands resting lightly on my shoulders. Her touch eased my fear a tiny bit.

"Ready?" she asked.

I nodded, and she said something I didn't quite catch.

A field of white light sprang up around us.

"Just in case of spills," Cassandra said as I flinched in surprise. "Ian wouldn't want you ruining his rugs."

Or his whole condo. I didn't welcome the reminder of the potential destruction—including my own. My next breath shuddered.

Antony leaned down and held the bowl in front of me. "Just put the flat of your hand against the surface."

I took another shaky breath. Then another. When I felt I could lift my hand without it trembling, I did as he'd instructed.

The liquid . . . metal. . . whatever was ice under my palm. It quivered for a moment, then flowed over my skin, engulfing my hand.

"Don't move," Cassandra warned.

She didn't have to worry about that. The touch of the demon stone held me frozen, not even breathing, as ice-cold fluid encased my hand and wrist. Somehow it wasn't smooth or slick like water or oil, but rather slightly rough as it flowed over my skin. Rough and freezing. My hand shone silver, like it should belong to an alien or a robot. Not like anything that belonged to me.

Creepy.

The stuff moved like some sort of living thing, questing for prey like a snake sliding through grass. The back of my mind chittered with fear. If it was the snake, I was the small, furry, vulnerable thing. But I stayed motionless, not daring to move as a thin trickle separated from the rest of the stone and started to flow toward my elbow.

Numbness spread up my arm as the demon stone paused,

trembling in place. Almost if it was thinking. The urge to bolt or burst into hysterics screamed in my mind as the cold surrounding my arm intensified to the point of pain. My teeth dug into my bottom lip and the hot salt of blood hit my tongue.

The thread of demon stone darted higher then paused again. I held my breath, unable to look away, wondering if it was about to flow right over me, choking me with cold. Wondering if the last thing I'd see would be silver flooding my eyes.

I couldn't hear anything else in the room over the roar of my pounding heart, but I got the impression that no one else was making a sound.

Then, just as I decided I couldn't take another second, the demon stone reversed direction and flowed back into the bowl, leaving my hand bare but freezing, the skin pale and blue as though I'd plunged it into ice water.

I gasped in relief, and everyone seemed to start breathing again at the same time.

"I guess that solves that," Cassandra stated with satisfaction. "You can take your hand back, Maggie."

I pulled my hand away from the bowl as fast as I dared. My skin started to redden, the return of blood and warmth like acid flowing through my veins.

The white light vanished, and Antony carefully carried the bowl back to the table and replaced the lid. I stayed where I was, rubbing my skin, trying to ease the pain.

"Radha," Cassandra said. "Perhaps you can help Maggie out."

Radha nodded and came to join us, placing both her hands around mine. A glow of green flowed around my arm and the pain increased exponentially for a second, making me whimper. Then it was gone.

"There." She smiled. "That should be enough."

I flexed my fingers. No pain, just a hint of pins and needles. "You're a healer, right?"

"Yes. When I'm not doing this." She gestured at the other four.

I craned my neck around to Cassandra. "How much time do you spend on 'this'?" The papers weren't exactly filled with stories of witches gone wild. Probably just as well. The normals outnumbered those with any sort of magical ability about five to one. There'd been a few points in history when witches had been persecuted, but now normals and those with magic got along as well as anyone could expect.

The rising temps and water levels of the early twenty-first century, as well as the upheavals of the following decades and the accompanying food and water crises had made a lot of other concerns seem petty. Humanity had remembered how to play nicely, and that attitude had largely stuck.

Not that that couldn't change in a heartbeat if witches started doing bad things on a large enough scale to raise the normals' fears.

I wiggled my fingers, trying to shake the last of the tingling away. None of the Cestis had answered my question. Guess I didn't have the right security clearance or something.

Right. New subject. "What would've happened if I failed the test?" I asked out of morbid curiosity.

"That would depend on how bad the taint was," Cassandra said, patting my shoulder. "Don't worry about it."

Easier said than done. Like it or not, I had to know how this thing that was after me operated. "The taint would make it easier for the demon to control me?"

"Yes. It helps them make a connection."

"Like a computer virus? A vulnerability waiting to be exploited?" I said more to myself than Cassandra. If that was the case, then I just needed the right antivirus. Good in theory, not so good in practice when it seemed the right antivirus was magic.

Lizzie nodded at me from across the table. "Close enough. The demon tries to take over your programming via whatever means it can."

"Lowered barriers. Right, Cassandra mentioned that already."

Something was nagging at the back of my brain, but I couldn't quite grasp it. I worried at the feeling for a few seconds but nothing became clear, so I let it go. We had more pressing concerns. Like Nat. And where the hell she was.

I straightened and turned my attention to Ian. "All right, I passed your test. Now what?"

"Lizzie will try and scry for Nat shortly," Cassandra said. "But first we wanted to talk to you."

I fought the urge to yell, "Can we just get on with it?" Nat was somewhere out there, and I didn't want to chitchat. But the Cestis held all the cards, so I had to play the game their way. Arguing the rules would just slow things down even more. "Talk away."

"Cassandra tells us you only have a basic knowledge of magic. Yet you killed an imp," Ian said in a tone that was distinctly principal-reprimanding-naughty-student.

"Beginner's luck," I said, keeping my own voice calm.

Antony frowned at me with his magnificent eyebrows. "Relying on such luck is dangerous."

Okay, this was wasting my time. Worse, it might be wasting Nat's, and we didn't know how much time she might have.

"Look, Cassandra already gave me this speech. I'm not going to run around setting fires, I promise. I really don't want anything to do with any of this."

"This?" Radha said with a rattle of bracelets.

I wiggled my fingers in the air. "You know, magic."

Four sets of eyebrows shot skyward. Cassandra just looked resigned.

"Why not? You have the power," Ian asked.

"Power has never done anything for me so far. In fact, it's caused nothing but trouble. My mother was hardly a good role model, and then I was bound to a demon. That demon is now hunting me, if you're all telling me the truth. Any sane person would be running away screaming at this point."

The five of them exchanged somewhat appalled glances.

"Yet here you are," Ian said.

I lifted my chin, meeting his gaze. "Let's get one thing straight. I'm here to find Nat, to make sure she's safe. I'll do your lessons and learn what I need to be able to protect myself, but that's where my interest ends. I don't want this." I looked at each of them in turn, hoping they could see I was serious.

Their expressions were blank, but their fields swirled in agitation. I got the feeling I might as well have been speaking Swahili.

"But you have a gift," Ian said eventually.

"Didn't you hear what I just said? I don't like magic." Not least because, if my gut was right, magic was going to lose me Damon. "As far as gifts go, this is one I'd be quite happy to return."

"You may change your mind about that," Lizzie replied.

I hitched a shoulder. "Maybe, but don't count on it. So, can we look for Nat now?"

"Why don't you wait outside?" Ian said. "We need to discuss some things that are Cestis' business."

Sit outside the principal's office and wait to see whether or not I got detention? I didn't think so. I stayed right where I was. "Nat's my friend, and I saw what Cassandra did already when she tried scrying. What exactly are you worried about me seeing?"

Ian locked eyes with me. "It wasn't a suggestion, my dear."

I turned to Cassandra, but her expression didn't give me a different answer. *All for Nat*, I reminded myself. For Nat I would put up with this. I bit down on my temper, and the hackles Ian had raised, and walked out the door. As it swung shut behind me, I heard Lizzie say, "But she's strong—" in an outraged tone before the thick wood and possibly an audio shield—or even magic—cut all sound.

I cooled my heels in one of Ian's rooms, plied with coffee and sandwiches and tiny little cakes by the same guy who'd opened the door. The food was welcome but didn't help stave off my temper. The longer I waited, the more I felt the desperate need to bite something other than a sandwich.

Checking for messages on my datapad was an exercise in frustration; nobody had seen hide nor hair of Nat.

I left another message on Nat's system and logged off. All I could do was sit and stew, my mind circling an endless loop between Nat, her weird behavior at the club, demons, the Cestis, Damon, and the problem with the game. Which proved to be even more frustrating. I couldn't come up with a new angle or idea on any of them, so I gave up, deciding to do some of my homework and check out the reading Cassandra had sent.

One of them was a treatise on demon lore. I didn't really want to know, but after my experience with the imps and the demon stone, I wasn't keen on having any more nasty surprises. I kicked off my shoes, curled up on one of the silk-covered sofas, and began to read.

About twenty minutes later, I was regretting the sandwiches. And not just because I'd been reading about demons. Nope, what had macraméd my insides was the sudden grip I'd gotten on that elusive thought that had been nagging at me.

I needed to talk to Damon.

But as soon as I reached for my datapad, the door opened and sandwich guy appeared.

"They're ready for you."

My teeth set. I liked Cassandra, and Lizzie seemed cool, but collectively, the Cestis attitude got on my nerves. I wasn't the type to jump just because someone else told me to, and the

Cestis seemed to want me to not only jump but do it cheerfully.

Still, giving in to my emotions wasn't going to solve anything, so I gathered my stuff and followed him back to the other room, wondering whether I should run my theory past the Cestis.

The snotty look on Ian's face as I walked in made me decide that Damon deserved to know first. I would deal with the Cestis to find Nat for now. Apart from that, I didn't owe them anything.

Nat's ring lay in front of Lizzie on the crumpled silk scarf. "Did you find her?" I asked.

Lizzie shook her head. "I can feel something, but I can't tell you where she is. I do think she's alive though."

My knees wobbled and I grabbed for the nearest chair, clutching its back until I was sure I would stay upright. "Good. Okay, that's good." I grinned at Lizzie, unable to come up with anything more to say as relief flooded through me.

"She's alive but I think she's in trouble. There's a real sense of darkness around her." Lizzie fiddled with one of the knobs of her hair and a long coil of red sprang free.

The relief drained away like someone had pulled the plug. Darkness? Did that mean danger? Was she hurt? I had a thousand questions but somehow knew Lizzie had no answers. "So what do we do about that?"

"I'll keep trying to narrow in on her, but you're going to have to look for her the old-fashioned way as well." Lizzie wound the stray hair around one finger.

"We are—I mean, I am." I didn't know whether Damon was still looking for her or not. "I'll keep trying." I was going to do some serious hacking when I got home. Go through her mail accounts, her data streams, her financials. She'd be mad as hell when she found out, but I'd rather have her mad at me than missing.

Lizzie stabbed a pin through her re-coiled hair. "If you

find anything, just let us know. Even a more specific area you think she might be would help me."

"I'm seeing Cassandra tomorrow anyway."

Tomorrow. It sounded like forever when all I wanted to do was find Nat now, now, now. But at least I knew she was alive. Or that Lizzie thought so.

I took a deep breath and told myself to focus on the good news. "Thank you for your help."

Lizzie nodded. "Are you sure there's nothing else you can think of right now?"

"I can give you the same list of places she hangs out as I gave Damon." Crap, that reminded me about my theory. I tried to keep it off my face. Damon deserved a warning before I brought a bunch of mystic magistrates down on his head. "But he's already checked all those places. Nobody's seen her."

"Nothing else she wears more than this ring?" Lizzie pushed the ring around the silk with a fingertip, frowning.

"That's her favorite."

"All right. I would like that list. Send it to Cassandra, and she'll pass it on."

"I'll do it now." I pulled out my datapad and shot off a message.

"Chill. Thanks." She leaned back and stretched, looking tired.

"I'm the one who should be thanking you."

That earned me another headshake. "Thank me when we find her."

I hoped I would have something to be thankful for when we did.

It was nearly nine o'clock, and the day had been a thousand hours long, so I headed home. I couldn't believe I'd started the morning in Damon's bed and close to happy. Part of me wanted to go to Damon and talk to him about my theory straightaway, but I needed some sleep and an hour or so with Nat's system, not necessarily in that order.

The apartment was still silent and empty when I got home. For once I wished I'd rescued another cat after Gran's old boy had died a few years ago. On second thought, perhaps I'd be better off with a dog. A witch with a cat was too much like the fairy-tale version of magic. And witches in fairy tales never came to a good end.

Definitely a dog.

And I definitely needed some sleep if I was pondering pets when I should've been looking for Nat.

I headed for Nat's room and opened her system.

Somewhere along the line, I must've fallen asleep, because the next thing I knew was the door buzzer jolting me awake. I eased up, my neck and back protesting from my unplanned nap facedown on Nat's desk.

I squinted at the time in the corner of the desk screen: 1:30 a.m. Who the hell was ringing my doorbell in the middle of the night?

I staggered out of the chair, letting out a groan as my back and neck squalled in stiff protest, and hit the intercom on the room panel. "Hello?"

"Maggie, it's me. Let me up."

Damon.

I stared at the intercom. What was he doing here? My heart started to pound, though I couldn't tell if it was from a crazy hope that he'd come to make up or excitement at the possibility that he'd come to tell me he had news about Nat.

Either way, I had to know. I buzzed him up.

"Tell me about demons again," he said as soon as I opened the door.

So much for here to make up.

I let him in and he strode into the living room. He still wore the clothes he'd been in at his house, though he'd added shoes. His hair looked like he'd been sleeping standing on his head, only I didn't think he'd slept at all. Stubble darkened his jaw, and the shadows under his eyes were just as black.

"What are you doing here?" I asked, hoping he still might have news of Nat.

"Tell me about the damn demons," he repeated.

No news then. This was going to be fun. I squinted at him, still half-asleep. "Don't you have a whole company of people to research this sort of stuff for you?"

His eyes narrowed. "I thought I'd ask an expert."

I laughed, the sound bitter. "Okay, if you think I'm an expert on demons, then you really are barking up the wrong tree. I already told you, I don't know much about magic."

"Cassandra must've told you something."

"A little," I said warily.

"Then tell me." It was almost a snarl.

I was tempted to snarl right back but kept my temper in check. I had a feeling he'd come up with a similar theory to mine.

"Sit down," I said. "Stop looming over me. I'm not going to turn you into a frog."

"I thought you said you didn't know about magic."

I rolled my eyes and pointed at the sofa. "Joke. I have no idea if frogs are possible. But you're kind of tempting me to find out. Sit."

Finally he obeyed—if you can call balancing on the edge of the seat, leaning forward and practically vibrating with energy "sitting."

Definitely worried about something. Which worried me. My pulse still bounced like a bumper car. Was it possible to go into adrenaline overload? Someplace where you passed through the fear and worry and strain and just went sort of numb? If so, I wanted to know how. I'd had enough of today's roller coaster.

"Where do you want me to start?" I asked, deciding I might as well sit too.

"Demons can possess people, yes?"

I rubbed at my neck, trying to convince my muscles they weren't actually steel. "Yes."

He twisted the watch on his wrist. "How?"

"Is the person volunteering?"

"No."

"Then their psychic barriers have to be lowered. The demon has to sneak in and take over before they can reject it."

"Fuck." A muscle flickered in his jaw.

I wondered if his neck was as sore as mine. I longed for coffee and some painkillers. "My thoughts exactly."

"Is that what happened to you?"

"No, I told you. My mother volunteered me without my knowledge or consent. What's this about, Damon?"

"I was thinking about the games."

Crap. So much for my horrible theory being farfetched. The ache in my neck spread down my back. "Me too," I admitted.

His eyes widened. "You were?"

"You *are* still paying me."

He sat back, and the atmosphere eased the tiniest of fractions. "I thought you would've had enough on your plate without worrying about Righteous."

"Not when it could all be connected," I said bluntly. "I think it has something to do with the static filter. Is that why you're here?"

This time the stream of curses that came out of his mouth was too rapid and too low for me to make out more than about a quarter of them. Those I could distinguish weren't pretty.

Fuck.

"Damon? Am I right? You think it's the filter too? That whatever it does to make the brain accept the VR also lowers the psychic barriers?"

He scowled. "It's ridiculous. Demons using a game to find people to trap. How do they even know about the filter? Or games?"

"Cassandra did say it would be watching me."

"But the first testers had issues before you got near a game."

"Got near Archangel, yes, but I've spent a lot of time with gamers and heard lots of conversations about game tech. It might've figured out it was a possibility." I hugged a cushion as I thought about just how many endless gamer gab-fests I'd sat through.

"It could hear what you heard?"

I shook my head. "I don't know. I told you, I don't understand how all this works. It might just be that those few testers had a tendency toward depression or something that didn't show up in your vetting and the filter set it off somehow. Coincidence, not demons in their case."

He scrubbed his hands over his face. "It still sounds ridiculous."

"Ridiculous but logical when you think about it. And it fits with the timing. I use a game with your filter for the first time and something weird happens. Then I get the chip and all hell breaks loose." My temples throbbed. I gave in and went to the kitchen, returning with two mugs of coffee and a roll of pain tabs. I swallowed three and passed them to Damon.

He gulped the drugs and the coffee, and then leaned back in his chair, staring at the ceiling. "It's not logical. The version Nat and Ajax's team were using had been rolled back to an earlier filter."

"Then I guess the demon got smart. Once it knew the loophole was there, it could watch and find it again."

"But if you're the one it was watching, it makes no sense

that the other testers were affected." He looked back to me, blue eyes challenging me to convince him.

I stuck to my guns. Solving the improbable was what I did. I knew the buzz that settled in your stomach when you found the right solution, the certainty. I felt it now. "Like I said, it might be coincidence with your early testers. It doesn't disprove the theory. And if Nat is connected to this, then it might have targeted her deliberately because of me. Do you have your people watching the other testers?"

He nodded. "Everyone is okay for now."

Thank God for that. I reached for my pendant, trying to think. "No one's using the games at Righteous?"

"I called a lockdown."

And no one argued with him when he called the plays. Right. Still, he'd done the right thing, which meant I was going to have to as well. "There's something else."

"What?"

I braced myself for an imminent explosion. "I'm going to have to tell Cassandra."

He shot to his feet. "What? No."

I stared up at him. "Excuse me?"

"You can't tell anyone. You signed the NDA." He folded his arms. Obviously for him, that was enough.

I wished it were that simple. "Damon, this is more important than a confidentiality agreement. We're talking about a demon. The more people it gets a hold of, the stronger it gets. If it gets strong enough, it comes through to this world, and trust me, from the little I do know, that's something we don't want to happen."

"You can't tell anyone. Not yet."

"Why not?" Was he really going to put his business first?

He threw up his hands. "Do you have any idea how many game systems we have out there? How many games?"

"You want time for damage control?" My voice rose about an octave as I stood. "Are you fucking kidding me? You need to get out there now and do a recall. Once you do that, it won't matter who I tell anyway."

For a moment he looked like I'd slapped him. In a way I had. I understood him. Understood how wrapped up his identity was in Righteous. And I'd just told him he could lose it all. But unfortunately, just like with me and my magic, he was going to have to suck it up.

His eyes blazed at me. "Not all of them have the filter. I just need time to identify which ones—"

I couldn't believe he was going to argue the point. "No. Just recall them."

"It could ruin me."

"A demon could destroy the entire world. You have to issue a recall. If you don't, then I'll send the story to the nearest vidnews stream and it'll be all over the net in about ten seconds. And I *will* be telling Cassandra."

He sank back down onto the sofa. "Why does she need to know?"

"Because she's part of—" I paused, trying to figure out how to describe the Cestis to him. They hadn't told me not to talk about them but I didn't want to screw yet another thing up. "She's a member of a group that deals with magical . . . issues. The fact that this demon could be hooked into a whole lot of people via games is something they need to know about."

He put his head in his hands. "I've worked damned hard to build this company."

"And I'm guessing you have a far better chance of keeping it if you're honest with people. If you try and cover this up, it'll end badly."

His expression was haggard. "We don't even know if it's true."

"Cassandra could help us find out. Or her group, maybe. They'd be able to tell if someone using a game had lowered barriers."

"You're suggesting I let a bunch of witches into Righteous?"

I thought about it for a moment. "No. I'm not sure they'd want to all be seen there in one place."

"Christ, what is this group exactly?"

"I can't tell you." He scowled and I held up a hand. "For one thing, I don't know much about them. I'd never heard of them until Cassandra told me."

"Yeah, but you're not the magical expert, remember?"

I tried not to let that cheer me up, the fact that he'd admitted I might not be an evil witch after all. We still had a long way to go, particularly if I couldn't convince him to come clean about the games.

"We could take a console to them."

Damon's face cleared for a moment. "Do they have chips?"

"What do you think? Look what happened to me when I got a chip. They could use a headset though. And anyway, they don't need to play the game, just observe someone who's playing."

"So we need a volunteer to play a game and potentially be possessed while a bunch of super-witches watch?" He looked as if he couldn't believe the words were coming out of his mouth.

But he'd hit on a good solution, even if he didn't believe it. "Something like that. Though I'm not sure super-witches is the right term for them. But I *am* sure they can do something to protect whoever shows them the game. It's either that or they can test your testers for demon taint."

"Not exactly flying under the radar."

"Probably not. This is the quickest way. I can call Cassandra now."

He dug his thumbs into his temples. "Do it."

I went to make the call. When I got back, Damon was still

leaning back on the couch, staring grimly at the ceiling. He lifted his head and raised an eyebrow at me.

"They can see us right now," I said.

"Where do we need to go?"

"Pacific Heights. Not too far at this time of night." I wanted to touch him, offer some comfort and get some in return, but my hands stayed by my sides. "Look at it this way—you got what you were paying me for," I said, forcing a smile.

I didn't even get a flicker of a dimple in return.

"This isn't exactly the outcome I wanted," he said. Our eyes met, and for a moment I wondered whether he was talking about more than just the game and the demon. Whether he might be sorry about what had happened to us.

But it wasn't the time to ask. I turned away from the window, and the man, and got ready to tell the Cestis how we might just have a demon on our hands who had figured out how to get all the power it ever wanted.

Chapter Seventeen

A GRIM-FACED Ian let us into his apartment. His expression didn't bode well for our welcome, so I positioned myself between him and Damon before I made the introductions.

"Ian Carmichael, this is Damon Riley."

Damon held out his hand, but Ian made no move to take it. "Let's save the introductions until we're all together. It'll save time," he said, sounding tired.

The other members of the Cestis were waiting in the room with the round table, looking somewhat more bleary-eyed than they had when I'd left earlier. Ian made introductions and everyone took a seat, this time two facing five.

"What's so urgent that we all have to get up in the middle of the night?" Lizzie asked cheerfully. She wore a skintight thigh-skimming mini in slinky black silica-silk that suggested she'd been out rather than home tucked in bed.

"We have a theory," I said slowly when Damon remained silent. "About the demon and gamers."

"Go on," Lizzie said

I launched into an explanation, hoping I wasn't losing them in the technical details of the filter and what it did. When I finished talking, they were silent, their expressions ranging from carefully blank to worried to downright curious.

Lizzie was the curious one, and she broke the silence. "You mean the demon can contact people through the games? That's kind of—"

"Horrifying," Cassandra interjected.

I had to agree. Worse, their reaction didn't seem to indicate that the idea was completely impossible. "We don't know if we're right. That's why we came to you. We need to test the theory."

Ian drummed his fingers on the table. "How exactly?"

"Could you tell if my psychic barriers were lowered while I was playing a game?" I asked.

Antony was the one who answered after another round of looks passed between the five witches. "Probably. Damon might be easier, given he's a normal." He looked at Damon. "You are a normal, right?"

Damon nodded firmly, mouth set.

Antony continued. "Good. You'll be easier. Maggie, you might be able to keep yours up by instinct just because you're thinking about it."

I glanced at Damon. I hadn't expected him to be the one who had to take the risk. Given his views on magic, I had no idea if he'd agree. "Will you try?"

He looked reluctant, shifting in his seat. Despite the clear unease, somehow he managed to seem like he was taking up a lot of space. Full on master-of-the-universe battle mode. Well, it was his company at stake.

"Will you be able to shield me from anything else that might be watching?" Damon asked.

"Yes," Ian said. "No demon will reach you within these walls." He frowned. "When was the last time you played this game of yours?"

"Not for a while," Damon admitted. "The last few weeks have been busy."

"What difference would that make?" Radha asked.

Ian peered over the rimless glasses perched on his nose. "We don't know how long this has been going on. He could already be tainted."

"So we test him," Lizzie said. "But it's a good point. The demon might've made contact with others." She looked directly at me. "Like Nat."

Okay, so Lizzie, at least, had fully grasped the situation. Still, I clung to the small hope that the Cestis would prove the idea wrong. "Nat only played the game in question once."

"Is there only one game with this filter?" Antony asked.

Damon shook his head. "There are other games with similar tech. But we've refined it in this new game. The older ones are less sophisticated."

"And did Nat play other games?" Antony said.

I nodded. "She's a semi-pro gamer. She plays Righteous games all the time."

"Plus she played at a Dockside club," Damon added. "If she was taking drugs or something, then she could be even more susceptible to the filter. Those clubs don't exactly have a reputation for keeping their tech clean."

I gave him my best "thanks a lot" look. But I couldn't argue the point. I had no idea what games Nat might have played at Unquiet when she'd been there without me. "If the demon had lots of people under its power, wouldn't you have noticed something by now? That would give it power, wouldn't it? So there should have been incidents? People doing whatever it is people possessed by demons do?"

Cassandra nodded. "She has a point. There haven't been reports of anything that would indicate demon activity other than the imps. And those attacks were focused on Maggie."

There was a rumble of thunder from outside the window and we all jumped. Mother Nature weighing in with sound effects. Just what we needed.

"What would indicate demon activity?" I asked.

"Usually the first signs are increased violence. Assault. Domestic violence. Crime spikes. That kind of thing," Radha said. "But I've heard nothing from any of the Bay Area healers that there's anything unusual happening."

Another clatter of thunder underscored her words. Lizzie flinched again, then giggled. "Maybe we can limit the timeframe a little. After all, the demon was bound to Maggie, so let's assume it only learned about the filter through her. When was the first time you played the game, Maggie?"

"The day I went to interview at Righteous. But there were game testers who were having some issues before then. That's why Damon hired me."

"What sort of issues?" Cassandra asked with a frown.

"We had some people testing the game who got depressed or anxious. There were a few incidents," Damon said. "But that was before I hired Maggie."

Cassandra's face relaxed. "So that could be unrelated, or it could be a different side effect of the game."

"This game has the latest version of the filter though. So maybe it reached some sort of critical point in how it affects people. I thought maybe that's why the testers started having problems, like maybe they were prone to depression or something beforehand and it made it worse," I offered.

Radha nodded. "That could be true. If this filter weakens their barriers—"

"Let's focus on Maggie for now. When was the first time you noticed Nat acting strangely?" Lizzie asked.

"After I had my chip removed," I said. "The next day or so. She said she'd been out gaming, and I thought maybe she was just tired, but she was acting oddly."

Lizzie bounced on her toes, the movement at odds with her serious expression. "My guess is the demon latched on to another familiar energy field as soon as it could after its bond to Maggie broke. If Nat had been using one of these other games, maybe her resistance was lowered. And if it got her then, who knows what it's done since. It could be getting stronger by the minute."

Damon held up a hand. "Wait. We don't even know if this theory is right yet."

"If a demon gets enough power, it can manifest in our world," Cassandra said. "The last time that happened—" She broke off and looked at Ian. He flipped his hand at her as if to say, "Go on." "The last time that happened here was a decade ago."

Her words landed like a gut punch. I couldn't breathe, like all the oxygen had been sucked from the room. "A demon caused the Big One?" Several hundred thousand people dead. My grandparents among them, even if Gran hadn't been an immediate fatality. Millions and millions of dollars in damages. Countless lives ruined. My home destroyed.

"A demon did all that?" My voice sounded distant—too high and too tight.

Cassandra nodded. "Yes. That's why the Cestis is currently based here. We're still cleaning up some of the mess. When it broke through, all sorts of things came with it."

I didn't even want to imagine. My fingernails dug into my palms, and I had to force myself to unclench my hands. I hadn't even noticed that I'd curled them into fists.

"We can't let it happen again," Antony said into the silence that had descended on the room. "Last time we got lucky."

"How did you kill it?" I asked.

"Not kill. Send back. The short answer is we didn't." Ian's voice was bleak.

I stared at him. A demon had come through to our world, and the Cestis hadn't been the ones who'd sent it back wherever the hell it had come from? Then what had?

"Excuse me?"

"It managed to fry itself when it got too close to an exploding substation," Antony said shortly. "Thank the powers."

I gaped at him. "It blew itself up? How——"

"This is all well and good, but we still don't know if we're right. We should focus on testing this theory," Damon interrupted. All six of us looked at him, but he didn't back down. "I want this tested. If you're going to ask me to recall half my products, I need proof."

"Right," Ian said. "That's reasonable." He rubbed his hands together. "Let's get on with it. I assume you have one of these game systems with you?"

Damon nodded toward the metal case he'd brought with him. "It'll take a couple of minutes to set up."

Everyone stood, most of the Cestis moving to circle Damon, watching what he was doing intently. I guessed none of them had ever gamed.

Lizzie came over to me instead. "I looked for Nat again," she said with a frown. "Still nothing but the darkness. More darkness. She's in trouble, Maggie. I'll try again after this. Maybe I can look for demon trace."

"What happens if it's possessed her?" I kept my voice quiet to keep myself from shrieking. *Nat.* If the demon had her, it was all my fault.

"That depends on how far gone she is. If it's only been a few days like you say, then she could be fine."

"And what happens if it's longer than that? Or if the demon has gotten to others via the games? Could it really build enough power to break through?"

Lizzie shivered. "Let's hope not."

"We're ready," Cassandra said from our left. "Lizzie, come help me shield. Maggie, you stand by Damon. You know how to get him out of that thing if we need to." She looked at the game system as though it might bite.

I did what she asked, and Damon settled himself back in one of the chairs. Across his lap lay a portable chip interface attached to a lead. He'd rolled up his sleeve to bare his chip.

As he reached for the lead, I grabbed his arm. "Wait."

"What's wrong?" he asked.

"It's just . . . ." I paused, feeling stupid. I was worried. Worried about this man who now had even more reason to never want to see me again after all this was over. "Are you sure you can shield him?" I asked Cassandra.

"Yes. He's safe."

I took a deep breath. "Okay." I let go of Damon's arm but leaned forward so my face was close to his. His eyes were shadowed and wary, and I wondered if he saw the same strain on my face. I wanted to kiss him, but I knew it would only confuse things more. "You so much as move a finger and I'm yanking you out," I said softly.

His mouth twitched slightly. "Just don't rip my arm off," he said, then snapped the lead in place and closed his eyes.

"Shield him," I snapped at Cassandra. She nodded. I couldn't see anything, but my skin buzzed as power flowed over it.

When the telltales on the console went green, I nodded at Ian. "Okay, he's in, and the game is active. Someone read him so we can get this damned thing over with."

"I'll do it," Radha said. She reached a hand toward Damon, resting it on his head.

I held my breath and waited.

After just a few seconds, Radha lifted her hand. "That was easy. I could slide right in."

"Good." I hit the button to shut the deck down.

"What happened?" Damon said, opening his eyes.

Cassandra patted his shoulder. "I'm sorry to say that your theory is correct."

"Not necessarily," Lizzie interrupted. "We don't know what his shields are like without the game. He might be someone who's naturally open."

Damon looked alarmed at the thought. "What does that mean?"

"Merely that you might be more receptive to magic than some people."

"How do we find out?" I asked, trying not to snap the words out.

"The easiest way is to get Radha to try and read you again. See if she can get in as easily a second time when you're not hooked into the game."

"Fine. Do that." He settled back in the chair and closed his eyes. His face looked relaxed, but his hands were clenched in his lap.

Radha raised her eyebrows but put her hand back on his head. Again it only took a few seconds before she sighed. "I could do it, but it was harder. I'd say the game definitely lowers the barriers. So the demon may have possessed others. It could be stronger than we think. Or here already."

"Fuck," Damon cursed at the same time as Ian said, "We'd know if it had come through."

"Maybe," Cassandra said. "With enough strength it could hide itself. And it could be anywhere."

"It has to be here in San Francisco if it wants Maggie," Lizzie protested. "I could scry—"

"And have the demon notice you? No." Antony shook his head. "Not a chance."

Damon was silent.

"You have to issue a recall on the games," I said to him. "Any that have recent versions of the filter."

His eyes were flat, face grim. "I know."

"I'm sorry." I couldn't even imagine what a recall might do to Righteous. Whatever happened, I was to blame.

"Sure you are." He rose. "If you'll excuse me, I have some calls to make." He headed for the door and I followed him.

"You're just going to leave?"

"No, I'm calling my lawyers and my PR team."

I caught his arm.

"What?" He jerked free. "I'm doing what you wanted, Maggie. But I worked hard to build Righteous. It's my life. Don't expect me to be happy when you make me burn it to the ground."

My throat was on fire, and guilt and pain warred in my gut. "Is it going to be that bad?"

"Who knows? Can't imagine that people will be that keen to play games that screw with your brain."

"Can't you fix the filter?"

"In time. Maybe. If I can afford to after this. Go back to your witch friends, Maggie."

"Don't go like this."

"I—" He cut off when a datapad started to ring. Mine, I realized, then scrabbled through my purse trying to find it.

Nat's voice on the other end of the phone sent a chill down my spine.

"Maggie?" The words sounded hoarse, as if she'd been crying. Or screaming.

"Nat, where are you?" I flicked the call over to speakerphone. Damon turned on his heel and moved fast toward the room where the Cestis were still gathered.

"Maggie, you have to come get me." Her voice hiccupped with a suppressed sob.

I tried to sound calm even though I wanted to throw up. "Tell me where you are. I'll be right there." Out of the corner of my eye, I saw Damon barrel back out through the door, five witches hard on his heels.

Cassandra reached me first.

"Tell me where you are, Nat," I repeated.

Beside me, Cassandra sucked in a breath, shaking her head at me. I ignored the warning.

"Nat? Tell me where you are."

"Vista Point. You know where."

Marin County. The other side of the Golden Gate Bridge. Too far away. "Are you okay?"

"Yes." Her voice still shook. "But you have to come quickly."

"Nat, what's going on? Tell me and I can help you."

"I'm sorry," she said.

"Sorry for what, sweetie? I just want to know where you are. We've been worried." I heard a quiver in my voice and paused, sucking in a breath, afraid that any show of nerves or stress on my part might send her running again.

"I didn't mean to. It was too strong."

"What was?" My hand gripped the datapad hard enough to hurt. Across from me, Damon was deadly still, his attention solely focused on the call. "Nat, are you sure you're okay?"

"I'm sorry," she repeated. "Just come."

The line went dead.

"Try the call trace," Damon said immediately.

My hands shook as I tried to hit the right combination on the keypad. "It's a public base. Right location though. Marin County."

"Okay, let's go get her."

"No," Cassandra snapped.

Beside her, Ian and Lizzie nodded. "It has to be a trap," Lizzie said.

"How do you know?"

"If she was free to come to you, she would. She said, 'It was too strong.' What else can 'it' be but the demon? That would explain the darkness I felt, if it's controlling her."

"Does it matter? I'm not leaving her there for some demon to amuse itself with. It's not her it wants anyway."

"Which is exactly why you shouldn't go anywhere near her. It's bad enough if it's been feeding from the games and has enough strength to make Nat do what it wants. It may have come through already if Radha is right. We can't let a corporeal demon rebind a witch. It would be near invincible with access to your power."

"I don't care. She's my best friend. My family."

"You're risking everyone's families if you go," Cassandra said.

"I don't care," I repeated. "You have no authority over me. I'm not part of your stupid Cestis and I didn't agree to live by your rules."

"That doesn't matter. If you break our laws, we will be the ones who judge you."

"Fine. Judge me. Do whatever you need to. After Nat's safe." Anger was building inside me, my skin shimmering with power.

Lizzie touched my arm. "Maggie, it doesn't have to be like this. We can go get Nat."

"You're all witches too. How is that any better?"

"The demon wouldn't be able to bind us as easily as you. We have defenses. And we've fought a demon before."

"But you didn't stop it. How would you stop it now?"

Lizzie's eyes dropped and she bit her lip.

And then I knew.

"If you have to kill Nat to stop the demon, you will. Won't you?" I stared into those so young-looking eyes and knew I was right. The Cestis would act for the greater good even if it meant sacrificing Nat. Well, maybe I was my mother's daughter after all, because for me, it was all about the personal, not some abstract "greater good." "This is my mess to fix."

Cassandra exchanged a look with Lizzie. "You need to calm down, Maggie."

"No, I really don't."

As though he agreed, Damon stepped up beside me.

Which only meant that Cassandra included him in the frown that transformed her face from Mrs. Claus to do-not-mess-with-me. "If you go like this, you're not going to be able to help her anyway. The demon will feel you coming and be waiting."

"Then I'll fry it."

"And what if it's come through? What if it's holding on to Nat at the time? What will you do then?

"You should listen to them," Damon said.

Apparently he was standing by my side but taking theirs. I glared at him, but he didn't flinch.

"They know what they're doing," he said.

"I think we've already proved that so-called experts have caused more problems than anybody in this situation," I snapped, then cursed myself silently as his face went icy cold. Me and my big mouth. Yes, Damon's team had come up with the filter, but it was my mother who'd first called whatever demon we were dealing with and given it a link to our world.

"I'm sorry," I said, but he had already stepped away, heading down the corridor and pulling out his datapad to make the calls that could destroy his life.

My heart cracked, but I couldn't worry about fixing me and Damon—or even trying to figure out if we *could* be fixed —while Nat was out there, waiting for me.

"She's clearly just going to do something idiotic if we make her stay here," Ian said, his words dropping into the tension-charged silence like the crack of a whip.

"I'm still here," I muttered.

"She is strong. We can use that," Ian continued.

"But the risk," Cassandra protested.

"The risk exists regardless," Ian said.

"What does that mean?" I demanded.

Ian hitched one elegant shoulder. "The demon could potentially overwhelm any of us if it's too strong. You're merely the easiest target because of your former bond."

"Doesn't that mean it's even riskier if you all come with me? You're the strongest witches in the country." I swallowed thickly. A demon with that sort of power . . . who knew what it could do to the planet? Maybe it could lead others through, turn the whole place into one big demon snack bar until all the humans were gone.

"This is why we need time to think," Cassandra snapped.

"Nat may not have time," I snapped back.

"Maybe. But you're no good to her if you just charge in and get taken too," Ian said. "We *need* to plan."

"You plan. I'm leaving." I started to move but Cassandra blocked me.

"No," she said. "Not yet. There are things you need to know."

"You're not seriously going to let her go alone?" Radha asked.

"She's right. If the demon has come through, we can't all be risked at once." Cassandra didn't look happy about what she was saying.

Lizzie grimaced. "But Radha is right. We can't send her alone. There's no way she'll survive it."

It must have been a measure of just how out of my mind with fear for Nat I was that this pronouncement didn't make me any less determined to go.

Cassandra nodded. "So we send one of us with her. Just one. The rest of us can prepare to be backup if we're needed."

"You only need backup if you think this plan will fail," I said. "If you think it's going to fail, I'm the most expendable."

"Merely a contingency plan," Ian said smoothly. "I'm sure you understand the need for those."

This whole conversation was taking too much time for my liking. Less chat, more action. "Okay, so I go. And one of you comes with me. That's settled. Can we move on to the part where you teach me how to kill a demon?"

"You only need to know how to kill it if it's managed to come through. Otherwise you just need to know how to free Nat. Demon stone will take care of that." Lizzie sounded as though she thought what she was saying was perfectly reasonable.

"Doesn't demon stone have to be magically contained? I don't know how to do that. Or how to un-contain it."

"Whoever comes with you can take care of that. You just have to get close enough to her to break the bonds. It won't be easy if the demon is controlling her."

"How do I do that?"

"We'll figure something out. There are spells to break bindings."

"And if the demon has come through? What then?"

"Then you—we—need to kill it. Or destroy its physical form, anyway. The shock of that will break the bonds it has with any humans."

"How?"

"Breaking the bonds requires changing the energy field temporarily. Like with you and the chip."

"You think I should tranq it and perform chip surgery?"

Lizzie grinned. "Only if you know what tranquilizers will work on a demon. It might work with the victims, but given we don't know who or where they all are, that's a little tricky. You need to change the demon's field."

"I'm sure that's not as simple as it sounds."

"Fire might do it. Or electricity," Antony said thoughtfully.

"Great, now I have to get it to stick its finger in a socket."

"We can check out the power sources around the park. There might be something you can use. Fire will definitely take care of its physical form though," Lizzie said. "Destroy that and it's back to its own plane. If Damon recalls the games, it can't gain power that way, so if we break its bond with Nat, it shouldn't be able to come back through."

"Lightning would work," Antony said.

"You want to teach a newbie to throw lightning?" Cassandra said. "Even if she has the ability, it would take weeks."

"She already called fire without knowing what she was doing. It's not that different," Ian countered.

"Even you can't do it reliably," Cassandra snapped, "and

the rest of us wouldn't risk even trying. We need another idea."

"Most other ways would involve her getting close to it. If it touches her, it can overwhelm her," Ian said.

"Sounds like I'd need a freaking missile launcher," I muttered. "Other options?"

Radha held out her hands. "Sheer force of will? You could change its field with magic and then kill it."

"How would that work?"

Radha looked at Cassandra. "Can she see the fields?"

Cassandra nodded. "She did during the lesson I gave her. But that's her only training."

"It will have to do," Radha said. She turned to me. "You need to alter the demon's field. Disrupt it. That would sever the connection to whatever it's using as a power source. The easiest thing might be to try and make the color you see it as change. It would take a lot of power though." She eyed me dubiously.

To save Nat, I was willing to try anything. "Just tell me what to do."

"With two witches, it should be possible," Antony said. "One to try and change the field and the other to try frying it. I'm willing to try. Who knows? It might just work."

Or we might just both die trying. I swallowed hard. I had moved into some crazy place beyond fear in my head, but my body still knew I was terrified. My hands wanted to tremble, and I wasn't sure I could take a step. But I had to ignore that. I had to hang on for Nat's sake. I could fall to pieces later, but now I had to focus.

"There are the daggers too, of course," Ian added.

What the hell? What daggers? "I thought you said I shouldn't let it touch me? Wouldn't using a dagger require getting close? And what kind of dagger can hurt a demon?"

"Ceramic daggers with demon stone cores. We use them on people who are possessed, mostly. A last resort to try and break a bond that doesn't give way to normal methods. It should work on a demon too, if you can find a vulnerable spot," Ian said.

"I don't even know what a demon looks like. How the hell am I supposed to know where it has a vulnerable spot?"

"They never look the same, but you'll know it's a demon. They're unmistakable. As for where to hit it, you won't know until you see what form it takes. But aim for soft and squishy: eyes, mouth, belly."

The longer we talked about it, the more ridiculous it sounded. But surely they wouldn't send me out there if they thought I had no chance.

"Okay," I said. "Enough with the worst-case scenario. Now tell me what to do if it hasn't come through."

They didn't let us leave for another hour or so. And with every endless second of every endless minute that ticked over, all I could think was that Nat was waiting. She was maybe hurting and broken. I did my best to focus on what the Cestis were teaching me, because it might just save Nat—and me—but part of my brain screamed at me to just go get her.

Eventually I put my foot down. "That's it. That's enough. We can't wait any longer. Antony, we're leaving. Grab the stuff."

The Cestis had produced a small mountain of weapons to use against the demon. Antony and I both had several of the demon stone daggers, which came in sheaths that were weirdly bulky, clearly designed to stop the daggers breaking and loosing the demon stone on something other than the demon if at all possible. They had some sort of spell on them too; they vibrated subtly under my tentative touch. None of these things made me want to strap the damned things around my body, but I had no choice.

Antony had added a huge gun to his arsenal. I refused to carry one. I'd only ever shot a gun on a range or in games. I didn't trust myself to not do more harm than good with one in real life. I'd accepted another, more mundane knife of the utility variety that Lizzie suggested might come in handy if Nat were tied up or something. Along with the weapons, we were both draped with enough amulets and protection to ward off just about anything. Or so I hoped.

Damon had spent most of the hour on the phone with his lawyers and avoiding me, but when I spoke, he rose. "I'm coming too."

"Don't be stupid," Ian said. "You can't help."

Damon's master-of-the-universe look descended over his face. "This is partly my fault. I'll stay out of the way, but I'm going. They need transportation, and they'll need someone to call the rest of you if something goes wrong."

It was clear that unless the Cestis were willing to actually physically restrain Damon, they weren't going to stop him.

"If something goes wrong, you might not be able to call," Ian said.

Damon shrugged. "I'll take the risk. I'm going."

Chapter Eighteen

I DIDN'T TALK as we drove through the quiet dark of the city. All the sensible people were safely in bed, not heading out into the night to fight a creature that part of me still didn't want to believe could even exist.

The mood inside the car was dark and silent too. Antony tried going over the plan until I told him to shut up before I had a panic attack. Damon just drove, his expression set. I watched him, watched the colors of the traffic lights and adscreens and buildings play across his face, but there was no change in the determined set of his jaw and mouth.

It took less time than I'd expected to reach the new bridge. Less time still to speed across the darkened bay to the headland, where the sky was ever so faintly starting to lighten.

The parking lot at the Marin County end was empty.

"Now what?" Antony said as Damon switched off the car.

I gripped one of the amulets Cassandra had festooned me with, hoping it would give me the strength to not crumble with fear and actually do what I'd come here to do.

My mouth was dry and I swallowed, licking my lips before I answered. "Now you and I walk. Damon stays here." I locked eyes with Damon, hoping he wasn't going to try some last-minute act of heroic stupidity like insisting on coming with us. Having Nat in danger was terrifying enough. The thin thread of control I was clinging to might just snap if I had to worry about him as well.

"If we're not back with Nat in forty minutes, then call Cassandra," I said to him. He nodded but didn't speak.

I looked across the parking lot to where the path into the park began. It was still almost totally dark. Almost anything could be lurking in the shadows around the first curve.

Nat had said I'd know where. I hoped I did. We hiked here regularly. And usually stopped to eat our protein bars in a pretty clearing a bit beyond one of the trailheads. It had to be there. *If I was wrong*—no, I wasn't going to think about that. It had to be the clearing. It would only take us about ten minutes to get there. And every minute I hesitated was another minute she was in danger.

I turned back to Damon for a long moment, trying to think of the right thing to say. I settled for just reaching out to touch his face. "I am sorry," I said softly. "Forty minutes, okay?"

His eyes closed and then opened, looking bluer than ever, though that couldn't be possible in the dim light. My heart lurched as I wondered if I'd ever see them again.

Finally he nodded. "Forty minutes. No longer."

"C'mon," I said to Antony, and we set out into the darkness.

The trail was rough and slippery underfoot after the night's rain. In the dark, it was like trying to tightrope walk in army boots.

"Can't you make light or something?" I hissed at Antony after I slipped for the forty-seventh time and he'd hauled me upright.

"I could, but the demon can sense magic. No point warning him we're coming."

"It knows I'm coming."

"It doesn't know that you're with me. Or that you know how to use your magic."

"I don't," I pointed out. "Besides it knows I fried its imp."

"We don't know for sure how much a demon sees or senses through the imps. Besides, if it could see, it should know you had no idea what you were doing."

That was hardly comforting. "I still don't."

"You will when the time comes. Lizzie's very good."

Lizzie had worked some weird voodoo on me during our preparation time to plant the knowledge on how to do various spells in my mind. When I'd asked why I had to bother learning from Cassandra if she could do that, she'd just laughed. Each spell was a one-off, apparently, and there were only a few that would work with whatever Lizzie was doing. I didn't feel any different, so I had no idea if she'd been successful. My head ached, but I put that down to tension rather than a barrelful of magic being shoved into my brain.

"I should go ahead, keep you in reserve," I said as we approached the trailhead. Antony nodded and moved behind me.

I regretted my suggestion as soon as he did. Now there was nothing between me and whatever waited for me. But that was the point. Antony was strong. A powerful, experienced witch. He had some chance of surviving and actually defeating the demon. Despite all the Cestis had done to prepare me, I'd accepted that I was basically cannon fodder. I probably wouldn't be getting out of this unharmed, or even alive.

Or at least I'd accepted that in my brain. My body wasn't so resigned.

My hand shook as I pointed ahead where a narrow secondary trail that I'd taken a few times branched away. "The main trail curves around here, and then there's a clearing. If you cut across using that trail, you'll be in some trees, out of sight but able to see."

I kept walking as his footsteps crunched off the path. I

wanted to run but wasn't sure whether it should be back to the car and safety or forward to Nat. So I just made myself keep moving, one careful but shaky step at a time, trying to be as quiet as I could until I reached the edge of the trees. I stopped there, hoping I was still hidden by the fading darkness.

Nat stood in the middle of the clearing, still dressed in the clothes she'd worn to Unquiet. Her bare arms were blotched with what I hoped was dirt rather than bruises, and her head was bowed. As I stared at her my heart began to thump so hard it hurt.

Nat. So close.

But still so far out of my grasp, because beside her stood a dark-skinned man. No, not a man. The demon. The shape of it subtly wrong, the colors of its skin swirling slowly as I watched. My skin prickled with terror.

Well, that settled one question. It was here. In physical form. Now we had to deal with it.

The demon's hand rested on the back of Nat's neck, but his eyes met mine across the distance.

"There you are," he said. "You're slow." His voice hissed and bubbled, resonating in ways that made my teeth ache.

"I wasn't aware I had a deadline," I said. I even managed to keep my voice from shaking.

"Natalia has been waiting for you. You shouldn't keep your friends waiting. Right, Natalia?" He shook her and she raised her head. In the now-gray dawn light, she looked pale, too pale. Her eyes were shadowed but they shone. It took me a moment to realize it was because she was crying soundlessly.

"I asked you a question," the demon hissed with another shake that snapped Nat's head back.

"Right," she said. Her voice scraped hoarsely but it held no emotion.

My right hand closed over the dagger handle at my waist. "Let her go." The words hurt my too-dry throat, but at least they were steady.

"I told her you would come. Come back to me," the demon said. I saw a gleam of teeth that on a person might've been called a smile. On the demon it was something distinctly not.

I fought rising terror, tightening my grip on the knife. "I didn't come back to you. I came for her. Let her go."

"If I don't?"

"I'll make you." I had no idea how, but I would try. For Nat. For me.

"How? You're weak. So weak you didn't even know I was there all those years. Why should I give her up? She's mine now. Just like you."

"I was never yours," I spat, taking a step closer. "Never." Part of me wanted to just run at him, to strike him down. But that would be suicide.

The demon gave me another of those sickening notsmiles, and the breeze across the clearing brought a sudden waft of rot. "Your mother didn't want you. She gave you to me. That makes you mine."

"Leave my mother out of this." I fought my anger, needing to think. Its energy field. I had to try to see its damned energy field.

I fought to clear my mind of rage and fear and denial, and suddenly a flicker of reddish black surrounded the demon, swirling like blood. The color flowed around Nat too, and my heart stuttered at the sight. Its field surrounded her. Engulfed her. I saw no hint of any color that could be her. That could only be bad.

"Such a pity Sara died," it said, then pushed Nat to her knees as easily as a man folding a piece of paper. She didn't resist, just knelt, shivering and blank. "She was amusing. But I couldn't risk her changing her mind."

It took a moment for me to realize what it meant. "You did it. You caused that accident." It had killed my mother. Taken what it had wanted from her and then destroyed her without another thought.

"Witches are so arrogant. They never think they'll lose. Like your friend in the trees."

Shit.

A gunshot cracked through the night, but the demon didn't react. Antony had missed.

Another shot, and this time the demon ducked as wild yowls came from the trees. I didn't even think, just bolted forward and grabbed Nat, hauling her up to her feet. A bullet whizzed just over my head as I heard the demon grunt. I ran, dragging Nat with me. She didn't resist, but she didn't move quickly either. I pulled her along, my shoulder straining as I headed for the trees.

The yowls in the woods grew louder, and an all-too-human scream joined them. My stomach roiled but I kept moving.

"Natalia, stop." The demon's voice rose from behind us and Nat froze. My arm wrenched with a fiery throb as I skidded to a halt too.

"Nat." I tugged at her, ignoring the pain as another scream came from the trees. A male voice filled with agony.

"Antony," I whispered. *Fuck.* Somehow I didn't think he'd be riding in to rescue us.

I yanked at Nat again. "Come on." She wouldn't budge, which made no sense. She was smaller than me, lighter than me. I should've been able to move her.

"I can't," she whispered. I turned back to the demon. Its left hand was clamped over its right shoulder, but otherwise it looked unhurt. Whatever the bullets in Antony's gun had been supposed to do, it hadn't worked.

"Natalia prefers to remain with me," the demon said as its energy field flared blood red. "In fact, she wants to help you understand why you should too."

"What do you—"

I didn't get to finish the sentence because Nat exploded into life beside me, her fist connecting with the side of my head. I fell backward, stars pinwheeling behind my eyes.

Nat crashed down on me, hands clawing for my face.

I grabbed for her wrists desperately as the demon's laughter rang in my ears.

"Nat. It's me. Stop."

She ignored me, struggling wildly. I managed to hold her off—just—but I wasn't sure how long I'd be able keep it up. I had the weight and height advantage, but I wasn't being fueled by a demon's will.

I twisted and writhed, trying to get on top of Nat as she fought me. Her knee hit my thigh with more force than I would've thought she could muster, and the pain arcing down my leg loosened my grasp on her hands.

Her right hand hit my face like a cannonball, fingernails raking my flesh. I screamed as I reached for her again. I had to stop her, had to break the connection with the demon. But first I needed her to stop trying to kill me.

I managed to catch her hand as she took another swing and then desperately twisted upright as she fought for freedom.

One of the daggers dug into my thigh, reminding me of its presence. It could break the connection, but I couldn't risk reaching for it while she was fighting me. So I did the only thing I could. Took a deep breath, then slammed my forehead into hers just as she'd taught me to do years ago when we first gamed together.

For one agony-fueled space of time, I wasn't sure that I hadn't knocked myself out. Only the pain told me I was still conscious. It took a few seconds to register that Nat was limp underneath me.

I pushed myself to my knees, swaying as I tried desperately to focus.

The demon had moved closer but stopped out of arm's

reach. "I can still reach her, still use her, even unconscious," it said.

"Really?" I snarled. "Try using her after this." I pulled the dagger out and it stepped backward, lip curling.

"Recognize this, do you?" I hoped so. If it knew what demon stone was, maybe it wouldn't just charge me and try to snap my neck.

"You could kill her, little witch."

"I know what I'm doing." I didn't, but I knew I wasn't leaving Nat under this thing's control for one more second. Radha had showed me where to strike, the blade needing to go deep before I snapped it to release the demon stone. Whispering a prayer to whatever damn god was listening, I raised the dagger and stabbed it into Nat's leg.

Nat screamed as the blade sank in, and I twisted it to snap it as instructed. Her body arched off the ground, the sound she made unearthly. The demon echoed the noise, shrieking in furious pain. The combination of their voices made my head throb and my ears ring.

"Hurts, does it?" I said viciously. "I have another one just for you." I left the broken blade where it was. Radha had warned against trying to pull it free if I had to use it on Nat. Blood flowed out of the wound as Nat fell back, deeply red and glistening in the rising sunlight. Too much? I couldn't think about it.

The other dagger was already in my hand as I stood to face the demon.

"You'll pay for that," it snarled. "You're mine."

"I don't think so." I focused on its energy field again. Freeing Nat had to have hurt it, but I didn't know if there were other people feeding it.

I had to try and change its field. Break the bonds.

"I had plans for you, but now I've changed my mind. Now you can just pay." It raised its hand and light flared, something slamming into me. I flew backward and landed with a bone-cracking thump, pain blooming through me.

I couldn't breathe.

"Maggie!" Damon's voice was a bellow that broke through the pain.

I sucked in air desperately and twisted toward the sound. What was he doing here?

The demon laughed. "A new toy. How interesting." It turned toward Damon, standing at the edge of the clearing, the gun in his hand pointed at the demon.

"Damon, get out of here," I screamed.

He looked from me to Nat bleeding at my feet and back again. "Where's Antony?"

I shook my head. "Go!"

The demon started forward and I scrambled up. Every inch of me hurt, but I lurched into motion to get between it and Damon.

"Take Nat," I said to Damon. "Go. Run!" The last word left my throat as a shriek.

The demon howled again, and a rush of hate and fear filled me. "Just like the imp," I muttered and held out a hand. I heard Lizzie's voice whispering in my ear and fire erupted around the demon, halting it in its tracks.

"Take her," I yelled at Damon. "She needs a hospital." I put all my will into the order. He jerked suddenly and his face went weirdly blank.

For a second I thought the demon had him, but then he sprinted to Nat. The pool of blood left behind as he lifted her made me stomach lurch. So much blood. How could she survive that?

"Is that all you can do?" the demon said mockingly.

I pivoted to face it, my world narrowing back down to the threat in front of me.

My hand shook as I raised the dagger. Maybe I could throw it and hit the demon. Maybe not. All that mattered now was buying enough time for Damon to get away and call for help.

The roar of the flames disappeared suddenly as they winked out of existence. In the sudden quiet, I heard the crunch of receding footsteps behind me.

Good. Damon was getting away. He and Nat should be okay.

If I could just hold off the demon.

I stared at the creature. The blood red of its field was fainter. Maybe it was weakening?

It didn't matter. I only had this one brief chance to try to kill it. Once it recovered from the temporary shock of my fire—which clearly hadn't hurt it too badly—it would come for me again. And then it would kill me.

I focused on the colors, focused all the rage and fear and will to survive into visualizing them as anything but red.

To my amazement, the demon staggered backward, shrieking again.

Triumph surged through me. It worked. I'd hurt it.

Then I saw the three imps running from the trees.

Fuck.

I was dead. One dagger couldn't take care of a demon and three imps.

I cast a look behind me, hoping against reason that maybe the cavalry might arrive. Instead I saw Damon standing frozen at the edge of the clearing, Nat in his arms. His eyes met mine and I knew something was wrong. He wasn't leaving. Was the demon stopping him, or had he decided to try and help? It didn't matter, really. I had to fight or we'd all die.

The imps surrounded the demon, looking up at it worshipfully like a sheepdog waiting for the release signal from a shepherd. The demon's expression turned savage, teeth bared in my direction, and suddenly I heard Lizzie's voice whispering again.

I had one last chance, now while they were all together.

"You want my power?" I screamed at it. "Have some."

Then I threw my arms skyward, looking with desperation up at the perfectly clear early morning sky, and called the lightning.

The world exploded with heat and light around me.

I ducked to the ground, covering my head with my arms as my ears rang and my skin flared with acid-bright pain like I was the one who'd been struck. Everything swooped and whirled around me, and I thought I heard howls and screams of rage through the ringing in my ears.

Then nothing.

Nothing but pain and a buzz in my head like several swarms of angry bees.

I opened my eyes slowly, wincing with every hard-fought fraction of an inch my eyelids moved. I turned my head equally slowly to where the demon had stood.

No demon. No imps. Just four piles of greasy, smoking ash like the ones outside Cassandra's shop.

I'd done it.

Killed it. Or at least sent it back where it came from.

Relief surged, pushing back the pain for an instant. Then it returned, with an additional side of nausea and tremors. But I had to get up. Had to help Nat and Damon.

Damon was still at the edge of the clearing, but now he was kneeling, cradling Nat close to his body.

I staggered upright and somehow managed to move the twenty feet to reach them, pain shrieking through me with every step.

Damon looked at me as I dropped to my knees beside them, gasping through the agony.

"I think she's dead," he said brokenly, and I stopped fighting the pain and let it take me away.

When I woke, I was, once again, in a hospital. A steady beep came from a machine beside the bed, and the air smelled of disinfectant and laundry powder. My head hurt, and I wanted nothing more than to close my eyes again, but the faces of the members of the Cestis standing at the foot of my bed stopped me.

Only four faces.

"Antony?" I asked as the memory of screams in the woods came back to me.

Cassandra shook her head, echoes of pain filling her eyes. "He didn't make it."

Tears welled as my throat tightened. The memory of more than Antony's screams crashed into my brain. I had to swallow hard before I could ask my second question, the one I didn't really want to know the answer to. "And Nat?"

"I'm sorry, Maggie." Cassandra's face was a study in sorrow.

I couldn't stop the sob that broke from my throat. Or the tears that followed it. They let me cry.

"I killed her," I said when I could finally speak. "I killed my best friend."

Radha shook her head. "No. The wound wasn't enough to kill her. It was the demon stone. She was too far gone. Nobody could have saved her."

"The demon stone I stabbed her with, you mean," I said bitterly. "That's just semantics."

"You tried to save her," Ian said. "You did save Damon."

"You might've just saved the whole world," Lizzie added. "You have to try and remember that, Maggie. That's important."

A world without Nat. My best friend since that first day Gran had brought me home to Berkeley. The nearest thing to a sister I'd had. It hardly seemed worth the price. I wanted to curl into a ball and disappear.

"Is Damon here?" I whispered.

Lizzie shook her head. "He hasn't been to see you. You've been asleep for two days. Radha and Meredith and Cassandra have been working hard on you." She looked kind of guilty. Guilty but smug. "You did it. You summoned lightning." She sounded a little awed.

"Trust me, it's not something I want to make a habit of."

"Hopefully you won't have to. Damon's company has recalled the games. The demon won't be able to get to anyone else that way."

I winced. "What was the reaction?"

"Scandal. Outrage." Ian shrugged. "He's a strong man. He'll recover. Rebuild. People don't change. They'll still want to escape into all the latest shiny toys."

I wished I could escape. Just slip on a headset and be someplace where none of the last few weeks had ever happened.

And never come back.

I closed my eyes as tears stung again.

"We'll let you rest," Cassandra said, one hand coming to rest gently on my arm. "Just rest. That's all you have to do now."

They let me out of the hospital the day of Nat's funeral. I took a cab straight to the service, made it through talking to her parents, who'd been told some of the truth but not exactly what had happened. They knew Nat had tangled with bad magic. They were pale and washed out with grief, but they thanked me for trying to help her.

The guilt almost brought me to my knees on the spot, but I'd been forbidden from telling them the full story.

The sun warming my back as they lowered Nat's body into the earth felt like a travesty. I shivered despite the warmth, wondering if I'd ever feel anything again but cold and sad and so very, very full of regret and guilt and shame. The Cestis were there, each of the four adding protection to the grave on top of the blessings of the priest.

I didn't talk to them. It was too hard. Magic had brought me nothing but pain. I didn't want anything more to do with it.

Not yet.

As I turned to leave, I saw Damon standing alone among the graves, about fifty yards back from the group of mourners, and knew my pain wasn't yet done. He hadn't come to see me in the hospital, hadn't called.

I knew it was over, but I still couldn't help the way my heart bumped when I saw him, the way I automatically moved in his direction. I wanted to talk to him, even if it was only to say a final goodbye.

"Hello, Maggie," he said as I reached him.

I tried to smile but my mouth didn't obey. My eyes burned from too many tears, and my hand throbbed where I'd gripped the white rose I'd brought to lay on Nat's coffin too tightly and been bitten by the thorns. "Hello, yourself."

He looked tired. The shadows under his eyes rivaled mine, and there were lines on his face that hadn't been there before. I wanted to reach up and smooth some of them away. Instead I clenched my hands and put them in my pockets.

"How are you?" I asked.

"Not great," he admitted. "I'm sorry I didn't come to see you. It's been . . . hard."

I couldn't imagine the chaos he'd been dealing with. Chaos I'd brought into his life.

"I didn't expect you to come," I said honestly. Hoped like hell, yes. Expected, no. "Is there any point in apologizing again?"

He looked away. "I'm sorry, Maggie. It's just too—" He stopped, cleared his throat, then brought that bright blue gaze to meet mine again. "Too much. The magic. Demons. Lightning from clear skies."

I understood. I didn't blame him, but oh, I wanted to change his mind. "That wasn't just me," I said. "I had help."

"The part where you made me leave was you though, wasn't it?"

"What?" I looked at him blankly.

"You told me to leave and I had to. You did something to me."

My heart plummeted. Had I? Made him do something against his will? The one person I wanted to trust me. The fight in the clearing wasn't exactly clear, just a blur of fear and pain and confusion. "I-I don't remember. If I did, I didn't mean to."

"I'm not sure that makes it better. If you did it without thinking."

"I was trying to save you. You and Nat."

"I know. I just—"

"Can't trust a witch," I finished for him. "It would've been easier if you'd worked that out before you made a witch love you."

His eyes widened. "Maggie—"

I shook my head. I had to finish this conversation before I cracked wide open and crumbled in front of him. "Goodbye, Damon. I am sorry. I hope you believe me."

I turned and walked away. One step became two, became twenty and then thirty. When I'd almost made it back to Nat's grave, I stopped, heart pounding. I didn't want to turn back, but I couldn't stop myself.

But there was nothing to see. Damon was gone.

I bit my lip, forced myself to look back at the grave. Lizzie stood back beyond the clump of Nat's relatives closest to the now-filled hole in the earth. She gave a little wave as I caught her eye, then drew an S in the air with one finger.

I knew what she meant.

I'd saved the world. It should mean something.
But it didn't. I'd saved the world, sure.
Problem was I'd destroyed my life in the process.
And I had absolutely no idea what to do next.

Want more Maggie and Damon?
Buy
Wicked Words

FREE SHORT STORY

Sign up to my newsletter and I'll send you TO CATCH A WITCH, an exclusive short story set in the Techwitch universe, plus you'll get all the news on upcoming releases and sales.

Go to www.mjscott.net to sign up.

About the Author

M.J Scott is an unrepentant bookworm. Luckily she grew up in a family that fed her a properly varied diet of books and these days is surrounded by people who are understanding of her story addiction. When not wrestling one of her own stories to the ground, she can generally be found reading someone else's. Her other distractions include yarn, cat butlering, dark chocolate and watercolour. To keep in touch, find out about new releases and other news, sign up to her newsletter at www.mjscott.net. She also writes contemporary romance as Melanie Scott and Emma Douglas.

You can keep in touch with M.J. on:
Instagram @melwrites
Twitter @melscott
Facebook AuthorMJScott
Pinterest @mel_writes

Or email her at mel@mjscott.net

Also by M.J. Scott

Urban fantasy

The TechWitch series

Wicked Words

Wicked Nights

Wicked Dreams

The Wild Side series

The Wolf Within

The Dark Side

Bring On The Night

The Day You Went Away (free prequel short story)

Romantic fantasy

The Four Arts series

The Shattered Court

The Forbidden Heir

The Unbound Queen

Courting The Witch (Prequel novella)

The Daughter of Ravens series (Coming soon)

The Exile's Curse

The Traitor's Game

The Rebel's Prize

The Half-Light City series

Shadow Kin

Blood Kin

Iron Kin

Fire Kin

Acknowledgments

Thank you to Sarah for reading and to the magnificent Lulus for always cheering me on and always being their for me. This year has been a tough one and I couldn't have gotten this far without all the love from many many people. Smooches to you all. Extra smooches to my Mum. And extra belleh rubs to Callie and Vesper for all the snuggles and purrs.

Made in the USA
Coppell, TX
14 June 2023